GREY HUNTER

THE BERSERKERGANG WAS on Ragnar now, in full flow. He smote left and right with awful power, the meat-cleaver sound of his chainsword on flesh telling him he did damage with every blow. He lost all track of time and sense of self, becoming an unleashed whirl-wind of death and destruction that smashed through the panicking mutants with all the fury of a Fenrisian thunderstorm. He lived only to kill, and he took action to preserve his own life only in so far as it would allow him to slay more. A few shells ricocheted off his armour. He ignored them. A few desperate mutants managed to land glancing blows before he sent them to greet their dark gods. He did not feel them.

More William King from the Black Library

• SPACE WOLF •

Science fiction adventure with Ragnar of the Imperial Space Marines.

• GOTREK & FELIX •

In the fantasy world of Warhammer, dwarf slayer Gotrek seeks a glorious death in battle.

• OTHER NOVELS •

A WARHAMMER 40,000 NOVEL

GREY HUNTER

By William King

This book is dedicated to the memory of Madge Blain

A BLACK LIBRARY PUBLICATION

First published in Great Britain in 2002

This edition published in 2004 by
BL Publishing,
Games Workshop Ltd.,
Willow Road, Nottingham,
NG7 2WS, UK

10 9 8 7 6 5 4 3 2 1

Cover illustration by Geoff Taylor.

A CIP record for this book is available from the British Library.

ISBN 1 84416 024 6

Distributed in the US by Simon & Schuster
1230 Avenue of the Americas, New York, NY 10020, US.

Printed and bound in Great Britain by
Cox & Wyman Ltd, Reading, Berkshire, UK.

See the Black Library on the Internet at
www.blacklibrary.com

Find out more about Games Workshop
and the world of Warhammer 40,000 at
www.games-workshop.com

IT IS THE 41st millennium. For more than a hundred centuries the Emperor has sat immobile on the Golden Throne of Earth. He is the master of mankind by the will of the gods, and master of a million worlds by the might of his inexhaustible armies. He is a rotting carcass writhing invisibly with power from the Dark Age of Technology. He is the Carrion Lord of the Imperium for whom a thousand souls are sacrificed every day, so that he may never truly die.

YET EVEN IN his deathless state, the Emperor continues his eternal vigilance. Mighty battlefleets cross the daemon-infested miasma of the warp, the only route between distant stars, their way lit by the Astronomican, the psychic manifestation of the Emperor's will. Vast armies give battle in his name on uncounted worlds. Greatest amongst his soldiers are the Adeptus Astartes, the Space Marines, bio-engineered super-warriors. Their comrades in arms are legion: the Imperial Guard and countless planetary defence forces, the ever-vigilant Inquisition and the tech-priests of the Adeptus Mechanicus to name only a few. But for all their multitudes, they are barely enough to hold off the ever-present threat from aliens, heretics, mutants – and worse.

TO BE A man in such times is to be one amongst untold billions. It is to live in the cruellest and most bloody regime imaginable. These are the tales of those times. Forget the power of technology and science, for so much has been forgotten, never to be re-learned. Forget the promise of progress and understanding, for in the grim dark future there is only war. There is no peace amongst the stars, only an eternity of carnage and slaughter, and the laughter of thirsting gods.

PROLOGUE

RAGNAR RACED FORWARD through the hail of enemy fire. Overhead, lightning split the night, turning the clouds an eerie electric purple. Moments later the thunder spoke, even its god-like voice unable to drown out the roar of small-arms fire. Rain the colour of blood, tainted by chemical pollutants and oxidised iron, pattered off his armour. Around him, lasfire ripped the night. Here and there grenades flared, bright as the lightning stroke and just as brief.

Ahead of him the fortress loomed, a massive structure of plascrete sheathed in steel. Once it must have been the local headquarters of the Imperial levies, or perhaps a sector house of the Arbites. Now, it answered to a different master. Banners bearing the hideous eye of Chaos fluttered in the rising wind. Someone had painted baleful runes down the building's bristling sides, creating an inscription in the language of evil gods. Was it a prayer or curse? Perhaps both.

The earth shook as Ragnar scrambled into position behind the tumbled remains of a wall. Shattered brickwork lay near him. Close to his hand he could see where stonework had run like water under the infernal blast of energy weapons. He smelled the air: it stank of explosives, chemicals and technical unguents from the huge machines all around. He caught the scent of his battle-brothers, all hardened ceramite and altered flesh of Fenris. He looked backwards and saw them racing forward through the night, man-like shapes, though larger by far than any normal man, garbed in powered armour inscribed with the wolf sigil of their Chapter. Bolters bristled in their massive fists. A few carried rocket launchers and other heavy weapons. They moved through the rain and the mud with perfect confidence, an unstoppable tide rolling towards the enemy fort.

Behind them, in the distance, he could make out the unimaginably huge shapes of the Titans. They looked like men but seemed the size of small skyscrapers, an impression heightened by the storm of battle, the clouds of dust and his own knowledge of how powerful the mighty war machines were. Beside them, all other armoured vehicles looked puny.

Now they loomed out of night and storm like ancient gods of battle woken by the thunderous drumbeats of war. The glow of their shields was faintly visible even amid the clouds of dust surrounding them. When their weapons fired, the muzzle flare flashed brighter than the lightning, throwing the entire war-blasted landscape around them into flickering relief for a few seconds. At their feet, lesser vehicles scurried, weapons blazing, sending salvo after salvo scorching towards the fortress walls. The earth around them spurted upwards as the massive guns of the fortress replied.

Ragnar breathed in the shuddering air. He smiled, showing two enormous protruding fangs. He could smell terror coming from the Imperial Guard units around them, and a dim distant part of him understood it. Many a night, as a boy on his home world of Fenris, he had lain awake shivering as he listened to the thunder's rumble and saw the lightning's flare. It was on such nights that wolves of war were said to come forth to hunt, and ancient terrifying beings bestrode the world.

The scene surrounding him might have been ripped from his boyish imaginings, but in reality was a thousand times more fearsome. Yet, now, he himself felt no fear. He felt alive, every sense stretched to the maximum, every tendon of his altered body taut and ready to spring into action. All around him the pack that were his brethren and his liege-men awaited his commands.

He poked his head up and surveyed the massive walls of the fortress ahead of them. So far so good. The small postern airlock the Scouts had reported was just ahead. Over it turrets bristled, but their weapons were trained on the distant attackers, distracted by the mass of Titans and armour, and the hordes of waiting Guardsmen. Mikko's Blood Claws were already in position, ready to swarm through the gates to take out the plasteel lock and hold the entrance at his command. A good leader, Mikko, Ragnar thought, about ready for promotion to Grey Hunter. He shook his head. Now was not the time to let organisational details distract him.

The heretical defenders were unaware of the closer threat. Good. For Ragnar, it was just a matter of crossing the fifty metres of killing ground and they were in.

Suddenly the landscape erupted. Tonnes of earth and broken paving hurtled into the sky. Ragnar flinched for a moment, wondering if they had been spotted. His body tensed in anticipation of explosions or raking fire strafing their position, but nothing happened. It had been a near miss, a miscalculated shot from the distant support force. Ragnar glanced back to make sure none of his men had been caught in the blast and saw no sign of it. He offered up a prayer of thanks to Russ and the Allfather. That had been a little too close for comfort, the sort of mistake that happened on a battlefield, all too often and all too fatally.

Brother Einar, Brother Anders and the rest of their Blood Claw packs had formed up around him. Their young faces looked tense, strained and eager for the kill. Briefly Ragnar wondered if he had ever looked as green as that to his superiors, and knew the answer was a resounding 'yes'. That had been a very long time ago though.

Brother Hrolf and his Long Fangs were in position now in the nearby crater ready to give them supporting fire if it was needed. The rest of his company's Grey Hunters stood ready to go in. Ragnar looked over at Brother Loysus. The Rune Priest had been assigned to his company for this mission by Great Wolf Logan Grimnar himself.

Ragnar's fingers flickered through his Chapter's handsign asking the priest if he was ready. It was too noisy for speech, and too close to the sensitive detection equipment within the fortress to risk the comm-net. Loysus gestured in the affirmative. A faint nimbus of light played round his fingers. Ragnar smiled grimly and then gave the sign. It was time to go in.

'Take out the door!' he told Mikko over the comm-net.

+Aye, lord!+ The youth's response was instant. Ahead of them, the bright bloom of explosive charges lit the night. The gate crumbled. Ragnar gave the gesture to move.

'Charge!' he cried.

AFTER THE SOUNDS of conflict, all seemed quiet. After the dreadful brightness of the storm-lashed night, the sunrise seemed almost dim. Carrion birds fluttered over corpses. Pariah dogs had emerged from their holes to drink the water puddled in craters. The priests went about their business, tending to the wounded, granting final rites to the dying, speaking words of encouragement to the living. Above the walls of the fortress the Imperial banner had been restored. Already work teams from the guard units were scouring the Chaos runes from the side of the building.

Ragnar sat in the silence, filled with the sense of gloom and anti-climax that often filled him after a battle, and took stock of the situation. The casualties had been light, all things considered. Ten Blood Claws wounded, six dead. Two Long Fangs lost to enemy fire. Four men missing. It was not yet known whether they were dead or if their locator beacons had simply been damaged. Doubtless all would become clearer as the morning progressed.

Ragnar suddenly grinned, trying to find something that would dispel his black mood. 'Mikko for Grey Hunter,' he said suddenly.

Old Brother Hrolf grinned back at him. 'Aye, he's about ready. So are Lars and Jaimie.'

Ragnar nodded. 'Talk to the brotherhood. See if they agree to accept them. If they are, I will perform the rites myself this evening.'

Strictly speaking, Ragnar had no need to consult anybody before elevating a Blood Claw to the ranks of the Grey Hunters. It was his privilege as Wolf Lord to make that selection, but only a fool discounted the opinions of his master sergeant, and the men who would have to fight alongside the newly raised Claw.

Initiation into the ranks of the Grey Hunters was an important rite for all concerned, not just for the men involved but for the company. It marked the passage from raw ferocious youth to something wiser, more battle-hardened, and above all, less likely to get his companions killed by his eagerness for combat. Blood Claws were furious young men; Grey Hunters had tempered their lust for combat with experience.

Ragnar saw the sergeant was looking at him, as were all the other warriors surrounding him.

'What is it?' Ragnar asked, already knowing what was coming. It was part of the personal myth that surrounded him.

'The tale is that you were never a Grey Hunter, lord.'

'Aye, that is so, more or less.'

'I thought it was impossible for a man to become Wolf Lord unless he had been initiated into the brotherhood, lord,' said Zoran, one of the newest recruits to the company, a man who had been transferred in from Fenris as a replacement for casualties. Zoran had the fresh-faced look of a Blood Claw who had only just been accepted into the Grey Hunters himself.

'I thought every man must undergo the rites to become a Grey Hunter, to be bound into the brotherhood.'

'I did not,' said Ragnar.

'How can that be, lord?'

'It's a long tale,' said Ragnar.

'We have all day,' came someone's voice from the background. Ragnar could see they were all keen to hear it, even those who had heard the story many times before. The sagas were one of those things that bound them together as a Chapter, part of what made them a brotherhood. Some of the Blood Claws had approached and were taking their places around the fire. Ragnar looked at their eager faces, and smiled sadly.

He plunged backwards into his memory, seeking the words that would, this time, enable him to tell the whole terrible tale correctly.

'It was a long time ago,' he said. 'In the days when Berek Thunderfist was lord of this company...'

ONE

'When will we ever get out of this bloody place?' asked Sven, a grimace of pure frustration twisting his cheerfully ugly features. Frost had gathered on his eyebrows, and hung like icicles from his sideburns. 'It's been nearly six months since Xecutor, and I am as sick of looking at bloody Fenris as I am of looking at your ugly face, Ragnar.'

Ragnar did not take the comment personally. It was just Sven's way. He understood his fellow Blood Claw's frustration. All of this training might well be improving his skills, but it was no substitute for action.

Briefly he wondered if the process that had turned Sven and himself into Space Marines had not done something to their minds and souls as well. He felt restless in a way he had never done before. He craved the excitement of battle and the thrill of combat in a way that he suspected was not entirely natural even for one of his warrior people. Or maybe it was that despite the leatheriness of their skins, and the few grey hairs that had started to appear in their hair, they were still Blood Claws at heart, with all of a young warrior's yearning for blood and glory.

He smiled and shook his head looking at their surroundings. All around them were the Ice Wastes of Asaheim, league after endless league of snowy desolation, broken only by the cold peaks of the Dragonfang Mountains. It was an environment in which he could not have survived ten years ago, back when he had been merely a lad of the Thunderfist tribe. It was so cold that even wrapped in the thickest of furs he would not have lasted an hour, and so desolate that if the temperature did not kill him, starvation would have. Most likely the ice fiends would have taken him before that happened. Now he found the place merely entertaining, a place to hone the skills he had been taught by his Chapter.

But then, ten years ago, his body had not been sheathed in the miraculous armour of the ancients, capable of shielding him from far more hostile environments than this. And ten years ago his body had not been transformed into a near tireless killing machine capable of eating lichen or the inhuman flesh of the ice fiends and their related folk. Ten years ago his unaltered eyes would have been snow-blind by now, rather than filtering out the glare. Ten years ago he would not have agreed with Sven in finding this little hiking trip quite so dull. Being back on Fenris after the Xecutor campaign had proven a bit of an anti-climax. He did not even feel a thrill of pride any more when he contemplated the armour runes that showed he belonged to Berek's company. Not much anyway. Not as much as when he had first been assigned to a proper unit.

Of course, back then he had never been off-world, had never embarked on the great ships that sailed between the stars, had not fought against men and daemons and monsters. Back then, he would have thought only gods capable of doing what he now found so lacking in challenge. How times had changed! Since then there had been Galt and Aerius and Logan's World and Purity and Xecutor and a host of minor campaigns he could not even be bothered to enumerate.

'There's nothing bloody funny about it, Ragnar Thunder-fist, or should I call you "Blackmane" like all the little cubs do?'

Having failed to get a rise out of him one way, Sven was taking another tack. It was a bit of a sore spot. Part of Ragnar wished he had never had that old wolfskin made into a cloak, it had been the cause of so much jesting from his old comrades. The new Blood Claw packs and even some of the older Wolves, the Grey Hunters and the Long Fangs, had taken it as a mark of Russ's favour. After all, it had been a long time since any man had killed one of the beasts while still in training and armed only with a spear. It was in fact considered near impossible.

Ragnar had pointed out the old monster had been sick and starving and he had killed it with a lucky blow, but that had made no difference. If anything, his un-Wolf-like modesty had gotten almost as much attention as the slaying. Perhaps he should have boasted about it, like Sven or anybody else would have done. He did not quite know why the fame made him so uncomfortable. Perhaps it was because he felt he was not worthy of it.

'You bloody daydreaming again?' Sven asked. 'Or can't you answer a civil question?'

'You'll find out when you ask one,' Ragnar responded, his nostrils dilating, catching the faintest hint of an acrid inhuman scent on the wind. He looked over at Sven to see if his friend had caught it too. Sven's marginally less keen nose twitched. The long moustache he had been cultivating since the campaign on Xecutor moved like the whiskers of some great hunting beast.

'You smell that?' he asked. Ragnar nodded.

'Ice fiend, I reckon. Not too close, not too far either.'

'Perhaps you're not quite so bad at tracking as I thought,' said Ragnar.

'We can't all have the razor keen senses of the blessed of bloody Russ,' said Sven. 'Maybe I should let you go and check this out on your own. After all, the cubs will give you all the credit for killing the beasts anyway. Even if I were to kill a whole bloody tribe single handed, while you stood back and applauded my fine bloody technique with a chainsword, they would praise you for it.'

Ragnar checked his weapons. Tracking down the ice fiends was the whole purpose of this expedition. They had been raiding along the coastal glaciers and slaughtering the mastodon herds. It was time they were taught a lesson. 'I think you're just jealous of my well-deserved reputation,' he said.

'I would be jealous if it was well-deserved,' said Sven. 'Unfortunately, all you do is hog the credit for my own heroic deeds.'

'Like I did on Micah,' said Ragnar, 'when I pulled you out of that squig pit, before they could gnaw you to death?'

'You always have to bring that up, don't you?' said Sven in a tone of mock gloom. 'I would have fought my way out in a few heartbeats if you had not interrupted.'

'Your plan was to choke the squig to death by thrusting yourself down its throat then, was it?'

'I was lulling it into a false sense of security,' muttered Sven, his eyes checking the horizon. Ragnar could tell he too had spotted the massive white shapes until now near invisible amongst the snows.

Sven made a few practice passes with his deactivated chainsword just to loosen up.

'I don't remember that being covered in the Codex Tacticus.'

'I am a brilliant improviser.'

'Apparently.'

'Well, what about it? I don't cast up all the times I have pulled your fat out of the bloody fire. What about that time on Venam? When I saved you from those heretics before they could chop you up with your own chainsword? You never bloody well hear me mention that, do you?'

'Not more than once or twice a day.'

Sven was in full flow now, not to be stopped. 'Or how about on that space hulk near Korelia or Korelius or whatever it was bloody well called – when I saved you from those tyranids? I never mention that, do I?'

'You just did.'

'Or what about that time–'

'Sven?'

'Yes.'

'Shut up.'

'Don't tell me to bloody well shut up, Ragnar bloody so-called Blackmane. Just because you have a head swollen to the size of a small bloody planetoid, doesn't mean I can't kick your–'

'No! Can't you hear it?'

'Hear what?'

'That!' There was a sound of cracking ice. Ragnar saw a crevasse start to open ten strides away.

'Glacier's breaking up,' he hissed, beginning to run forward, as the crack splitting the ice came nearer.

'I would never have noticed,' said Sven sarcastically.

'Quite probably,' said Ragnar, racing forward and leaping over the gap. Sven was a few strides behind him, but leapt fractionally too late. It was obvious that he was not going to make it across the widening gap, and was going to tumble down, Russ alone knew how far. Ragnar leaned out and grabbed his friend's outstretched hand, tugging him forward and sending him sprawling in the ice beside him.

'Siding with the ice fiends now, eh?' said Sven around a mouthful of snow.

'No – just saving your life yet again.'

'So you say. I was doing fine before your sneak attack sent me sprawling.'

'Going to wedge open the crevasse with your thick skull, were you? Best use for it, most likely.'

Sven bounded to his feet and cast a casual glance over his shoulder, checking on the distance separating them from the ice fiends. Several hundred strides lay between them still. It looked like the fiends were waiting to see whether the crevasse took them. 'Yours is the only head around here big enough to fill that hole,' said Sven cheerily.

The ground beneath their feet started to move again, as the glacier shook. 'Maybe we should get off this frozen river of ice before it swallows us both up,' said Ragnar.

'Well, looks like the only way out is through them,' said Sven, gesturing to the approaching ice fiends.

'And your point is?'

'Just giving you directions in case you get lost again,' said Sven, turning and racing towards the approaching creatures. Ragnar followed him, the snow crunching under his ceramite boots and splashing off his greaves, his breath clouding the air like steam. The ice fiends bellowed challenges. The two Blood Claws answered with whooping war-cries. As they closed the distance Ragnar realised how big the creatures were. They were almost twice his height. Long white fur covered their bearish bodies, massive yellowing tusks protruded from the gaping caverns of their mouths. Long dagger-like claws tipped the three digits on each paw. Their faces were a startling combination of humanoid and beast. Their yellowish-red eyes gleamed with a malign and bestial intelligence and a glittering malevolent hatred of all not their kind. There were close on ten of them, all male, a pride of hunters. Ragnar knew they would fight until either they were dead or their prey was. There was no more insensately ferocious life form on the surface of Fenris. Unless it was Sven, he thought.

Ragnar thumbed the activation rune of his chainsword and it roared to life. He sprang into the ice fiend pack, chopping right and left. His first blow took off a taloned hand and sent blue blood spurting to stain the snows.

Briefly and incongruously a screed of information placed there by the tutelary engines back in the Fang blazed across his brain. He recalled that the blood of an ice fiend contained different chemical elements from human blood, designed to prevent it from freezing in the winter chill of the arctic wastes. He also remembered that it was poisonous, just as the creature thrust its stump into his face and a deadly searing jet of the stuff spurted into his eyes.

Ragnar was grateful as the translucent second lid dropped into position over his eyeball. Even so, the pain was immense as the corrosive stuff began to eat away at the specially hardened flesh. He shook his head to clear it away and a massive impact sent him sprawling into a snowdrift. Gratefully he scooped up a handful of snow to wash the poison ichor from his eyes. From the scents of the beasts and the sounds of their heartbeats he could tell there were none within striking distance. He could hear Sven leaping among them, chopping away with his blade, preventing the beasts from getting at him.

'Just as I thought!' he bellowed. 'Leaving me to do all the work, while you have a bloody kip in the nice soft snow.'

Ragnar retracted his second eyelid and wiped his eyes. The stinging had started to diminish as his enhanced body adapted to the poison. He saw Sven carve a ruinous path through the ice fiends, hacking left and right with his mighty chainsaw-edged blade. It looked like his fellow Blood Claw was going to do just what he claimed and take out the entire pack all by himself, when one of the beasts grabbed the Space Wolf from behind, immobilising his arms. Another knocked the chainsword from his grip with a buffeting blow.

Ragnar leapt forward, burying his own blade in the back of the beast that held Sven immobile. It let out an ear-splitting howl and dropped the Blood Claw as it clutched its wound. Ragnar hacked again, smashing his blow into the creature's neck and beheading it. He could hear Sven scoop up his blade. A moment later they laid into the beasts with their potent weapons. Chainsaw blades ripped through fur and flesh. Blue blood flowed. The beasts kept coming, filled with the insensate savagery of their kind, determined to kill the human interlopers.

The Space Wolves matched savagery with savagery, and brute strength with superior speed and weaponry. Within heartbeats Ragnar carved up two of the fiends, severing limbs and spilling ropy intestines. In five heartbeats he could see that more than half of the ice fiend pack was dead. Even so, the monsters kept fighting. Their claws scrabbled against the hardened ceramite of Ragnar's armour with a hideous keening screech. Their foetid breath stank in his nostrils. The reek of their blood and fur and internal organs began to overwhelm all other scents.

Ten heartbeats later it was over. All of the ice fiends lay dead or dying. One of the wounded lashed out at Ragnar even on its dying breath. He avoided the stroke easily and sent it to hell with a flick of his blade.

'Fierce buggers, aren't they?' said Sven, rotating the blades of his chainsword in a snowdrift to clean it.

'I've seen worse,' said Ragnar scooping up a handful of clean snow to wipe the alien blood from his armour.

'Well, they won't be killing any more bloody bondsmen, that's for sure.'

'You have it there,' said Ragnar quietly. He felt an obscure melancholy start to sneak over him now that the excitement of the battle was over. The creatures had not presented much of a challenge after all, and in death had started to look slightly pathetic.

'Useless beasts,' said Sven. 'Not even good to eat.'

'I suppose not.'

'Cheer up, Ragnar. You'd think it was you that had taken your death wound, not them.'

Ragnar attempted a smile, wondering at the change in his mood. Such things were becoming rarer and rarer as his body adapted to the changes that becoming a Space Wolf had wrought, but still they sometimes took him off guard. Suddenly, his eye caught sight of a distant flickering, as something massive dropped through the white clouds to the south-west. A moment later, he heard the sonic boom of the approaching aircraft.

'Looks like we've got company,' he said.

'Help has arrived. Too bloody late as usual. I've done all the work. You'll get all the credit.'

Ragnar reached down and wadded up a snowball. A second later he snapped it into Sven's face. So swift were the Blood Claw's reflexes that his comrade almost evaded it despite Ragnar's speed. Almost.

'Sneak attack, eh?' said Sven. 'Well, there's only one bloody response to that.'

A moment later, a snowball smacked off Ragnar's armour, and then a second.

They were still fighting when the Thunderhawk's landing skids dropped into the snow nearby.

Ragnar was surprised to see Sergeant Hakon emerge from the hatch of the gunship. He thought the veteran had returned to Russvik to take charge of training once more. The old Marine was even more grizzled-looking now than when Ragnar had first met him, five years before. His face was still a patchwork of scars, his eyes still chips of blue ice. His hair and long sideburns were pure grey. His canines were monstrous fangs. He surveyed the two Blood Claws for a second and the fighting stopped.

'You're wanted back at the Fang,' he said.

'We're flattered that you came all this way to get us,' said Sven. Over the past few years, they had all lost some of their awe of their leader. 'Has our liege Berek Thunderfist decided that he needs a bigger audience when the skalds sing his bloody praises?'

'You should watch your tongue, youth,' said Hakon, 'or Lord Berek might rip it out. He always had a bit of a temper that one. Or I might do it myself, if you don't show some respect for your elders.'

Hakon's voice was a flat and flinty as ever. Sven's cheerfully ugly face lost some of its cheeky expression at the sergeant's tone. Perhaps he had not quite lost all awe of the old man, Ragnar thought.

'Why have we been summoned?' asked Ragnar. It was not every day that a veteran sergeant and a gunship was dispatched to recover two Blood Claws on a hunting expedition.

'It's not just you,' said Hakon. 'Every Wolf on the planet has been called back to the Fang.'

'Every one?'

The sergeant nodded.

'Must be something big,' said Sven.

'Aye, youth, must be. Such a thing has not happened since you and your friends discovered that Chaos nest under Daemon Spire Mountain, and that was the first time that had happened in over a century.'

'It's nice to know we've brought a bit of excitement into your otherwise dull lives,' said Sven.

'Get in. You're not the only cubs I have to pick up today,' the sergeant said.

Ragnar followed Sven into the innards of the armoured gunship and strapped himself in.

'Who's he calling a bloody cub?' muttered Sven. 'About time we were made Grey Hunters, that's what I think.'

'Do you have an idea what all this is about?' asked Aenar Hellstrom brightly from across the hold. His oval face looked almost obnoxiously young and cheerful. Aenar was part of the most recent intake of Blood Claws to Lord Berek's company. A whole new pack of them, the second Ragnar had seen since his own acceptance by Lord Berek. Looking around he could see a couple of other members of the pack – the saturnine Torvald and the massive brute everyone just called Troll.

Sven grunted, not wanting to reveal his ignorance to one of the cubs, as they thought of the youngsters. It would not do. After all, he and Sven and Strybjorn were veterans of sorts, the oldest Blood Claw pack, and Aenar and his ilk had not even been off-planet yet. Aenar whooped as the Thunderhawk shuddered and roared its way through a patch of turbulence. *Was I ever like that,* Ragnar wondered with all the world-weariness of his extra five years? *It's a wonder that Hakon did not shoot me.*

Ragnar exchanged knowing glances with Sven who looked as if he were about to cuff the younger Blood Claw. Ragnar glanced around the inner cabin of the Thunderhawk. It was indeed a strange mix the gunship had picked up on its trip around the wastes. Along with Hakon there were other veterans, Long Fangs bearing the insignia of three different great companies, Grey Hunters, Blood Claws, even a Wolf Priest who had been scouting for new aspirants along the ridges near the glacier valley. It seemed like a fair cross-section of the Chapter had been abroad, about their own business in the winter-bound lands of the northern continent.

Hardly surprising really. Most had probably been doing the same as him and Sven, keeping their skills sharp by hunting, tracking, climbing mountains, practising winter world survival strategies. It was part of the routine for most of the Wolves when at home on Fenris. Those not involved in mandatory duty rosters were left free to pursue their own interests, unless of course some emergency came up.

What could be going on, Ragnar wondered? What was so important that all of these warriors had been recalled to the Fang? Had the Thousand Sons returned? Had a nest of Chaos worshippers been uncovered? Or was it something else – a summons to battle beyond the stars? He fervently hoped so.

Ragnar took a deep breath and began to murmur cleansing prayers to Russ. He needed to calm his mind, and be ready for anything, to be certain that whatever the challenge was, he could meet it. In a way it did not really matter what awaited them back at the Fang, he would find out soon enough, and be ready. It was his sworn duty as a Space Marine and a bondsman to Berek Thunderfist and Great Wolf Logan Grimnar. It was his duty to Russ and the Emperor and the spirits of those who had gone before him.

He felt a great calmness pass over him, as the ancient words of the prayer triggered responses programmed deep into his body's central nervous system. At once he felt both at peace and alert. The beating of his double hearts slowed. His breathing became deeper and more relaxed, his mind clearer and calmer. It was becoming easier, he thought. The more he practised these ancient rituals, the more effective they became, and the quicker he got results.

'You'll soon be as god-bothering as Lars was,' said Sven. Instantly a vision of their old comrade, killed by a monstrous ork warlord on Galt, sprang into Ragnar's mind, dispelling the serenity that filled him. Lars had

been a strange fey youth, perhaps marked for the Rune
Priesthood had he lived. Ragnar knew that he himself
had little in common with him. He doubted he was
going to hang himself from the tree of life to gain mystical knowledge. As far as he knew, he possessed no trace
of psychic powers.

Rather than laughing, Aenar greeted this remark with a
look of even deeper respect. He was one of the ones who
had started calling Ragnar 'Blackmane', after the skin of the
great wolf he had killed during his initiation quest. Ragnar
felt he could do without looks like that. They made him feel
a little too responsible for his liking. Sven saw the look too
and shook his head disgustedly.

'Ragnar slew all ten ice fiends,' he said with heavy sarcasm.
'I stood and watched his splendid bladework.'

'Really?' asked Aenar breathlessly.

'No, you idiot. He bloody well did not. He spent most of
the fight wiping the tears from his eyes. Tears of envy at my
god-like bloody prowess I might add.'

Disbelief scribed itself on Aenar's face. Sven shook his
head in disgust again, leaned back, closed his eyes and
started to snore. Outside through the portholes, Ragnar
could see the wolf-marked face of the moon, glimmering
against the jewelled blackness of the sky.

No matter how many times he saw it, the sight of the
Fang always astonished Ragnar. The massive peak, thrusting clear of the atmosphere, was the home of his Chapter.
It was said to be the highest mountain in the Imperium,
one of the greatest natural wonders, and Ragnar had
never found any reason to doubt this. It dwarfed all the
lesser peaks, the way a wolfhound might dwarf a terrier.
Within its hollowed core lay one of the mightiest
fortresses in the galaxy, the central and most important
base of one of the oldest and most renowned of all Space
Marine Chapters.

A thrill filled Ragnar when he contemplated it. In
ancient days the place had been home to the man-god,
Leman Russ, primarch of the Chapter, and the Emperor's

mightiest bondsman. From here he had set out to distant Terra and fought against the traitorous factions of the Horus Heresy. Here he had overseen the transformation of the first generation of Fenrisian warriors into the very first Space Wolves; he had given his own blood and genetic material to ensure it. This was the place that every one of the thousands of warriors who had become Space Wolves over the past ten thousand years called home. In the time since their founder's disappearance, the Wolves had done their best to live up to his legacy.

The Thunderhawk screamed down the Valley of the Wolves, towards its landing site, passing over fields worked by the thralls of the Chapter, and over the mines and refineries that kept its warriors supplied. In the hellish glare of the venting gas jets, Ragnar saw the massive metal pipes clinging like enormous steel vines to the mountain sides. A cloud of dark smoke rose from the towering metal chimneys to wreathe the ridges of the great mountain. Abruptly the gunship decelerated, slowing from fantastic velocity to a standstill in a few dozen heartbeats.

Ragnar, like everybody else, was thrown forward against the straps of his restraining harness. Sven opened one eye and looked around.

'I see our pilots haven't improved any with practice,' he said, and closed his eye once more.

The Thunderhawk landed on the hydraulic platform and descended into the depths of the Fang.

Ragnar emerged from the gunship into the great landing bay. All around. Space Wolves and thralls stood frozen in amazement. A great booming blast echoed through the cavernous hallway, seeming to disturb the clouds that had formed under the vaulted ceiling.

Servitors – half-man, half-machine – halted, red warning lights blinking on their craniums, and gazed around in wonder. Ragnar himself paused, half wondering if what he was hearing could be real. Every nerve of his body thrilled and responded to a knowledge imprinted deep in his brain by the teaching machines. This was the Horn of Doom, sounded only in moments of the gravest crisis to the Imperium and the Chapter, a signal calling every man to battle.

'Excellent,' muttered Sven. 'Some bloody excitement at long last.'

TWO

RAGNAR GLANCED AROUND the Great Hall, drinking in the sight of the Chapter's meeting place. Amid the barbaric splendour of its trappings the Wolf Lords and their retinues had already begun to assemble. All of the great captains present within the Fang had already made it to the chamber. Judging by their grim faces, they had been consulting with Logan Grimnar, and knew about whatever was going on.

Berek Thunderfist stood ready, flanked by Morgrim Silver-tongue, his skald, and Mikal Stenmark, his chief lieutenant, and captain of his Wolf Guard. Ragnar, Sven and Hakon moved to take their place in his retinue, along with nearly a hundred other warriors of Berek's company. There were none of the usual greetings, backslappings, taunts and boasts. Ragnar could smell the acrid taints of tension, suppressed anxiety and excitement in the air.

He studied Berek closely hoping to glean some hint of what was to come.

If he had expected to discover anything he was disappointed. Berek looked much the same as ever. He was a massive man, his broad open features no different from usual. A smile, part self-satisfaction, part genuine friendliness, hovered on his full lips. His human hand toyed with his striking mane of long golden curls, before moving to smooth his neatly trimmed beard.

The ancient power gauntlet that replaced the hand he had lost in battle with Khârn the Betrayer flexed unconsciously. A faint aura of lightning crackled across its surface, filling the air with the taint of ozone. It was from this he took his nickname, and not from some connection with Ragnar's own clan, as he had once supposed. As always, the Wolf Lord looked relaxed and a little too pleased with himself.

Ragnar pushed the thought aside. If any man here had reason to be justifiably proud it was Berek. He had come victorious out of more than a score of legendary close combats with the Imperium's deadliest foes. He had led the expeditionary force to Kane's World and destroyed the foul Temple of Khorne there. He was one of the most successful field commanders in the Chapter's history and was talked of by many, not least himself, as a possible successor to the Great Wolf when that time came.

Ragnar had reason to be grateful to the man, and he was. It was just that it sometimes seemed to him that there was a flaw in Berek, hidden too deep to be noticed, yet which you could occasionally sense, as you could sometimes feel the presence of danger only by instinct. It was true that Berek had never lost a battle, but Ragnar suspected the body counts in the staves of his saga told a different tale. Berek led men to glory but it was often purchased at a high cost in Space Wolf blood.

Ragnar shook his head, wondering if the flaw was in him. No one else seemed to think this was a failing. Many Blood Claws clamoured to follow Berek, desperate for the glory that being in his company promised. Ragnar had himself, if truth be told. The Wolves were never afraid of the sight of their own blood if it gave them a chance to prove their valour but…

Ragnar glanced around at the other Wolf Lords. There was Egil Ironwolf. Another mighty man, older by far than Berek.

A silver crescent of hair descended from the sides of his bald head, and his beard hung in a dozen pleats. Great furrows crinkled the leathery skin of his face. His clear blue eyes surveyed the scene with a cold ferocity unusual even in a battle-brother.

Often appearances were deceptive; the brethren aged at different rates depending on how their bodies responded to the genetic alterations that transformed them into Space Wolves. In this case they were not: Egil was older even than Logan Grimnar although he looked as hale as a man half his age. It was said he had weathered over seven standard centuries in the service of the Chapter.

Gunnar Red Moon was proof of the variability of the ageing process. If it were not for the length of his mighty fangs, he could easily have been mistaken for a Blood Claw. His skin was fair and his complexion as clear as the newest initiate's. He was slender by Space Marine standards, with a fragile haunted fey look that made him resemble an apprentice skald more than the battle captain he was. You could never have guessed by looking at him that this was the man who had torn off an ork warlord's arm and used it as club to beat it to death when his chainsword had failed at the battle of Grimme Field. As with Egil and Berek, there was a grimness about his manner that told Ragnar nothing about what was going on.

Before he could inspect the other Wolf Lords, the great iron gates sealed with the rune sign of Logan Grimnar were thrown open and the Great Wolf himself strode into the chamber, flanked by his retinue of priests and skalds. Also in the retinue were two figures Ragnar had not seen before, a tall slender man and woman garbed in ornate grey tunics with golden epaulettes on their shoulders. Their heads were shaved and tattooed and wrapped round with grey scarves bearing runes of a strange design. From their gold buckled belts hung holstered laspistols and scabbarded rapiers. From their necks hung golden chains bearing the sign of an eye flanked by two rearing wolves.

'Navigators,' he muttered, the knowledge rising from deep within the caverns of his subconscious. He felt a brief sense of wonder. He knew that a small clan of Navigators from House Belisarius had a sanctuary within the Fang. There was an ancient friendship between the House and the Chapter, and it was a right granted to them by Leman Russ himself, in the ancient days before the Empire. The family had the exclusive right to guide the starships of the Space Wolves' fleet through the immaterium. In return, it could call upon the services of the Chapter when it required them. Ragnar considered why the Great Wolf had required their presence at this meeting. It could only mean one thing – the Chapter's fleet was about to be deployed somewhere, which meant most likely that the Chapter was going off-world.

The Great Wolf strode to a raised podium in the centre of the chamber. He was a massive man, grizzled and ancient-looking, but who moved with the electrifying speed of a much younger warrior. He raised his massive axe in the air. Instantly all went silent.

'Brothers,' he said, his deep powerful voice filling the chamber effortlessly. 'The Shrine of Garm has fallen to heretics. The Spear of Russ has been taken.'

Instantly there was a gasp of horror. Ragnar saw expressions of disbelief and outrage on the face of the older Wolves. Somewhere within him he felt a visceral response to the Great Wolf's words and he was surprised by it. Another legacy of the tutelary engines, no doubt. A heartbeat later knowledge flooded into his mind.

Garm was the site of one of the holiest of all the Space Wolves' shrines. Indeed, the world had taken its name from Garm, mightiest of the First, one of the Wolf Lords who had risen in the service of Russ himself during the founding of the Chapter. The cairn marked the spot where he fell in battle with Magnus the Red, primarch of the Thousand Sons, during the battle that had freed the planet from the domination of the traitor Marines. It had been a desperate moment, when Russ stumbled and the evil one had stood triumphant over him. Garm had snatched up Russ's spear and launched himself to his primarch's defence.

Using Russ's mighty weapon he had wounded the Chaos primarch, a feat considered near impossible by mortal man. The furious Magnus had burned him down on the spot with evil magic, but the hero's death had given Russ time to recover, and drive off the lord of the Thousand Sons.

The cairn had been raised by Russ himself with his own hands, in tribute to the first and greatest of his followers. The primarch caused a jet of cold blue flame to mark the spot, and laid his enchanted spear on the cairn, asking his old friend's spirit to watch over the weapon until he returned to claim it. It was a place where one could still sense the presence of the primarch on certain wild stormy nights. It was also a place that had been sacred to the Thousand Sons, and the two Chapters had fought many a battle over it. Never had it been allowed to remain in the hands of the heretics. It was an insult to the honour of the Space Wolves and it was not to be borne.

As for the Spear of Russ, it had been forged for the man-god by the folk of Garm, greatest artificers of the factory worlds of this sector. They had taken the fact that Russ himself had laid it in the shrine as a pledge of friendship with his people, and they had protected it ever since – with help from the Wolves of Space, of course.

'The Shrine of Garm has fallen and we are going to take it back. No slave of Chaos will be allowed to sully it. The holy site must be cleansed with fire and blood. The Spear of Russ must be waiting for our lord on his return if the prophesies of the final days are to be fulfilled.'

Ragnar found himself joining in the roar of approval that followed. In the scents of his battle-brothers he could detect nothing but anger and outrage.

'What happened?' shouted Berek Thunderfist.

Logan Grimnar's voice boomed across the chamber.

'The tale goes thusly! One hundred days ago the master of the Order of the White Bear refused to pay his tithe to the Imperial governor of Garm. He foreswore his oath of allegiance and sent the heads of the tax collectors back to the palace on plates. It was a sign for a general uprising.

Apparently the governor was a venal man who had set taxes at ten times the level required by the Ecclesiarchy, using the money to live in luxury and fund a network of spies, informers and strong-arms. He was hated by the folk of Garm, who rose against him urged on by an apostate priest known as Sergius. Civil war raged across the surface of the planet. Many of the industrial brotherhoods, including the Order of the White Bear and the Silver Mastodon, declared for Chaos, and are now trying to summon aid from the Eye of Terror. Now Chaos seeks a beachhead on one of the greatest foundries and arsenals of the Imperium and if it is not opposed it will seize it and fortify it. If this happens, the enemy will control one of the main routes between Fenris and the Eye of Terror, and one of the most sacred sites in the long saga of our brotherhood will have fallen forever into the foul claws of Chaos. Can we allow this?'

'No!' roared the massed ranks of Space Wolves as one man.

'Can we stand back and allow the Spear of Russ to be held in the foul talons of the evil ones?'

'No!'

'Will we allow this call for succour and vengeance to go unanswered?'

'No! No! No!'

'The Wolf ships will sail between the stars to Garm. There we will join forces with the Imperial fleet gathered to free the world from the shackles of Chaos and the taint of heresy. We will teach the slaves of darkness what it means to sully the honour of our Chapter. You have one hour to pre-pare yourselves for departure!'

Pausing only long enough to acknowledge the approving roar of his followers, the Great Wolf swept from the cham-ber. A couple of heartbeats later, Ragnar found himself joining the throng racing towards his cell to gather his gear and personal effects and make ready for the long journey between the stars.

'So, it's off to bloody war we go!' said Sven loudly as they left their cells. For all his complaining tone, his manner and scent spoke of happiness and excitement. They raced through the corridors of the Fang, heading to the great hangar bay in which the shuttles waited, carrying the kit-bags that held their personal possessions. 'The bold Space Wolves must save yet another world from the denizens of the dark.'

'It is the task the Emperor has set us,' said Ragnar, echoing the fulsome tones the Wolf Priests used when preaching their sermons. 'And we will not fail Him! There will be foes to smite, plunder to take, and new worlds to tread. Who could ask for more?'

'Maybe a bite to bloody well eat,' said Sven. 'I don't fancy eating grubs and worms and tree bark again like we did on Galt.'

'The fleet is going,' said Ragnar, as they leapt into a drop-tube and drifted a thousand metres down into darkness. 'And I am sure it will be well supplied.'

'What do you know about Garm? And I don't mean all the stuff the bloody ancient machines taught us about the holy shrines either. You are always studying the archives about old battles. Know anything?'

Ragnar thought for a moment. Garm had been the site of more encounters with the Thousand Sons than any other world in the sector. Since his encounter with the Chaos Marine Madox, he had taken a personal interest in such things. He had read as much as he could about it, for he felt certain that he would encounter the heretical Traitor Marines once more.

He flexed his knees to absorb the shock of landing and bounded out into the corridor once more, kitbag over his shoulder. Sven raced along by his side, keeping pace easily, despite Ragnar's longer stride.

'It is an industrial world,' he said eventually. 'Part forge, part hive. Dark clouds of pollutants fill the skies. Steel citadels cover the surface. Each is ruled by an industrial order, sworn to serve its own master. Each master is sworn to serve the governor, and the governor is sworn to serve the Imperium.

'The members of the orders represent only a small fraction of the population. Each owns its own factories and foundries and the services of the clans who work there like thralls. Every man, woman and child has a lord.'

'Sounds more or less like bloody Fenris.'

'On Garm, the distinctions between classes and castes are much more strict. Obedience is demanded and expected. Disobedience can be punished by death.'

'Doesn't sound like the system is working too well at the moment.'

'Perhaps it is.'

'What do you mean?'

'If a lord becomes a heretic, all of his followers will too. If a lord becomes a rebel, so will his people.'

'Why should they obey a rebel or a heretic?'

'Just because he is an oath-breaker does not mean that they are too. Besides, they may know no better.'

'They must be bloody stupid if they can't work that out for themselves.'

'Wait until you see for yourself before you judge.'

'Yes, oh wise one. You sound more like a bloody priest every day.'

'You're the one who asked me about Garm.'

'I'm sorry I did, your holiness.'

They emerged into the hangar area. Already companies were forming up to take shuttles, one for each company present, one for each ship. Each of the great companies was assigned its own vessel for the duration of the campaign. Each would carry its supplies and equipment and thralls, containing everything it needed to keep that company on the field.

These shuttles were different from the one he had taken when he had accompanied Inquisitors Sternberg and Karah Isaan on the starship *Light of Truth*. They were smaller, more streamlined and much more heavily armoured. They bristled with weapons, and looked more like large Thunderhawks than normal spacefaring vessels.

As Ragnar watched, a Rhino armoured personnel carrier roared up the ramp and into the interior of the shuttle. It was swiftly followed by another and then by squads of bikers. Ragnar glanced around and saw several thralls in power-loader exo-skeletons carrying massive crates on the tines of their mechanised armour. One by one they disappeared within the depths of shuttle freighters and emerged without their loads.

All through the hangar hall hundreds of thralls loaded dozens of shuttles. Some of the vessels, less well armoured than the others, were used only for carrying stores to starships. Ragnar was suddenly aware of the scale of the operation going on around him, and how well organised it was. Most of the Chapter was already on the move, ready to make the leap between the stars, mere hours after their supreme commander had given the order.

'Hope we get our own bikes this time out,' said Sven. 'There's nothing I bloody like more.'

'I think you have ork blood in you,' said Ragnar, thinking of the awesome greenskin warriors and their fondness for loud fast machinery.

'I've had plenty of ork blood on me,' said Sven and laughed as if he had said something funny.

As he and Sven clambered up the ramp into the interior of the shuttle, the duty sergeant, Hakon, as fate would have it, called out their names and checked them off a list.

'Not taking any chances on leaving anybody behind, sergeant?' asked Sven, cheekily.

'If we didn't make this list some of you would probably sleep through the Horn of Doom and miss the ship. And we couldn't have that now, could we? Now get on board and less of your lip.'

'Aye, your lordship,' Ragnar bellowed and narrowly avoided the sweep of Hakon's boot. Grinning, he and Sven entered the innards of the shuttle. It was warm and dark and smelled of oil, weapons, ceramite and the exhaust fumes of vehicles. Lubricants had pooled in the well-worn floors. Ragnar made his way up a set of stairs balustraded with wolf-headed gargoyles and moved through a series of bulk-head doorways till he found the take-off chamber containing the other Blood Claws.

A quick check told him everybody was present. Strybjorn as well as the boys of the new packs. They looked at him and then Sven with a mixture of excitement and anxiety written on their faces. He realised that some of these youths had never been off-planet before. Casting his mind back, he managed a surge of sympathy for them. He recalled his own first voyage into space in the company of Sven, Strybjorn, Hakon, Nils and Lars. An unaccountable sadness filled him when he thought of his dead companions and the dead inquisitors who had accompanied them, particularly Karah Isaan, for whom he had felt an un-Space Wolfish fondness.

'What's it like, travelling through the immaterium?' Aenar asked enthusiastically.

'Bloody horrible,' said Sven. 'The ship shakes and vanishes and you hear the howling of daemons and dead men outside its walls. Your stomach feels like it's about to jump up your throat and romp off down the corridor all by itself. Your bowels get weak and loose and–'

'Sven is just describing how he always feels when he faces any danger,' said Ragnar. 'You'll be fine.'

'Hark to Ragnar, the bloody hero,' said Sven. 'I'll have you know he wouldn't be here now if I had not pulled his bloody bacon from the fire a dozen times.'

Before Ragnar could reply, red warning runes glowed along the walls, and they heard a great air-horn blast. In the distance, Ragnar could hear massive airlock doors clang shut.

'Strap yourselves in,' he said. 'We're taking off.'

Ten heartbeats later, the shuttle shuddered into the air, and headed for the distant sky. What waited for them beyond it, Ragnar wondered, feeling an ominous sense of foreboding.

THREE

RAGNAR WATCHED THE approach of the *Fist of Russ*, Berek's ship, through the porthole of the shuttle. On first inspection, it was a disappointment. Seen from close up it was smaller than the *Light of Truth*, the first starship on which he had travelled, though it looked more densely armed and armoured. Around the ship, shuttles and Thunderhawks came and went. Judging by the loops and flare of landing jets, many of the gunship pilots were merely testing their vessels, performing shakedown trials before hurtling into the docking bays of the mothership.

Briefly Ragnar considered whether, when he finally made the rank of Grey Hunter, he would apply for pilot training. He found the idea attractive, and mentioned it to Sven.

'Does this mean you want to bloody well skive off from hand-to-hand fighting? Typical.'

Ragnar considered this for a moment, as he watched a Thunderhawk hurtle by so close that he could make out the pilot's features through the armour glass windows.

He must be doing that deliberately, Ragnar realised, matching velocities exactly so that there were only a few dozen metres per second difference in the speeds of the two vessels.

'No. I still want to be in the front line. I just quite fancy being able to fly one of those things.'

Sven looked at him as if he were mad. 'If the Emperor had meant us to fly, we would grow wings along with our second hearts.'

'Don't be stupid, Sven. That's like saying if He meant us to be able to fly between the stars we would make warp jumps instead of farting.'

Sven laughed. 'There are some people I wish could do that.'

The *Fist of Russ* came ever closer. The rune sign of Berek's company was visible on the side, a massive silver hand clutching a lightning bolt. 'Do you think our lord and master could have had that painted any bigger?' Sven's tone was affectionate, but showed an awareness of their captain's besetting sin.

'Not without having the ship made bigger,' Ragnar replied.

'I wager he would do so if he could.'

'Or if he thought Sigrid Trollbane was having it done,' added Strybjorn. Ragnar looked over at the Grimskull. His former enemy must be a little excited. He did not usually take part in Sven and Ragnar's good natured mocking of their chieftain.

There was a faint sense of motion as the shuttle rotated for docking. Ragnar saw massive dish antennae rotating on the side of the *Fist of Russ*. Above it, on the jutting tower where the ship's bridge was situated, was another symbol. It was not in the familiar runic script of Fenris but showed flowing Imperial characters surrounding a winged man.

'What is that?'

'Don't know,' said Sven. 'I thought you were the scholar around here.'

Sergeant Hakon overheard them, as he made his way down the steel corridor. 'It's the sign of House Belisarius.'

'Who are they?'

'Navis Nobilitae. Navigators.' Ragnar remembered the two slender foppishly garbed figures he had seen with Logan Grimnar back in the Fang.

'How come they have their sign on our bloody starships?' asked Sven.

'Because without them these starships would not be going anywhere,' responded Hakon curtly. 'They guide us through the immaterium. Without them–'

'I know what a Navigator does, sergeant. I am curious to know why our ship bears their sign. Does it not belong to the Chapter?'

'I sometimes wonder whether the teaching engines managed to drive anything into that thick skull of yours, Sven. Ragnar, did they do any better with you?'

Hakon was being unfair, Ragnar thought. The teaching machines had placed enormous amounts of information within their brains but that did not mean you instantly had access to all of it. Sometimes, trying to find what you needed to know was like being lost in a great library, looking for a single volume. And, of course, sometimes the information was simply lost, forgotten or never transferred at all. Like most of the ancient machines owned by the Chapter, the tutelary engines were not entirely reliable.

Still, it was worth a try. Ragnar closed his eyes and invoked the mnemonic prayers he had been taught, concentrating on the image of the winged figure, the name Belisarius, and the concept of the Navis Nobilitae. As if from a great distance concepts drifted up, like half-forgotten memories suddenly recalled by the stimulus of a scent or a song.

'They are our allies,' he said eventually. 'Our pact with them dates from the time of Russ, from the Dawn Ages, before even the founding of the Imperium.'

'Very good, Ragnar,' said Hakon. Sven grimaced sourly at this. Obviously his grasp of the process of mnemonic prayer was not quite so good as Ragnar's. 'They are sworn to guide our ships and to provide twenty-four of their best pilots to serve the Great Wolf. In return we are sworn to come to their aid should they summon us, and to provide sanctuary in times of need. Their chieftain has a bodyguard of Space Wolves, just as our lord has a retinue of Navigators.'

'Why do we need twenty-four bloody Navigators?' said Sven. 'The Chapter has only fifteen great ships. One for each company. Three in reserve.'

'Slow as ever, Sven,' said Hakon. 'Replacements and reserves are always needed – with Navigators as much as with ships. More so, for there are times when men need to rest and ships do not.'

As Hakon and Sven talked, other images and ideas flowed into Ragnar's mind. He realised he had never given consideration to a lot of things before now, to the level of support that stood behind every Space Marine. It was not just thralls and mechanicians they needed, but Navigators and crews. For he realised that the crews must be raised from the folk of Fenris and trained by those who preceded them on the great ships. In a moment, he became conscious of the fact that he and his battle-brothers were merely the tip of a great spear, the cutting edge of a huge organisational structure intended to send them into battle anywhere in the Imperium.

Out of the porthole he caught sight of glittering lights, so distant as to be little brighter than stars, each in reality a huge ship. In another moment the giant sphere that was Fenris came into his field of vision, remained there for a moment, and then vanished as the shuttle entered the vast metal cavern that was the hangar deck of the *Fist of Russ*.

As they moved through the ship to their assigned cells, Ragnar could not help but contrast his experience on the Space Wolf ship with his first experience of an Imperial starship, the *Light of Truth*, and with that of the transport which had eventually brought him back from Aerius to Fenris. On those ships most of the crew had been conscripts and convicted criminals, either sentenced to serve punishment for some crime or press-ganged by a naval shore party. Most of them had been chained to their machines, and harshly disciplined by their officers.

The folk of the *Fist of Russ* were free men, proud to serve the Chapter, permitted to come and go as they pleased. They looked on Ragnar with awe but no fear. They did not expect the lash for the slightest infringement of discipline, real or imagined. They were an elite among spacefarers and knew it. All of them showed the mark of Fenris. They were tall men, mostly blond, rangy and fierce-looking. They wore grey tunics that bore the sign of the wolf, and went armed and ready to do battle, if need be, in defence of their ship. They moved with a purposeful stride, certain of what they were doing.

The *Fist of Russ* smelled different too: cleaner and more efficient, more like the air of Fenris. There was no taint of pain and torment in it. Obscurely, Ragnar felt proud of his Chapter. This ship was just another one of the myriad of small but important things that separated his people from the other arms of the Imperium like the Inquisition. The thought stayed with him as he marched to the cell he had been assigned.

His cell was small and steel walled. It had a porthole that looked out into space, and a small terminal that allowed access to the ship's datacore. There were racks for his weapons, and stands for his equipment. A hard bed filled one corner. He tossed his kitbag into the chest bolted to the floor and stowed his wargear before making his way over to the terminal altar.

It was slightly different from those he was used to in the Fang but still recognisable. A small cube of metal topped by a circlet of hologems surrounding a small brazier for the machine incense. A long brass umbilical connected the machine to the data cavity in the wall. Two rearing metal wolves, bolted to the tabletop, flanked it and held it in place.

Ragnar squatted cross-legged before the altar. He lit the small block of machine incense, tapped the ivory keys and spoke the words of invocation. His fingers worked through the invocation sequence to summon the knowledge spirits of the datacore. In answer, the altar shuddered, the air shimmered and a glowing sphere of light sprang into being over the glowing hologems.

Ragnar's fingers flickered over the keyboard. In answer, the ectoplasmic nimbus of light before him swirled and a picture of the *Fist of Russ* came into being. It was a small but perfectly accurate facsimile of the mighty vessel he had seen from the shuttle. In answer to another catechism, the machine spirits showed images of the other craft. To Ragnar's surprise they were all different.

Logan Grimnar's *Pride of Fenris* was similar to the *Light of Truth*, a grim warship far larger than the *Fist of Russ*. Egil Ironwolf's was of the same type, if marginally smaller. The others ranged from one half to one third the size of those ships, and showed many subtle differences. In answer to his questions the spirits whispered facts about the fleet. Most of the ships were old. The Chapter had captured many of them in battle during ancient actions millennia ago. Some had become Chapter property more recently.

The *Iron Wolf* for instance, had been taken during a battle against a rebel fleet when Egil's own ship, the original *Iron Wolf*, had been crippled. The Chapter had claimed the battleship as plunder, and refused to return it to the Imperial fleet, an act that apparently still caused problems in certain quarters. Ragnar could not for the life of him understand why. On Fenris these things were simple: when you captured an enemy's ship it belonged to you or your liege lord. It did not matter if your foe had stolen it or claimed it in battle with someone else.

Apparently, certain factions within the Imperium thought differently. Ragnar was worldly wise enough to know that strangers had strange customs, and that not everybody held to the law as it was adhered to on Fenris, but he could not help but feel sorry for anyone who sought to claim the Chapter's spoils back from it.

Ragnar wondered what it must be like to have command of your own ship, to be a Wolf Lord like Berek Thunderfist?

To be in charge of your own company, to be considered a hero by your Chapter, and a legend in your own time, particularly by yourself. To a Blood Claw like himself it was an almost unimaginable position. Aside from becoming Great Wolf, it was the highest position anyone in the Chapter could aspire to.

Of course, it was rumoured that Berek was not content with it, that he desperately wanted to be Great Wolf. Ragnar wondered if that was one of the things that made him a Wolf Lord with his own company. Would anyone with the drive to reach such heights be content to stop there, one rung below the ultimate achievement?

It did not seem likely that Logan Grimnar would die soon. At least not of old age, but then few Great Wolves had ever died in their beds. There was always the possibility when the Chapter went into battle that even the highest ranking could become a casualty. If that were the case, perhaps Berek would achieve his ambition.

As a lowly Blood Claw, Ragnar was not privy to all of the scuttlebutt that passed around the ranks, but even he had heard discussions of Berek's ambition and his rivalry with Sigrid Trollbane, who was seen as his chief competitor for the Wolf throne. Ragnar had also heard of brawls and duels being fought between men of the two great companies, a shadow of the tension that lay between their chieftains.

A shadow fell across the altar. Ragnar looked up to see Sven standing in the doorway of his cell. 'You never bloody well stop, do you! You'll go blind if you spend all your time staring at a hologlobe.'

'At least I'll know something about what's going on.'

'You think that's important? All a Space Wolf needs is a foe in front of him and a weapon in his hand.'

Ragnar considered his friend, knowing that Sven was serious. Sven had many virtues but imagination was not one of them. Now that he had adjusted somewhat to the changes wrought by his transformation into a Space Marine, he seemed genuinely content to be one of the rank and file. He had no ambition greater than becoming a Grey Hunter, and no desire stronger than to cleave the foes of the Chapter. Ragnar was suddenly aware of the difference between the two of them.

He did like to know what was going on around him. He did want to be more than a sword in the fist of the Great Wolf. Was he ambitious himself? Was part of the reason for his ambivalent feelings towards Berek Thunderfist, that the Wolf Lord's ambition reflected his own? Ragnar did not know. He just felt that in some way he was growing up into someone different from the vast majority of the Blood Claws around him.

'Maybe so. But it never hurts to know why and more importantly how you are going to get to your foes.'

'You think too bloody much, Ragnar. You need beer.'

'Is there any on this ship?'

'This would not be the *Fist of Russ* if it did not have a stein of beer in it.'

'Hopefully there is more than one.'

'As fate would have it, while you were weakening your eyesight communing with the spirits of knowledge, I was performing a vital reconnaissance mission. I have located the feasting hall and uncovered the location of a barrel at least.'

'Then like true Space Wolves, let us boldly seek our objective.'

'Best be prepared. Doubtless there are several scurvy knaves who will seek to stand between us and our prize.'

'Then we shall teach them the folly of their ways! Lead on!'

THE FEASTING HALL lay deep within the bowels of the ship. Around the tables was a scattering of Blood Claws. It seemed that they were the only ones without duties to perform before the ship made its jump through the immaterium; the crew and the rest of their brethren were busy. Ragnar and Sven helped themselves to steins of ale.

Ragnar sat down on a bench next to Aenar, Torvald and the hulking Troll, along with several other members of their pack.

Ragnar felt a little envious. Most of his early comrades had gone to the 'grave'. He pushed that dark thought away. Doubtless soon these bold lads would know the feeling too. The rate of attrition among Blood Claws was terrible. By the time they made Grey Hunter it was likely that only half of the young warriors in front of him would still be alive.

Sven took a place opposite them. Overhead in an ancient cogitator a countdown tolled off the minutes and seconds before the ship would be on its way. There were several hours yet to go.

'Have you heard anything about where we are going?' Aenar asked. Torvald was leaner and shaven headed with a bleak but humorous face.

'Ask Ragnar,' said Sven. 'He is the scholar around here.'

'That's because it takes a brain to be a scholar, and Sven is hampered by his lack of one,' said Ragnar, before sharing his knowledge.

'It would be just my luck for it to be some hellhole or other. I was cursed at birth, you know.' Torvald was given to complaining bitterly about some curse that had been placed on him at birth. His mother had offended a witch or something. Ragnar was not entirely sure. The tale changed a little every time Torvald told it.

'I hear that a full ten companies are being sent out,' continued Aenar.

Ragnar nodded. The maximum number of companies ever deployed in the field at once was eleven. One company always had to be left out of a campaign, so if all the others were wiped out it meant the Chapter would continue. Such an event had happened only three times in the Space Wolves' history, but happen it had. To have ten companies dispatched to the same place at the same time was most unusual indeed.

'Garm is an important place,' said Ragnar. 'The shrine there is almost as sacred as those in the Fang.'

A familiar scent told Ragnar of the arrival of another old companion. 'Look who has finally decided to join us,' said Sven. Ragnar looked round to see his old rival and comrade

Strybjorn Grimskull approaching their table. He seemed even broader and more muscular than ever, and his deep-set eyes studied them all with a habitual wary, appraising look.

'I thought I would give you the pleasure of my company,' said Strybjorn, without cracking a smile.

'When does that start then?' said Sven. 'I've known you for years and it's never been a pleasure.'

'Very funny,' said Strybjorn grimly. He nodded at Ragnar. There had been tension between them since before they became Space Wolves. Strybjorn had been part of the raiding party that had wiped out Ragnar's entire clan. Not even the fact that they had saved each other's lives and fought together against deadly foes since then had entirely removed it.

'All ready for Garm?' he asked. The younger Blood Claws roared enthusiastic affirmatives. Sven nodded. Ragnar shrugged.

'You don't seem all that keen, Ragnar.'

'I'm keen enough. I just want to learn more before we go in.'

'What is there to know?' Sven asked.

'What sort of foes we will be fighting, for one thing,' said Ragnar.

'How many of them there are,' added Strybjorn.

'How well equipped they are–'

'That's easy,' interrupted Sven. 'Our foes will be flesh and blood, just like us only less tough. There won't be enough of them to go around the rest of you by the time I am finished with them. Their equipment will be like ours but less destructive since we are Space Marines, and have the best bloody gear in the galaxy. If you have any other questions, I will be pleased to answer them.'

'Thank you, Sven,' said Ragnar ironically. 'It's hard to understand why you haven't been made a Wolf Lord already, seeing as how your confidence must inspire the men.'

'He inspires me,' growled Strybjorn sarcastically. 'Inspires me to wonder how it's possible for anyone so thick to be a Space Marine.'

'I didn't think intelligence was a requirement,' said Sven too quickly to realise what he was saying. 'I thought it was courage and ferocity.'

'I think all three might prove useful,' commented Ragnar.

'We'll see,' said Sven. 'Once the shooting starts all the knowledge in the world won't make any difference, it's down to skill with chainsword and bolter.'

Sergeant Hakon strode into the hall. He looked at them and said, 'It's nice to see that some folk have nothing better to do than sit around and drink beer and boast.'

'It's a great life being one of the Emperor's chosen, sergeant,' said Sven.

'The Emperor chose you to fight in his name, not sit around like drunken farmers. Get back to your cells and check your gear, then strap yourselves in for the warp jump.' His words were fierce but his tone belied them. He knew as well as they did that their gear was already stowed and checked.

'Any word on what we can expect when we get there, sergeant?' asked Aenar.

'War,' said Hakon. 'Now off to your cells. Move!'

FOUR

THE ECHO OF the warning klaxon faded. They had left the immaterium. Ragnar shook his head. This time the disorientation of emerging from the warp was greater than any he had experienced. His whole body tingled and his senses shrieked. He felt as if he had been stretched on a rack. He had heard that no two warp jumps were ever the same, but this was the first time he had ever received such definitive proof of it. The whole ship had shivered like a whipped beast for what seemed like days. The hull had shuddered as if some evil god had smote it with a hammer.

Here and there he could make out new dents in the armour plate of the walls. He had no idea what could have made them, and he was not sure he wanted to find out. He was just glad they had arrived.

The ship suddenly shook once more. He was tossed forward and had it not been for his restraining harness, he would probably have fallen, Space Wolf reflexes or no. What was going on? The alarm horn sounded, a long ululating blast that every fibre of his being responded to. The ship was under attack!

What had happened? Had some monster followed them out of the immaterium? Had they encountered pirates or a Chaos fleet? Even as these thoughts flashed through his mind, the air above the terminal altar flickered and the face of the Navigator, the tall slender woman he had seen earlier with Logan Grimnar, appeared.

'All crew: we are being attacked from vector alpha-alpha-twelve by enemy craft, presumed to be traitors. They are attempting to prevent us achieving orbit around Garm. In His name, they will be denied.'

Despite the pounding of his hearts, Ragnar forced himself to keep calm, unhooked himself from the restraint harness of his bunk and hurried across to the altar. This was his first real opportunity to witness a space battle, and he was determined not to miss it. After all, it might easily also prove his last. He might die here in an instant, the ship surrounding him vaporised by the terrible destructive energies being unleashed all around them.

Ragnar crouched before the altar terminal and made the invocations. The holosphere shimmered and became a three dimensional representation of the space around the *Fist of Russ*. Blue teardrops represented the ships of the Space Wolf fleet. The red points of light must be the enemy vessels. Other distant points in a lighter blue were, doubtless, ships belonging to another Imperial force.

The lights flickered and an eerie booming sound vibrated through the air. It was either the ship's shields absorbing an attack, or a power drain caused by the primary armaments being activated. His hands danced across the keyboard runes, his invocations to the spirits of information came so fast as to be almost garbled. Suddenly he achieved what he was aiming for, a pure unfettered communion between himself and the machine. Ragnar hooked himself into the flow of information passing through the ship's central nervous system. This was the same tide of data that the pilots, gunners and Navigators responded to. In his case, there was nothing he could do to alter the flow. He could only watch enthralled, his eyes riveted to the holosphere, as the *Fist of Russ* raced into battle.

He could see that the sky was filled with ships. A monstrous red sphere represented a space hulk. Amazement filled him. Those evil structures got everywhere, drawn to battle and war as inevitably as vultures to carrion. How did they manage it? Did some daemon god guide them? He dismissed the thought and concentrated on the work at hand, plucking information out of the datastream.

He could see that the Chaos ships were mostly huge battleships and cruisers. Massive, heavily armed, not particularly manoeuvrable, but then they did not need to be. They relied on the terrifying hitting power of their weaponry. Superficially they bore a resemblance to the Imperial warships they had once been, but over the millennia they had altered and mutated just like their crews. One of the Chaos ships had peeled off and was closing determinedly on the *Fist of Russ*. Other enemy cruisers appeared to be doing the same with the remaining Space Wolf craft. It was a challenge to which there could only be one response, although Ragnar was not sure it was the correct one.

Had he been in charge of the Fenrisian fleet, he would have grouped his ships in order to concentrate their fire power against a single foe and engaged the enemy one at a time, picking them off individually. Instead, the great ships were responding like Fenrisian warriors challenged to single combat, pairing off with their chosen foes, and making ready for battle. It was like watching a battle of dragon ships back home on the world ocean of Fenris.

Ragnar smiled savagely. It was all very well coming up with a superior plan, but a field commander has to work with the troops he has available, and take into account their likely response. In the case of the Space Wolves, this was entirely predictable. They would fight their duels, and only then, with victory achieved, would they go to each other's aid. Ragnar shook his head. The pride of a Fenrisian warrior was a great strength as well as a weakness. Fortunately it

appeared their foes felt the same way. Either that or their
captains were so insane that they no longer had a grasp of
sound tactics.

He studied the oncoming ship as more details became
available. The image expanded to fill the holosphere. It was
incredibly large, a massive structure of metal and ceramite,
crudely riveted together. Massive cables snaked across its
side, spitting sparks as they overloaded. It reminded Ragnar
of the carnivorous fish of the Fenrisian sea: a barakuda or a
ripper. Massive turrets lined the upper dorsal spine. Some of
those weapons already belched fire although the range was
too great for them to do much damage. The heretics were
not ones for conserving energy.

At this range, the *Fist of Russ* had superior weaponry. Its
nova cannon was capable of doing huge damage. Ragnar
could tell that their pilot's strategy was to keep as much distance as possible between the two ships and use the
Imperial vessel's superior ranged capability to pummel the
foe into submission.

For the moment, as far as he could tell, it appeared to be
working. Energy bolts chipped away at the screens surrounding the enemy vessel. Whenever they made contact,
the shields flared and brightened. Sometimes a pale blue
glow spread across the energy barrier like ripples on a pond.
Sometimes huge thunderous sparks of energy danced along
the side of the heretic ship, turning armour to cherry red,
molten slag.

It was a thrilling sight but somehow dissatisfying. This
was not how combat should be. A Space Wolf should be in
the thick of battle, smiting his foe, not watching the discharge of mountain-shattering energies on a holosphere.

It appeared that the heretic captain was not about to sit
still for the Fenrisian's tactics. He turned his vessel head on
towards the Space Wolf ship, and suddenly the sensors
recorded an enormous discharge of energy from the rear of
the vessel. Readouts raced into the red. For a moment, it
looked like one of the *Fist's* shots had hit the reactor or done
some other critical form of damage. Any second, Ragnar

expected to see the enemy ship fly apart, wracked by a terrible explosion.

It did not. Instead it began to lurch forward, moving with ever-increasing velocity, closing the gap between the vessels with a speed that the *Fist of Russ* could not match. The heretic crew were overloading their engines, taking an awful risk with their drives in order to close with their foe. Mouth dry, Ragnar watched as the gap closed. Surely soon the Chaos cruiser would be in range to annihilate the *Fist of Russ* with one blast of its awesome batteries.

The *Fist's* pilot had anticipated the enemy's move, and the Imperial ship veered erratically on an evasive course, which only let their opponent close the distance quicker. The enemy ship opened fire. The *Fist of Russ* shuddered under the impact of multiple blasts.

Red warning lights blazed on the cell wall, a klaxon sounded loudly. The steel of the deck vibrated beneath Ragnar's feet. He could hear bulkheads slam shut and the hurricane roar of air being sucked out into the void of space. He felt the ambient temperature leap as a whole section of the hull must have been reduced to slag.

The holosphere winked out. The lights flickered and died. For a moment, the only sound was the twisting of metal and the eerie whine of the great fans that circulated air within the ship spinning to a halt. Darkness filled the cell. Ragnar could smell panic in the air. If the *Fist of Russ* lost power, they were dead, a sitting duck to be reduced to their component atoms by the enemy's next blast. This was not the way he had expected to meet his death.

He bounded to his feet and made ready to race into the corridor. He was not sure what he was going to do, but every instinct in him revolted against sitting quietly and awaiting doom. Every fibre of his being demanded that he do something, anything, in the face of inevitable death. The beast within him howled its protest against such a fate.

A heartbeat later the lights flickered back on, dimmer, partially extinguished in places. The holosphere glowed and returned. In it, Ragnar could see that the *Fist of Russ* had swung around and was arcing towards the enemy ship. Its image looked very damaged. The heretics continued to fire, although sporadically, without the super-violent intensity of their opening salvo, and, even as Ragnar watched, that firing ceased, like the last few raindrops of a storm pattering sullenly into the ground. Even so, the *Fist of Russ* boomed and echoed and shuddered under the impact a few seconds later.

What was going on? An instant later the answer smacked Ragnar in the face. The Chaos worshippers were going to board them. They were going to try and take the crippled Imperial vessel as a prize. Ragnar found himself thanking Russ for the savagery and greed of the heretics. They were offering him a chance at a warrior's death, rather than a simple annihilation. An instant later, a broadcast across the comm-net made him even more grateful. It was the booming jovial voice of Berek Thunderfist, filled with confidence and a wild joy in being alive.

+All Wolves report to the forward bore-tube. We are going to teach these Chaos-worshipping scum a lesson.+

Ragnar paused for a last glance at the holosphere and saw exactly what he expected. The *Fist of Russ* was now driving directly towards the enemy cruiser, moving at full speed, ramming velocity.

Sparks of light lit the corridor as a crewman frantically tried to weld closed a blazing power conduit. Ragnar raced along, to be joined by Sven. The other Blood Claw had a chainsword in one hand and a bolt pistol in the other. He looked ready for trouble.

'Well, Ragnar, are you ready to teach the heretics a bloody lesson?' Sven asked jovially. He sounded for all the world like a man engaged in some enjoyable recreation, not one trapped on a crippled starcraft racing towards an inevitable collision with a much larger foe.

'I most certainly am. How about you?'

'They will not find a better bloody teacher. I wonder if old Berek has a plan or whether he is making this up as he goes along.'

A massive fist emerged from a doorway and clipped Sven around the ear. It was followed by Sergeant Hakon. 'The Wolf Lord undoubtedly has a plan, just like he has more brains in his arse than you have in that empty cave you call a head. I have followed Berek Thunderfist out of far tighter scrapes than this! Now follow me! Battle awaits!'

The sergeant took the lead as they barrelled along the corridor. Ahead of them someone had opened a postern gate through one of the bulkheads. As they reached it, Strybjorn emerged from a side corridor. He too was armed and ready for combat. In his mind's eye, Ragnar tried to visualise how close they must be to the enemy ship and found that he did not have a clue. The *Fist of Russ* shuddered once more, like a man in the grip of breakbone fever, as another blast smashed into it. For a moment, Ragnar found himself tumbling through the air, as the artificial gravity failed, then training took over, and he cartwheeled, kicked himself off the walls and followed his comrades through the postern at increased speed.

He felt as if he was swimming, pushing himself off the floor or ceiling or wall and hurtling headlong down the corridor like a diver. He could see that the others had holstered their weapons to give themselves a free hand to control their direction or take advantage of any rungs or other handholds. Out of the corner of his eye, he caught sight of other company members doing likewise as they moved along parallel corridors. It seemed like every Wolf on the ship was responding to Berek's command.

Sven and Hakon had disappeared from sight The corridor ended in a steel ladder, metal rungs set in the wall. He cartwheeled again to bring his legs around and absorb the impact, then piked forward, grabbed a rung and pulled himself upwards. Above him he could see Sven's boots. Below him he could sense Strybjorn duplicate his own manoeuvre.

Ten heartbeats later he emerged into a long gunnery hall. Sweating men rammed massive cartridges into the maws of huge weapons. Teams of gunners responded to the bellowed instructions of their officers. Each of the weapons was larger than a Rhino APC, and most impressively, Ragnar knew these were among the least of the guns mounted by the *Fist of Russ*. At a signal, one of the gunnery officers pulled a massive lever, and a weird halo of energy surrounded the weapon as it discharged. The smell of ozone filled the air. The *Fist of Russ* was fighting back. An instant later, he had passed the weapon and joined the rest of the company in the forward boarding hall.

Ahead of him, Berek Thunderfist stood astride the mount of another great gun, flanked by Mikal and his Wolf Guard, the toughest, bravest and most highly honoured warriors in the company, each a veteran of a hundred frays. It was Ragnar's ambition to one day be worthy of joining them, but he knew he had a long way to go. You had to be a Grey Hunter of at least ten years of very distinguished service to be invited to join that select group. It had been made very clear to him on numerous occasions that they were almost as far above a lowly Blood Claw, as Berek Thunderfist himself.

Astonishingly, the Wolf Lord looked as if he was enjoying himself. His lips were split by a wide grin, revealing his enormous fangs. His booming laughter echoed round the chamber, filling all who heard it with confidence, dispelling all fears.

'Greetings, brothers!' he roared. 'In approximately two minutes and four seconds, assuming we are not all blown to hell in that time, we will make contact with our opponent. They undoubtedly think they are going to board us, and take our ship as a prize. We shall teach them a different lesson. Our ship is now aimed directly at them. The boarding beak is in position. As soon as we make contact, we are going through. The enemy is an Acheron-class cruiser and I think we can assume the schematics have not changed all that much since the Second Gorechild War. We will fight our way into the heart of the heretic ship and detonate its power core with thermo-charges.'

A roar of approval greeted this bold plan.

'The charges will be set on a variable fuse, length to be decided by the man who plants them. As soon as they are activated we will return to the *Fist of Russ* and break away. We are Space Wolves. There should be plenty of time for us to take a little stroll and kill a few Chaos worshippers on our way back. If not, if we run out of time, I will see you all in hell.'

Ragnar realised that despite Berek's jovial tone, their mission was a desperate one. It would require them to fight their way through a host of deadly warriors to the heart of an unknown vessel. There was very little chance that they would be able to make their way out again, once the charges were set. And yet, it was a plan that allowed them a chance at glory. It certainly beat being blasted into non-existence by the Chaos ship, or the ignominy of being taken captive.

'In the unlikely event that our mission fails, I have ordered the crew to arm the self-destruct sequence of the *Fist of Russ*, so one way or another we will take these bastards into hell with us.'

And assuring that there is no retreat possible either, Ragnar thought. He was reminded of those Fenrisian warlords who would burn their ships on the beaches when they arrived on a hostile island, telling their men and their foes alike that there was no retreat and no way out save through victory. It was all a very desperate gamble, yet still it appealed to him.

Which was probably why he found himself cheering like a madman along with all the others.

FIVE

SUDDENLY, THE *FIST OF RUSS* decelerated. There was a thunderous clash of metal. A rumbling vibration passed through the deck as the beaked boarding prow cleaved through the armoured hull of the enemy vessel. Ragnar held his breath involuntarily, knowing that this was one of the most difficult of all special manoeuvres. The *Fist's* captain had just a few seconds to exactly match the velocities of the two vessels or the impact would destroy them both. The grinding sound continued.

The absolute tip of the ship, a great neutronium bit, the hardest substance in the known universe, smashed through solid duralloy and steel, chewing through metal like a drill through soft wood, creating a route for them into the heart of the enemy vessel. The Space Wolves stood ready. Ahead of him, Ragnar could see Berek check the sensor on his wrist. It was doubtless set to locate the impulses of the Chaos power core. Near him, several of his Wolf Guard hoisted weapons in one hand, and massive square thermo-charges in the other. Nearby he saw Hakon and the members of his own squad checking their weapons as automatically as he was doing.

All around him, metal creaked and shuddered as the reinforced bulkheads absorbed the strain of the impact. From somewhere came the smell of blazing chemicals. Overhead, a power cable spurted a jet of sparks. It was like being trapped by an enormous accident. He breathed deeply and recited litanies of calm, determined to push the image of the two ships colliding and crumpling out of his mind, of him and his brothers being crushed to a bloody pulp.

Suddenly, the motion ceased. Ragnar knew this was an illusion created by the two vessels' velocities now being perfectly matched, but it was an illusion so compelling that it might as well have been true. Ahead of them, the neutronium bit ceased its rotation. There was a hiss and a spurt of steam or smoke as the two vessels joined and pressure attempted to equalise.

A barrage of new scents assaulted Ragnar's super-keen senses: the bitter smell of the polluted machine oil the heretics used, the odd scents created by their strange machines, all of it mingled with the weird undercurrent of unnatural life that was the hallmark of Chaos.

Ahead of them the light was dimmer and more reddish than on the *Fist of Russ*. Already the Wolves of Berek's company were racing through the boarding tunnel towards it. When his turn came Ragnar joined them.

They emerged into the Chaos ship. It was like entering a different world: everything looked colder and darker. The machinery seemed simpler and much more massive, evidently patched and repaired with whatever came to hand, stuff salvaged from wrecks and looted craft. It looked as if it were given the bare minimum of maintenance by tech-adepts who just did not care. Despite this, there was moulded metalwork done with amazing if insane skill. Embossed daemon heads leered above archways. Moulded metal claws tipped every lever and door handle.

It was madness – what kind of tech-priests would spend their time crafting ornate casings and not pay attention to the spirits they contained?

The hellish lights illuminated corridors speckled with rust and marred by huge holes and dents. The sometimes sour, sometimes sickly-sweet scent of Chaos and mutation was stronger, carried everywhere by the monstrous ventilation ducts.

Quickly, the Wolves spread out. Every sergeant had linked his locator to Berek's through the comm-net, just as his own was linked to Sergeant Hakon's. Berek and his Wolf Guard were already racing deeper into the ship. There was nothing to do but follow them.

Almost immediately they emerged into a large hall, in the centre of which loomed a massive gimbal mounted weapon. All around it milled a group of Chaos crewmen, armed with a motley assortment of weapons, led by a huge scaly-skinned mutant whose stalked eyes emerged directly from his forehead. In one hand he brandished a massive cleaver, in the other a large antique-looking gun. The crewmen were clad in what might once have been a mixture of uniforms but were now simply tattered rags. They were like an army of beggars who had garbed themselves in the tattered remnants of some defeated army.

Before the Chaos worshippers could respond, the leading Wolves were in position, blasting them with a withering hail of fire. It was a testimony to the mutants' toughness that it took a number of direct hits from bolter shells to put them down. Ragnar saw the leader keep coming, despite the fact that one of his arms had been blown off, and a bullet had passed right through his forehead, and blown half his brains right out the back of his skull.

'Bloody mutants don't need their brains to fight,' muttered Sven.

'Just like you,' Ragnar replied. He took aim with his pistol and put a bullet through the huge creature's right eye. This time it tumbled and fell, a look of blank incredulity on its brutal face, as if it could not quite understand what had happened to it.

Ragnar felt the beast stir within him, and howl with rage and battle-hunger. He fought down a rising tide of excitement that threatened to overwhelm him. It was difficult; for him, as for many Space Wolves, combat had an effect comparable to the most powerful stimulant drugs. He felt exalted. The constant flow of stimuli fed his emotions. All of the new scents and sounds, the thunder of battle, the roar of weapons, acted to feed the frenzy, as did the scent of excitement coming from his battle-brothers.

There was nothing to match this feeling. It wiped away fear, and nervousness. It increased the keenness of his senses to near unbearable levels as he scanned his surroundings for threats. There was nothing to quite compare with the feeling that your life lay in your own gauntleted hands, and that you lived or died by the keenness of your perceptions, the quickness of your reflexes, the strength of your sinews and your skill with your weapons.

Briefly, some distant detached part of his mind wondered whether this might be one of the flaws of his Chapter, a legacy of impetuousness and ferocity left by the gene-seed of Russ. Not that it mattered. He drank in the nectar of battle, sweeter than any wine.

The bolt pistol kicked in his hand once more. Before he was fully conscious of it, he had shot another enemy. A flash of pallid greyish skin caught from the corner of his eye, a blur of movement, and too quickly for the conscious mind to process it, he had spotted the threat and acted to remove it.

Like a tide of steel and ceramite, the Space Wolves raced through the Chaos craft, heading towards their goal. At their head ran Berek and his Wolf Guard. Occasionally, Ragnar would catch a glimpse of his leader in action. It was as awesome as it was revealing. Berek was a warrior of the utmost deadliness. In close combat, nothing could withstand his fury and the ancient power of his thunderous fist. He smashed through the Chaos worshippers like a steel-prowed ship cleaving a stormy sea.

Somehow, without understanding quite how it happened, Ragnar and his squad found themselves in a different corridor from the rest of the Wolves. He had vague memories of a rush from a side door, a massive bull-horned enemy barrelling into him, and a swift, savage hand-to-hand battle that ended with the enemy dead at his feet. He could remember the stink of the monster's tainted blood, and the feel of its taloned fingers on his throat as it strove to hold him in place and smite him with a power axe. He recalled vividly how his own counter-stroke had taken its hand off at the wrist, and how the corpse had seemed to dance across the floor as it tried to resist the impact of the bolter shells exploding in its chest.

He looked up and saw Sven grinning at him. His bulldog features held the same look of fierce joy that Ragnar knew must be on his own face. He grinned at Ragnar and mouthed, 'Good fighting.'

Ragnar could only agree. Now all worries and fears had fallen away. The fact that they were fighting their way ever deeper into a vessel filled with deadly enemies meant nothing. The fact that even if they reached their objective they had little chance of escape before those terrible charges detonated meant even less. Now there was only the moment, the turbulent sweep of battle and the deadly thrill of combat. Ragnar felt truly alive, running along the edge of existence.

Sergeant Hakon paused to glance at the locator on his wrist, pursed his lips and indicated that they should proceed down the corridor. Filled with excitement, Ragnar took the lead, knowing instinctively that Sven and Strybjorn were at his heels. The whole Blood Claw pack trotted in single file.

The corridor widened and gained height. Huge girders reinforced the ceiling over their heads. More daemon heads leered down. Foul altars depicting monstrous creatures marked the sites of controls. Metal stairs led up to balconies above. Ragnar kept his eyes peeled knowing that this would be a good spot for an ambush. He noted the metal doorways in the walls. Their hinges were massive. They were made from reinforced steel that looked like it had been stripped from the turret of a tank. Enormous pipes snaked along the walls. Large regulator wheels protruded from the joints where two or more of them met.

In the distance small-arms fire echoed down the corridor. It seemed like the battle continued unabated. Ragnar risked a quick glance over his shoulder to see if he should take the passage leading towards it, but Hakon shook his head. It appeared that in this massive hull, echoes were just as deceptive as they were anywhere else. He nodded acknowledgement and strode forward.

Briefly he considered what must be going on around him. All throughout this monstrous craft man and mutant were engaged in a life or death struggle. Judging by what he had seen so far, Berek had not encountered stiff resistance. Unsurprising, really, since the last thing the heretics would have expected would be for their prize to assault them. They were about to learn what it meant to do battle with Space Wolves.

Briefly, another image intruded into Ragnar's mind, of the Chaos worshippers, unaware of the attack, pressing ahead with their assault on the *Fist of Russ*. He pushed the thought aside of what would happen if the Wolves were successful in blowing up the ship, and then returned to their own ship, only to find it held against them. That was a bridge they would burn when they came to it, as Sven would say.

From up ahead, he caught sight of the bright muzzle flash of bolters, and heard the unmistakable howling of battle-cries. He picked up his pace, emerging onto a high metal balcony that looked down onto some sort of vehicle storage hangar. Beneath him Ragnar could see row upon row of massive tanks, studded with spikes and stained with vile insignia of Chaos. The coarse glow of the ceiling lights bathed the area in ruddy light, illuminating the fierce battle that was taking place.

A group of Space Wolves was pinned down behind one of the tanks, surrounded on all sides by bands of howling mutants, cut off from Space Wolf support. Ragnar smiled. As fate would have it, he had emerged on the balcony above and behind the largest group of mutants, putting him in the perfect position to attack them from the rear and ease the pressure on the embattled Wolves. Not one of the creatures had noticed him yet. He touched the grenade dispenser on his belt and allowed a few of the lethal metal eggs to drop into his palm. He set the fuse of the first and tossed it, lobbing the rest in quick succession.

Huge explosions rent mutant flesh. Gobbets of enemy meat flew in all directions. Tainted blood sprayed their cover. Almost out of grenades Ragnar opened up with his bolt pistol. Moments later, he was joined by Sergeant Hakon and the rest of the Blood Claw pack who added their contribution to the hail of fire.

The heretics were thrown into utter confusion, suddenly finding themselves under assault by an unknown number of foes from an unexpected direction. They were brave though, Ragnar had to give them that. Some of them turned, seeking the source of the danger. One of them, a massive mutant, a giant really, twice the size of all the others, bellowed instructions to his fellows. Ragnar saw him grab one of his men and push him roughly forward. The fellow fell flat on his face and for a second, Ragnar had a clear shot at the leader. He took advantage of the moment, and snapped off a burst of fire that took the leader in the head, below the helmet. The mutant's face exploded, and for a second his torso stood there, still waving encouragement to his followers, before toppling forward onto his sprawling minion who let out an enormous, demoralising scream of terror. It was too much for the other mutants, who scattered in all directions seeking cover from the menace at their rear.

Ragnar saw the opportunity he had been waiting for. He ignited a flare and leapt up from behind the cover of the balcony's metal banister, and sent a fixed-beam transmission on the comm-net to the trapped Space Wolves. The flare stick crackled in his hand, and Ragnar felt his gauntlets heat slightly.

+You down there! There is a way out of the trap! Get your sorry arses up here quickly! Look for the flare!+

He put every ounce of command he could into his voice, hoping that whoever was down there would have enough sense to respond.

They did. As Ragnar had hoped, they were quick to see a way out of their predicament. Instantly, as a pack, they broke from their cover and headed in Ragnar's direction, storming through the remains of the broken mutant band. Ragnar felt a thrill of pride. He had just helped save the lives of some of his battle-brothers.

A massive hand smote him on the shoulder, and knocked him back down into cover. Ragnar snarled and turned to see Sergeant Hakon glaring at him. 'You did well there, Ragnar, but there's no sense dancing around making a target of yourself with that flare.'

Ragnar suppressed a growl, and forced the beast back down within him. He could see the sense of the sergeant's words. He had let his own exaltation blind him to the harsh realities of the situation. He nodded and Hakon grinned. He gestured at Ragnar to toss the flare back down the corridor. He did not want Ragnar to throw it in any direction where the retreating Wolves might see it, and be misled. Ragnar obeyed. Hakon nodded. 'Right. Let's give the Wolf Lord and his retinue some covering fire, shall we?'

The Wolf Lord, Ragnar thought? Was that who had been down there? Ragnar thought he might not have used such a peremptory tone if he had known. He shrugged, thinking there was nothing he could do about it now, then leapt up into a shooting crouch and sent another burst of fire into the oncoming Chaos horde.

SIX

RAGNAR COULD SEE now that the men coming up the stairs were indeed Wolf Guard. Normally he would have been able to recognise them by the heavy Terminator armour they wore, but now they were garbed in the standard armour of Space Marines. Doubtless there had not been time to don their wargear when the order to ram was given. Not that they seemed to mind; they were all of them large, fell-looking men, grinning at the prospect of a good fight. Ragnar could smell no anxiety, despite the closeness of the call, only keenness and a desire to shed blood once more.

Sensing eyes on him, Ragnar turned and saw that Berek was looking at him. He realised that the Wolf Lord knew exactly who it was who had so insolently called orders to him. He forced himself to meet Berek's gaze, and to his surprise saw that the Wolf Lord was grinning as he strolled over to him.

'That was quick thinking, lad,' he said, 'and you have my gratitude. The company might have been building a funeral pyre for Berek Thunderfist this very day if you had not intervened, and I am not yet ready to greet my predecessors. I will not forget this, Ragnar.'

Ragnar was even more surprised that the great Wolf Lord had remembered who he was, and felt a surge of pride at this acknowledgement. Berek turned to Hakon and bellowed, 'It's good to see that you have taught your cubs how to bite, Hakon. Now, let's get on with this.'

Ragnar risked another glance at the veterans of the Wolf Guard. He was surprised that he could count only five of them, including Morgrim and Mikal Stenmark. Surely, the rest of those powerful warriors could not be dead? Morgrim caught his glance and seemed to read his mind.

'Our force was cut in two by the ambush,' said the skald. His speaking voice was hoarse and rough and quiet, completely at odds with the clarity and range of his singing. Ragnar noted that silver hair framed his long lean face. His eyes were a strange gold colour. 'The others were driven back through the doorway by a hail of fire. I am certain they have joined up with the rest of our force.'

Ragnar nodded, considering this. He was not entirely sure of the wisdom of the Wolf Lord's decision to lead the vanguard of his force into battle. No one could doubt his bravery but… He shrugged. It was not for him to judge the likes of Berek Thunderfist. If the Wolf Lord chose to lead his troops in the traditional Fenrisian manner that was his business.

Morgrim clapped him on the shoulderpad of his armour. 'No time for wool-gathering, boy. We better get to the heart of this tub before the heretics realise what we are about.'

With that he lengthened his stride, and followed the rest of Wolves into the depths of the ship. Ragnar followed, knowing that he had got all the praise he was going to get for his exploits.

They emerged into a larger gallery. Looking down into the vast space Ragnar could see a massed horde of Chaos warriors assembling, far too many to fight. Like the others he ducked back into the shadows to avoid being seen. He was astounded by the size of the vessel on which they moved and fought. Brought up among the barbarian islanders of Fenris, the word 'ship' had certain connotations in his mind. It conjured up an image of a dragonship, one of the longboats made from the hide and bones of the monstrous sea-going lizards his people hunted. They were perhaps fifty strides long with benches for twenty oarsmen on each side. To some part of his mind, that still was a ship.

This was something else. It seemed larger than any structure ought be, bigger even than one of the vast starscrapers he had seen on Aerius. Entire islands from the world sea of Fenris could have been lost within it. It was a labyrinth large enough to swallow the entire island on which he had grown up.

Ahead, Berek had gestured for them to stop. Ragnar paused just quickly enough to avoid bumping into Sven's back. 'What are they saying, Morgrim?' Berek asked.

'They believe about ten thousand warriors have boarded their ship and are trying to take it from them. They are making ready to repel boarders,' said Morgrim, amusement was evident in his soft voice. The Wolf Guard laughed quietly. The Blood Claws joined in, more to take part than because they understood the joke. It dawned on Ragnar that Morgrim must have patched himself into the heretics' own comm-net and must be able to understand their twisted language. For the first time he understood how very useful this skill was to have. If they survived this, he would ask Morgrim how he had managed it.

'They plan to sweep through the corridors en masse, catching us in the jaws of a trap.'

'We must hurry on then,' said Berek, 'and find the power core before they pin us down again.' He sub-vocalised orders into the comm-net, giving instructions to all of the other squad leaders on the sealed command channels. He spoke so quietly that not even Ragnar's hyper-acute hearing could pick up the words.

Mikal Stenmark checked the sensor unit on his wrist. 'We are not more than five hundred metres from the power core now, Lord Berek.'

'Aye, Mikal, so I can see, but who knows how long it will take us to get there? Those five hundred metres are by the straightest route. These corridors might wind for leagues before we get to the core.'

'Then best we start soon, lord,' said Stenmark cheerfully.

'My thoughts exactly, Mikal. Let us be moving before those Chaos worshippers down there realise we're here and try and treat us to a tasty meal of hot bolter shell.'

Judging by the roars and bellows from below, the heretics would be only too happy to oblige. Ragnar could see some sort of cloaked priest or officer was whipping them up into a frenzy. There was a sense of ominous power about the man that Ragnar had come to associate with sorcery.

As they moved, Morgrim kept up a running commentary that let Ragnar follow the flow of the battle. It now looked as if the crew of the *Fist of Russ* had managed to stall the Chaos intruders, and it appeared as if the confused heretics were doing their best to hunt down the Wolves who had boarded their own vessel. They were under the impression that they were under attack by a much larger force than was actually the case. As he listened to the skald, Ragnar deduced that Berek had ordered his company to split up into their component squads and spread as much mayhem as possible, to perform hit and run attacks, and avoid becoming bogged down in firefights they could not possibly win.

As he listened, Ragnar became aware of countless tales of heroism and valour. It appeared that Varig's squad had managed to trap a huge warband of heretics by attacking it from two sides at once and blowing up both ends of a corridor with demolition charges.

Hef's lads had managed to extricate themselves from being encircled by a hugely superior Chaos force by crawling out through the airvents, leaving proximity fused mines to destroy the heretics when they eventually investigated their abandoned position.

Ferek's squad had managed to fight all the way to one of the magazines before being driven back by a withering hail of fire from the defenders. It was possible that if they had succeeded they might actually have been able to blow themselves and perhaps the ship to the other end of the galaxy, so Ragnar was relieved they had failed. There was such a thing as being too enthusiastic, he decided.

The heretics were well and truly confused. As they raced along near abandoned corridors, Morgrim gleefully quoted a Chaos commander claiming to have encountered forces numbering in the hundreds, while Hef reported that the two wings of the Chaos force were being caught in their own crossfire, confused by the smoke of the explosions.

It appeared that in situations like this there were advantages to being a small, compact, well-organised and disciplined force. Ragnar was not sure how much longer their luck would hold but right now things seemed to be going better than he would ever have imagined possible.

He looked over to see if the other Blood Claws were paying attention. In the flickering light of the glow-globes, he could see Aenar looked both worried and exalted in equal measure. His eyes were wide and his mouth hung half open. A frown of near ludicrous concentration marred his brow. He was obviously intimidated by being under the eye of the legendary Wolf Lord as much as at being caught up in his first shipboard action. Torvald looked surprisingly calm under the circumstances, gazing around with a sardonic expression fixed firmly on his face. If not for his scent, Ragnar would never have guessed that he was as nervous as Aenar. Strybjorn looked as grim as always, his brooding features carved from rock. Sven grinned cheerily back at Ragnar. Hakon looked relaxed and confident.

Up ahead Ragnar could see a greenish glow. The scent of the air changed. It tasted now of ozone, and there was a charge to it that made the hairs on the nape of his neck rise. As they emerged into the power core of the Chaos ship he half expected to see that they had entered the boiler room of some mighty steam engine. He was not entirely disappointed.

Enormous cast metal engines towered above them, disappearing into the shadowy recesses of the cavernous ceiling far above. High atop each of them was a huge steely sphere clutched by a massive brazen claw set on a copper spike. As the sphere rotated, greenish lightning flickered across its surface. Every now and again, there was a thunderclap of noise, and a lightning bolt leapt from the sphere to impact on the massive metal tower in the centre of the room. At the top of this tower rotated the largest of the moving spheres, all but invisible behind the curtain of power bolts that danced across its surface. The thunderclaps almost drowned out the roar of the great engines.

On the nearest engine Ragnar could see rotating cogwheels, the smallest of which was larger than his body, the biggest of which was the size of a dragonship. They were fouled with rust, and dripped oil. Occasionally from a massive pipe a burst of superheated steam emerged with a noise like a huge kettle whistling. Ragnar wondered whether even the Chaos engineers who had built this strange device could know exactly what every component did. Maybe. He heard Mikal mutter, 'How can this work? This is not a power core. It's more like a factory.'

'This is the power core, my friend,' said Berek. 'Unless my sensor is totally malfunctioning.'

'It looks like no core I have ever seen.'

'I doubt that you have seen every form of power core in the galaxy, old friend.'

'You are right, Wolf Lord, yet… it is all so alien, so strange.'

Ragnar could see what the man meant. His skin tingled. There was something in the eerie radiance from those machines that made his flesh creep.

'The thing is unshielded and seems to use tainted fuel,' said Morgrim. 'No wonder so many of the crew are mutated.'

'It will be scrap by the time we've finished with it. Oleg, Korwin, set those charges. The rest of you keep your eyes peeled and your noses twitching. This is a big place, but I doubt the Chaos worshippers have left it unguarded.'

As if in answer to the Wolf Lord's statement, a bellow of rage filled the air. Ragnar turned and saw an enormous heretic, garbed in some sort of soiled uniform, a crab-like pincer on the end of his right arm. The mutant glared at them in fury, bellowing instructions to several squads of burly followers.

'Looks like we've another bloody fight on our hands,' said Sven, diving behind the cover of the nearest large machine. Ragnar followed him, a hail of bolter fire sparking off the steel plates of the floor behind his feet. 'At least the Chaos worshippers are good for something.'

'More than can be said for you,' said Ragnar, ducking low around the corner and snapping off a shot with his bolt pistol. The shell whizzed past the ear of a charging heretic. His comrades returned fire, forcing Ragnar back into cover.

'That wasn't very clever, Ragnar,' said Sven. 'You might have lost your head. No great loss admittedly but–'

'You lot follow me!' barked Sergeant Hakon, rushing down the corridor away from the central aisle.

'I think the sergeant has an idea,' said Sven, as Strybjorn, Aenar and Torvald headed off in Hakon's wake.

'Probably means to circle this generator and flank the heretics,' said Ragnar.

'I worked that out for myself,' said Sven, rushing after the rest of the squad.

'It's sometimes hard to tell.'

Ahead of them a large flight of metal stairs rose along the side of the structure, disappearing out of sight around its curved bulk. It was a maintenance walkway, designed to give access to the core, but it could be used for other things. Hakon led the Blood Claws up the stairs. Moments later, Ragnar found himself circling the structure with a good view of the battle spread out below him. The Wolf Guard had taken up position behind several of the smaller Chaos engines and blasted away at an oncoming tide of heretics and mutants. They shot with a calm precision, making every shot count, keeping up a hail of fire that twice the number of Chaos worshippers would have been hard pressed to match. Many deaths rewarded their efforts, but not enough. For every foe who fell there was always another to take his place, and they were closing the ground with the outnumbered Wolf Guard swiftly.

'Grenades!' ordered Hakon. Instinctively Ragnar obeyed, squeezing the frag grenade dispenser on his belt. A small oval egg of death dropped into his palm. He set the timer for three seconds and lobbed it into the oncoming mass of heretics. Heartbeats later the rest of the Blood Claws did the same. Severed limbs flew everywhere as flesh was ripped to gobbets. Mutant blood and bile flooded the floor. Incredibly, several of the huge wounded creatures kept coming despite having lost arms or legs. Ragnar could see one armless giant roaring with rage more than pain racing towards Berek. Another missing both legs pulled itself onwards with its arms. One less wounded hopped forward, the stump of one leg leaving a stream of blood behind it.

The remaining heretics glared around to see where the attack had come from until their pincer-clawed leader roared orders and they advanced forward once more. Ragnar readied himself for another salvo of grenades when he became aware that the metal platform on which they stood was vibrating. Shots raised sparks around his feet. He glanced up and saw that another group of heretics had emerged onto a higher platform on the side of the great machine opposite them. They were pouring bolter fire down onto the Blood Claw position. It seemed Sergeant Hakon was not the only one with an idea of sound tactics.

Ragnar saw Aenar fall. An exploding bolter shell had sheared away a chunk of ceramite from the shoulder pad of his armour, exposing red raw flesh below. The young Blood Claw tumbled forward onto his hands and knees. Ragnar made a grab for him, catching him before he could go over the edge of the platform. Aenar looked up at him and smiled weakly. Ragnar glanced around. Sven and the others were already returning fire on the heretics above them, but it was a one-sided battle. They were too badly outnumbered.

Ragnar helped Aenar to his feet. Blood from the wound splashed his armour, but the flow was already starting to slow down as Aenar's re-engineered body began to heal itself. Holding his wounded comrade with his left arm, Ragnar snapped off a shot with his right, as they headed back round the corner and out of the enemy's line of sight.

Now he sensed the metal staircase vibrating with the weight of many booted feet, and he caught the acrid stink of mutants nearby. Apparently they were not the only ones who had decided this ledge would make a good spot for an ambush. Either that or the heretics had guessed they would use it for an attack position, and had divided their forces, one part to pin the Blood Claws down, while the other part closed.

He glanced at Aenar and saw that he too had heard the approaching enemy. As gently as he could Ragnar let go of the wounded man and drew his chainsword. He was going to need both weapons if he was going to keep his companions from being overwhelmed. A quick glance at Aenar reassured him. The younger Blood Claw slapped a synthiflesh plaster on his wound, and proceeded to seal the breach in his armour with repair cement. Behind him, the other squad members were backing into view, keeping up a continuous rain of fire on their attackers. Ragnar wondered if they were aware of the new threat approaching, or whether they were too distracted by the firefight. Not that it mattered; it looked like it fell to him to do something about it.

He sensed the heretics were already nearing the head of the stairs, and would soon emerge onto the platform. There was nothing for it now, but headlong assault. He rushed forward and leapt into the air, letting momentum carry him downwards. As he did so his stomach lurched. Below him he could see dozens of hideously mutated faces leering up at him.

SEVEN

RAGNAR TWISTED IN the air, kicking both feet into the chest of the lead heretic. Not even the mutant's massive musculature could protect it from the power of the blow driven with all the force created by his running jump, augmented muscles and the carapace's hydraulic systems. Ribs snapped, and the heretic was propelled back into the ones behind it, sending them tumbling back down the stairway. At the same time, the force of the kick killed Ragnar's velocity and allowed him to land nimbly on the stairs.

One swift look told him the situation. The mutants were in disarray; one of them had been driven completely off the edge of the stairs and sent tumbling to the hard metal floor below. Another had saved himself by clutching onto the guard-rail as he went over, and now hung on like grim death with one hand, as his legs and free arm flailed for purchase.

Ragnar brought his chainsword down, severing fingers and sending the wretch crashing downwards to join his fellow in death, then sprang forward once more while the mutants were off-balance.

With one stroke, he severed the head of the leading heretic; another stroke split his body in two. Pressed back by falling bodies, the mutants were unable to bring their close combat weapons to bear effectively. Ragnar struck again and again, using his superior elevation and momentum to great effect. The chainsword reaped heretic lives like a scythe swathing corn. The bolt pistol in his left hand spat death into the faces of the mutants beyond.

He could see one or two of the bolder mutants trying to press the ones in front forward. He aimed at them through the gap, blasting one heretic skull to fragments. He chopped at the enemy in front of him. It managed to parry, barely, with its power axe. The teeth of Ragnar's chainsword screeched against the metal pole of the axe, sparks rose where metal met metal. Ragnar twisted his blade round, moving it over the obstruction and burying it in the heretic's throat. A swift left-right movement had the head hanging by a flap of neck muscle. A kick sent the near-decapitated body tumbling headlong into the heretics behind.

It was too much for the mutants. Hampered by the press of their numbers and the falling bodies of their friends, they knew they were no match for the ferocious reaver striding among them. At that moment, Ragnar was a sight to make the bravest heart quail. Covered in blood and brains, moving almost too fast for the eye to follow, slaughtering half a dozen Chaos worshippers in as many heartbeats. The survivors turned to flee back down the stairs. It was then the killing really began. Ragnar pounced like a wolf springing on its prey, smashing his blade through the heretics' undefended backs, severing spines, rupturing spleens, painting the stairway with blood.

The screams of his victims encouraged the remaining mutants to run faster, panic more furiously. They smote each other in their desperation to get away, tripped over the bodies of those they had backstabbed, and stunned themselves as they fell headlong down the stairs. Ragnar saw that he was not going to be able to overtake them quickly enough to kill them all. Instead, he holstered his chainsword and snatched up a bolt pistol from one of the fallen. Pistol in each hand, he braced himself with a leg on either side of the banister and slid down, blasting away with both weapons. Firing into the panicking mass, every shell took its toll, slamming into tightly packed bodies and exploding to cause the maximum damage.

On the way down Ragnar managed to overtake a few of the fleeing Chaos lovers and put shells into them. They fell, hampering their brethren more. Seeing the bottom of the stairs coming, he braced himself and hit the ground rolling, still firing, his superhuman reflexes and quickness of eye enabling him to hit with more than half the shots. At the end of the roll, he dropped the traitor's pistol and unsheathed his chainsword once more, leaping into the fray like an unleashed god of war.

His blade described an enormous arc, cleaving flesh and bone, sending the wounded reeling. His bolt pistol finished off the fallen. A downward stamp of his armoured boot broke a neck. A red haze dropped over his vision now. All of his foes appeared to be moving with painful slowness. He saw one heretic frantically trying to draw a bead on him with a bolter, dropped to his knees out of the line of fire and sprang forward, bearing down onto another heretic, carrying it forward as a shield of flesh, feeling its body flex and spasm as its fellow's bolter shells ripped into its body. Then when his animal keen nostrils told him he was within striking distance. He tossed the heretic's still twitching corpse at the shooter and followed it through himself.

The heavy body sent the mutant with the gun sprawling. A look of panic crossed its fur-covered bestial features. A kick to the taloned hand sent the weapon hurtling into the distance, a downward stroke sent the heretic to hell.

The berserkergang was on Ragnar now, in full flow. He smote left and right with awful power, the meat-cleaver sound of his chainsword on flesh telling him he did damage with every blow. He lost all track of time and sense of self, becoming an unleashed whirlwind of death and destruction that smashed through the panicking mutants with all the fury of a Fenrisian thunderstorm. He lived only to kill, and he took action to preserve his own life only in so far as it would allow him to slay more. A few shells ricocheted off his armour. He ignored them. A few desperate mutants managed to land glancing blows before he sent them to greet their dark gods. He did not feel them.

He stormed through the survivors hacking and chopping at exposed flesh, blasting with his pistol at point blank range. A god-like sense of exaltation filled him. He ducked and weaved beneath blows, struck with the speed of a lightning bolt. Nothing slowed him down, nothing stopped him.

Suddenly all was still around him. He glared around looking for new prey, and saw only a few wounded. Those who had fled had managed to get out of his sight. He stood panting, blood dripping from his armour and his blade, and bared his teeth. A triumphant howl erupted from his throat and echoed eerily throughout the halls.

The rest of the squad headed down the stairs. Aenar was on his feet once more, moving under his own power. He held a bolt pistol in his unwounded hand, his right arm held stiff by his side. Behind him came Sven, Torvald and Strybjorn. Sergeant Hakon brought up the rear. Aenar and Torvald looked at him with something like awe. The sergeant looked grimly satisfied. Sven grinned cheerfully.

'Bloody hell, Ragnar,' he said. 'You might have left some for us.'

Ragnar realised that the sounds of shooting in the distance had stopped. Did this mean the Wolf Lord and his bodyguard were dead or triumphant, he wondered? Hakon seemed to sense his mood. They began moving around the huge metal structure, back in the direction they had last seen their company's leader.

As the battle site came into view, Ragnar saw that the Wolf Guard had wreaked even more havoc than he had. Dead mutants lay sprawled everywhere. Berek Thunderfist sat atop a pile of corpses inspecting the severed head of the Chaos leader. The mutant's face looked more daemonic than human. Curved ram's horns emerged from the forehead. The lobeless ears were pointed. Sharp fangs filled the wide mouth.

Several more squads of Wolves had entered the power core and had obviously moved in support of their leader. High atop the various metal towers, Wolf Guard magnetically clamped their demolition charges into place.

Berek looked up. 'Just in time, Hakon,' he said. 'We're almost done here. It's time to head back to the *Fist*.'

The Wolf Lord rose to his feet and discarded the mutant's head without a second thought. He looked over his assembled troops, as if gauging their level of injury. 'You've done well, men,' he said. 'But this was the easy part. It took us twenty-seven minutes to fight our way in here. But now we know the way out, I think we can get back in around half that time.'

He gazed up and saw that all of the Wolf Guard had finished and were coming down from their perches. 'We have fifteen minutes to get back to the *Fist*. Don't get bogged down in any firefights. Don't get carried away killing any heretic scum. Don't stop for loot. The *Fist of Russ* will make its withdrawal in exactly fifteen minutes from when I activate the detonators. I am giving the signal now. *Let's go!*'

Berek pushed a command button on the back of his armoured fist. Ragnar heard a weird eerie cry echo over the comm-net. Everybody knew it was time to be on his way. As one, the Wolves turned and raced from the power core of the doomed ship.

Ragnar glanced at the chronometer superimposed on his vision by the systems within his armour. It was set on a countdown now, ticking off the minutes and the seconds till the charges detonated and the Chaos cruiser was blown to pieces. Thirteen minutes and twenty-six seconds to go.

'What happens if the mutants find the bloody charges we left behind? Think they can defuse them?' Sven panted next to him.

'No. First they will have to work out what we were doing. Then they will have to find all the charges. Since they were proximity shielded that means they'll have to carry out a visual search – they won't show up on sensors. Then they will have to defuse them all. I doubt that can be done in the remaining thirteen minutes or so.'

'Let's hope so, and let's hope that they don't set a few off trying to disarm them either. That will cook our goose as nicely as any Chaos bloody ambush!'

'You're just full of good cheer today, Sven.'

'Somebody has to bloody well keep morale up around here.'

Ragnar looked around. Aenar looked a little pale and he weaved as he ran. Perhaps his wound was worse than it appeared.

'You all right?' Ragnar asked. Aenar grinned weakly.

'He will be fine,' said Hakon. 'Just you keep your eyes peeled for any mutants. Last thing we want is to be cut off in this metal maze when the *Fist of Russ* breaks free.'

'But sergeant,' said Sven, 'we are Space Wolves. Shouldn't we be seeking a hero's death?'

'Nothing heroic about getting yourself blown up, boy. Stupid, yes. Heroic, no. Not that I would expect you to be able to tell the difference.'

Sven grinned cheerily. If it was not for his scent, Ragnar would never have guessed that he was as nervous as he himself. From up ahead came the sounds of battle.

'Ambush!' said Hakon.

'Good, a bloody battle,' said Sven.

Nine minutes and forty-five seconds. Ragnar wasted a second inspecting the corpses. They lay sprawled everywhere, mingled with the dead bodies of a few Wolves. The mutants were an odd bunch. Most looked normal save that their flesh was covered in boils or warts or their hair had fallen out in clumps. Some had scaly skin or fur. Some were more bestial with bird-like talons instead of hands and feet. Some had faces where the flesh had run together like melted wax.

Ragnar saw a couple of the Wolves collecting gene-seed from the fallen, driving the armoured punches into the chests of the dead, twisting the collar on the top of the punch to open and close the grabbing claws, ripping the tiny tentacled egg from the chest cavity. Even as he watched, the punch's claws enfolded the gene-seed completely and sucked it into a stasis tube, to be hooked onto the collector's belt. Another ten seconds gone, he thought. Best be moving.

Morgrim Silvertongue had broken comm-silence. He had hooked himself into the Chaos net and was translating orders from the enemy leaders as they passed down the command chain.

'Most of the mutants are scouring the ship for us. It looks like they are thin on the ground in this area because they think we've already passed through it. No – Some of them are reporting they have sighted us here. Sounds like their leader is ordering his troops back to meet us. I don't think they have quite worked out what we are doing yet. We've confused them.'

'From what I have seen, that's pretty easy to do,' said Sven.

'Don't underestimate them,' said Ragnar. 'They may look stupid, but they are fierce warriors. A bit like yourself actually.'

'Ha bloody ha!'

Eight minutes and fifteen seconds.

'We're not going to make it,' muttered Aenar. 'Leave me. You'll make better time without me.'

'We are not going to do that,' said Hakon. Ragnar could see that Aenar was right though. Their progress was slower than they had anticipated. Chaos patrols were everywhere and more seemed to be appearing by the second. Even if they had no idea what was going on, the mutants were still capable of getting them all killed by simply being in the way. Right now, Berek's bold plan was not looking quite so good.

In his mind's eye, Ragnar saw the demolition charges exploding, vast yellow fireballs ripping through the hull, incinerating everything that got in their way. He saw his own life ending in fire and pain and terror. He pushed the thought aside and concentrated on the task at hand. He could smell mutants ahead. Within his skull, the trapped beast howled with bloodlust. If it was going to die, it wanted to take as many foes as it could with it.

Ragnar did his best to fight down the impulse. Charging headlong into battle now might be satisfying but it would not save them. It would be better to avoid a confrontation unless there were so few mutants they could rush right through them.

'Take the fork to the right,' he heard Berek say. The heretic stench came from the left. It seemed that the Wolf Lord was thinking the same way as he was. 'And pick up the pace, we don't have all day.'

The steel plates beneath their boots rang as they ran faster. Five minutes and fifteen seconds to go.

'You think Lord Berek can defuse the bombs the same bloody way as he activated them?' asked Sven nonchalantly. Ragnar thought he recognised this corridor, thought he could pick up the scent trail of their earlier passage on the way in coming from somewhere nearby.

'Why? You thinking of asking him to pause the countdown for a few seconds so you can have a rest?' Ragnar responded, sniffing the air. Yes, they definitely had passed near here before. How much farther could it be to the *Fist of Russ*? He checked the locator on his armour. The signal said it was only five hundred metres, but with all the twisting and turning of the ways, who knew how long that would take?

'I might. I may need my strength for the last sprint at this rate.' From somewhere behind them came the sound of bolter fire, heavy and hard.

'Your powers of prophesy are greater than I thought,' said Ragnar.

A signal cut in on the comm-net.

+ This is Hef here. Looks like the mutants are about to overtake us, and in force. Must be several hundred of them coming up this corridor.+

Ragnar looked at Sven. His ugly face showed dismay. Hef's squad were the rearguard. If the enemy had made contact with them then they were not too far behind. Perhaps they were going to have to turn and make a stand here. Once again the vision of those searing yellow flames licking through the corridor leapt into Ragnar's mind.

+Do you need support?+

Berek's voice was calm and full of confidence even with the flatness the comm-net imparted. He might as well have been asking whether they wanted a beer.

+No, Lord Berek. We can hold them here for a minute or so, I am certain.+

Even over the net, Ragnar could hear the bolter shells whizzing around Hef. He heard the stutter of the Marine's answering fire. It was eerie because a split second later, like an echo, he could hear the weapon's original roar. The signals on the comm-net travelled faster than sound.

Moments later came the sounds of explosions and the death howl of a Space Wolf. It sounded like Hef and his squad were achieving the heroes' deaths they sought. Another image flashed into Ragnar's mind, of an onrushing, irresistible horde of Chaos worshippers, racing to overtake them, brushing aside Hef and his pitiful few as if they were not there. He dismissed it, even as the sounds of combat receded behind them.

Three minutes and thirty seconds to go.

'This does not look good,' said Sven, looking at the twisted wreckage of the corridor around them. Someone had been using heavy weapons here. Part of the roof of the corridor had come down, leaving only a crawlspace, barely wide enough for one man. It was impossible to tell how far it might run, or whether it would become too narrow for them to pass through. Ragnar wondered whether it would be worth seeking an alternative route. Maybe they could double back and find another corridor. They had thought this would be the easy way. It was definitely the route they had come by. The scent trail was unmistakeable.

Not that the decision was his to make. The rest of the squads had already disappeared into the dark maw. Only Varig's squad was behind them. The distant sound of fighting had stopped. Ragnar could sense the mutants coming inexorably closer.

'Move, Ragnar!' commanded Hakon, putting his hand on Ragnar's shoulder and forcing him down to his knees. Briefly and instinctively Ragnar resisted, and then realised that by his hesitation he was putting more than his own life in jeopardy, he was endangering his comrades too. He dropped to all fours and crawled forward into the steel lined tunnel.

Two minutes left. The thought was chilling.

EIGHT

RAGNAR DIVED HEADLONG into the narrow tunnel of wreckage. He felt instantly claustrophobic; the walls seemed to press in all around him. He felt their steely embrace constricting the shoulder pads of his armour. Ahead of him, he caught the reassuring scent of his pack, and could make out the movement of men crawling swiftly towards their destination. Behind him he could hear Hakon encouraging the remainder of the force into the tunnel. He guessed the sergeant was going to go last.

Far off in the distance Ragnar thought he could hear the sounds of battle erupt again. Perhaps a few of the rearguard yet lived and had managed to spring a surprise on their attackers. A huge explosion, like a cluster of grenades all going off at once, mingled with the death howl of a Space Wolf, told him this was true. After that there was quiet for a heartbeat and then the triumphant roars of the enemy. The sense of darkness and impending doom increased.

Ragnar crawled on. The walls narrowed around him, scraping against the sides of his armour. It was as if they

87

were gripping him tighter, trying to prevent his escape. He knew this was an irrational fear. He could hear the sounds of men moving ahead of him, some of whom were far larger than he. The tiny daemon of fear whispered at the back of his mind though. The walls were unstable – what if they collapsed further? What if they were collapsing even now? He was going to be trapped, unable to move further. Unable to shift at all and in exactly one minute and thirty-two seconds the whole ship was going to explode. Part of him wanted to simply freeze and huddle down in fear, to cover his head with his arms and wait for the inevitable end.

He fought back, using his own thoughts to fight his fears, as if they were a chainsword and terror was a monster. Even if the walls were collapsing he must go on. That was the only way he was going to get out. The Emperor would not aid him if he would not help himself. He needed to move, not cringe. He was no coward. If he did not do so, he was dooming not just himself but his battle-brothers.

He had never felt anything like this clawing claustrophobic fearfulness before. Perhaps it was because the tunnel was so dark and dank and narrow. Perhaps it was because they were in this alien ship. Perhaps it was because of the pressure of the clock constantly ticking towards death. Perhaps it was some flaw in his own psyche, unrevealed at the Gate of Morkai, or developed since his transformation into a Space Wolf. Perhaps it was some combination of all of these factors. He knew that what he was doing now was far more difficult than fighting those mutants earlier had been.

He forced himself to crawl on, to put one hand in front of the other. He ignored his accelerating heart-rate and the sweat that broke out on his brow.

One minute and ten seconds to go.

Suddenly, blessedly, there was light ahead. He heard the soft movement of men raising themselves to their feet and stretching their limbs into a run. He virtually sprang forward the last few remaining metres, emerged into the light in a half crouch, and sprinted forward towards the welcoming hatchway of the *Fist of Russ*.

Thirty seconds to go.

All around him he could hear the familiar welcoming scents of the company's own ship.

Twenty strides took him there. He sprang through and looked back over his shoulder to see that Sven and Torvald were moving forward, supporting the reeling Aenar. Sergeant Hakon and Varig's squad were racing closer. He could hear Berek shouting into the comm-net, giving orders for their departure. Already the great doors in the bow were swinging shut. Ragnar wanted to shout out 'No!'. It seemed unfair that the others should be cut off now. He wanted to try to hold the gateway open with his bare hands, but he knew that even his superhuman strength reinforced by the hydraulic systems of the armour would not be enough.

Then suddenly Sven and the others were through. Sergeant Varig was last, leaping through a gap that was only just wide enough for him to get through and which snapped closed an instant later. He was strangely aware of the consummate judgement Berek had exercised when giving his orders. The Wolf Lord had left just enough time and no more for the rest of the squad to get through. What if something had gone wrong, Ragnar wondered? Nothing had, praise be to the Emperor.

There was a grinding, tearing noise. The *Fist of Russ* shuddered and shook as if in the grip of some giant daemon's claw. Fear surged back into Ragnar's mind. What if they were trapped? What if the *Fist* could not break free? What if the strain of trying to get away tore the ship apart? Then there was nothing he could do now except pray.

Twenty seconds to go.

He pressed his face against one of the reinforced portholes and looked out. For a moment it was misty; droplets of moisture congealed, hardened then vanished on its surface. He could see that the enemy ship had already receded a hundred metres behind them.

Ten seconds.

Were they far enough away, or would they be caught up in the blast? What if the charges malfunctioned? What if the Chaos ship was not destroyed?

He recognised these thoughts as the last remnants of his claustrophobia-induced terror. He knew that there was nothing he could do now, that if death came all he could do was face it like a true son of Fenris. He pushed the phantoms from his mind and watched the receding vessel. He noticed the vast chasm in its hull that represented the point of impact with the *Fist of Russ*.

Five seconds to go.

As they pulled faster and faster away, Ragnar realised that compared to the huge size of the enemy cruiser, the impact rent was not quite so large. The Chaos ship seemed as large as a floating iceberg, an indestructible mountain of armoured metal. Even as he watched he saw the enemy vessel's turrets, bristling with enormous weapons, begin to swing to bear on the *Fist of Russ*. They were moments from being blasted into eternity.

Time slowed. The tension was almost unbearable. It seemed to be a race between whether the heretics' weapons or the explosion of the power core would send them to their fates. Ragnar fought down the urge to close his eyes and pray to the Emperor. Whatever happened, he wanted to witness it.

Four seconds to go.

Looking back, he saw humanoid figures being swept out into space. Their eyes bulged. Their mouths opened in silent bellows of rage and fear. Of course, when the *Fist of Russ* had pulled away, they had left a huge gap in the walls of the cruiser. It was decompressing. The air was being sucked out into the vacuum and anything that wasn't strapped down was going with it, and that included any mutants in the area. Doubtless, bulkheads were even now being slammed closed within the ship.

Three seconds.

One of the largest turrets seemed to be pointing directly at the *Fist of Russ*. Was it his imagination or was there a hideous infernal glow visible deep within the barrel of the weapon? He felt the lurch of the ship as the *Fist of Russ* continued to accelerate away.

Two seconds.

It was not his imagination. The hellish weapon system really was activated, and it was pointing their way. He knew that there was no way the Space Wolf vessel could take a hit from such a thing at this close a range and in its crippled state. He bared his teeth in a snarl of rage and defiance, at one with the wolf spirit within. All around him he smelled the fury and rage and tightly controlled fear of his battle-brothers.

One second.

The *Fist of Russ* lurched to one side as the pilot took evasive action. An enormous beam of coruscating radiance flashed past in the darkness of space. It had missed by mere metres, a hairsbreadth in terms of space combat. Ragnar's gaze strained out into the darkness, waiting for the explosion his whole body had become keyed up to expect. As far as he could tell, nothing was happening. He could see nothing. Had the demolition charges failed to go off? Had there been some mistake with the timer? Had the mutants against all odds discovered and disarmed them? What was going to happen now?

Their ship was crippled and directly under the guns of the vastly superior foe. It would only be a matter of seconds before the enemy gunners made the necessary corrections to their arc of fire, and the devastating beams of energy would play over the *Fist of Russ* snuffing out all of their lives. It seemed that all of their hard work had been for nothing. They would have been better off remaining aboard the Chaos cruiser and meeting a hero's death in battle. Now they were destined to be swatted like bugs. Their deaths would have no meaning whatsoever.

Then the whole shell of the Chaos ship seemed to expand. Great gouts of plasma burst out of every orifice, every turret, every airlock, every porthole, every point of weakness on the hull. The slow expansion of the ship continued. It was like watching a pigskin being inflated to bursting point. Slowly the huge structure of metal began to buckle and twist. The process accelerated as large chunks of the hull were blown into space and the fiery inferno within was revealed. Ragnar thought he saw a few tiny humanoid figures being vaporised but it might have just been his imagination.

The chain of explosions came faster and faster, larger and larger until they all merged into one vast cataclysmic and final eruption. The whole enemy craft vanished, consumed by a fireball brighter than the sun, a sight made all the eerier by the silence in which it happened. Ragnar half expected to feel the *Fist of Russ* rocked by the shockwave, to hear a vast rain of debris clatter into the side of the ship, but they were already too far away. He braced himself for the thunder of the explosion, then realised he was being foolish. There could only be silence in the vacuum of space, even at the death of so mighty a ship. He realised that he had been holding his breath, and that the silence within the boarding chamber was as intense as the silence outside its walls, then he heard Berek Thunderfist speak.

'We built a suitable pyre for our brethren. What say you, brothers?'

The roar of the Space Wolves was deafening. Ragnar joined in giving vent to all of his joy and relief as well as his pent up fury and grief. He realised that Sven was slapping him on the back, and that Sergeant Hakon had been hoisted on the shoulders of the squad and was being tossed into the air by his followers.

'We bloody well did it!' bellowed Sven, and Ragnar could only slap his shoulder pad in agreement.

'Silence all!' bellowed Berek, and instantly all was quiet. All eyes turned to their chieftain. He stood there posed, one hand cupped over his ear, obviously listening to a voice coming over the comm-net. He nodded his head twice then grinned.

'It appears that we were not the only ones who were successful in our mission. We have been joined by the forces of the Imperial Grand Crusade. The Chaos-loving scum have been driven off. We are victorious this day.'

This time the roar of acclamation was even more deafening than the first. Berek was hoisted onto the shoulders of his Wolf Guard, and stood there legs apart, braced on the shoulderpads of two of the mightiest of his warriors, looking as completely relaxed as if he stood on the metal deck of the ship. Ragnar was aware how much this was a pose, intended to impress, to project an image, but he did not mind. Berek had shown himself to be a worthy and successful battle leader. He was entitled to his foibles.

Now the warrior chieftain gestured for quiet. 'We must lift a stein and toast our dead brothers. This calls for ale!'

The third cheer was loudest of all.

'THIS IS THE bloody life!' said Sven, swigging down another tankard of ale. 'We gave those mutants what for. Although I must confess there were times when I had my doubts…'

Ragnar looked at his friend closely, wondering whether this was the ale talking. This was pure Fenrisian lager, containing ribaldroot, a herb that suppressed the Space Marines' usual ability to metabolise poisons, even alcohol, and allowed them to get drunk. It was not like Sven to admit to having doubts, or even admit to thinking about anything, so this was quite a confession.

'There were times when I felt the same way myself, to tell the truth. We cut it a bit fine on the run out!'

'Well, thank Russ that the Wolf Lord bloody well knew what he was doing better than we did.'

'I'll drink to that,' said Ragnar, suiting action to words. 'Things went pretty well, in our first action of the new campaign.'

'Aye, they did. You know this was my first boarding action?'

'Mine too, if you don't count that space hulk back at Koriolis.'

'I mean ship to ship, blade to blade, right into the fray, you idiot. I remember the hulk too. Who could forget it and those genestealers?'

Ragnar saw that Aenar was looking at them wide eyed. Torvald was poker-faced but Ragnar could tell from his scent that he too was impressed and hanging on to every word.

'You fought genestealers?' queried Aenar.

'No – we went up to them and gave them a big hug and a hearty hail fellow well-met,' said Sven, pausing to take another swig of beer. 'Of course we fought them, idiot boy! What else would we do?'

'I meant you've really seen them, and boarded a space hulk as well?'

'Haven't you ever listened to Sven's boasting, back in the Fang?' Ragnar asked, not unkindly. The beer was making him feel mellow.

'I don't think I have ever heard him talk about it.'

Ragnar considered this. Actually, he did not think he had ever heard Sven talk about this in front of the others either. Perhaps it was not surprising. The trip to the space hulk, along with their whole quest for the ancient eldar talisman, had affected all of the survivors deeply. It was not something they ever talked about with anyone who had not been there. There had been too many deaths, and too much strangeness. Now under the influence of the ale, and the warm camaraderie that came with shared survival, it seemed easier to talk about it.

He let Sven tell the tale, only correcting a few of his more outrageous lies about his prowess in battle when they arose. He did not see how it was possible for anyone to take Sven's claim to have slaughtered twenty stealers in single combat seriously, but Aenar obviously did, and Torvald at least listened with a straight face.

Ragnar looked down into his beer. He remembered how he had frozen in that fight and had been saved by Sven. It was a secret shame he had never mentioned to anybody, although he kept finding it threatening to erupt from his lips now. It brought back memories of how he had almost frozen back in the tunnel of wreckage back on the mutant ship. He continued to think about this, brooding so deeply that he did not even notice that Sven had finished his tale until he felt a poke in his ribs with an elbow.

'You all right there? You're looking a bit green about the gills. Can't hold your ale, I suppose, just like I always bloody suspected.'

Ragnar glanced around and saw that Aenar and Torvald had gone off to get more drink. 'I was just remembering the fight,' Ragnar said, almost defensively.

'And a bloody good one it was too.'

Ragnar realised that Sven was not the man to discuss his doubts and fears with, no matter how good a friend he was. He would have to wait for another time. Perhaps when he next saw Ranek, the Wolf Priest. After all, listening to such confessions was part of the old priest's duties. Not for the first time though sitting amid his friends, his comrades and the members of his pack, Ragnar felt alone. How could that be, he wondered? How was it possible to feel this way amid the camaraderie and the drinking and the loud singing? He glanced at the high table, where Berek sat, surrounded by his Wolf Guard, smiling and jesting and looking completely at ease. Had the Wolf Lord ever felt this way, Ragnar wondered? Somehow, he doubted it.

His eyes travelled a bit further and came to rest upon Sergeant Hakon's scarred and sinister face. He saw the old warrior was looking at him thoughtfully and he wondered how long the sergeant had been doing so. It sometimes seemed like Hakon could almost read his thoughts. Ragnar hoped he could not read his current ones, or the black mood they were bringing on. He looked away and saw Aenar and Torvald returning clutching several more steins in each fist.

He reached up and grabbed one and swigged it back, hoping to drown out the bleakness with beer. Aenar slammed the remaining steins down on the table.

'I owe you that beer for saving my life,' he said with drunken seriousness.

'You owe me nothing,' said Ragnar. 'It was my duty to a fellow Space Wolf.'

The words sounded a little hollow to him, but the others did not seem to notice.

'It wasn't nothing to me,' said Aenar. 'I owe you more than a beer, and I won't forget it either.'

Sven belched loudly. Ragnar looked at him and laughed.

'I have never seen anybody fight like Ragnar did against those mutants blocking our path,' said Aenar. 'It was like watching a berserker from one of the old sagas.'

Ragnar considered this. Was this another source of his black mood. Was he a berserker? He was not sure he liked the idea. In the old tales, such warriors were always coming to dark fates brought on by their insatiable lust for battle. He was not at all sure he wanted to be like them.

'Drink up,' said Sven. 'When Ragnar's in this mood, he could turn a village fair into a funeral.'

NINE

'LOOKS LIKE WE'LL be seeing bloody Garm soon,' said Sven, glancing down at the chessboard.

'How do you work that out?' asked Ragnar, considering his next move. Aenar's hand hovered over his dragonship, preparing to move it forward to take the most advanced of Ragnar's thralls. Was he really going to fall into such an obvious trap? The youth was a better player than he looked, although nowhere near as good as Torvald or Ragnar himself. 'You've been saying the same thing every day for a week.'

Sven squinted down at the pieces. 'Aren't you going to jump that thrall and take the other three pieces behind it?' he asked Aenar innocently.

'We're playing chess, not draughts,' said Aenar, moving his hand away from the board and frowning thoughtfully.

'My clan never played chess back on Fenris. Draughts is a man's game.'

'Funny,' said Ragnar. 'I thought it was for folk too thick to understand chess. And you haven't answered my question. What makes you think we'll be dropping on Garm soon?'

'I've been talking with the crew.'

'We all have. They don't seem to know any more than the rest of us.'

'Don't kid yourself,' said Sven. He grinned broadly. 'Some know more than others. Just like us.'

'And some of us, like you, know less than others, on account of not having a fully working brain.'

Aenar was watching the byplay between the two of them worriedly, as if he actually thought they might come to blows. It showed how green he still was, Ragnar supposed. Back on Fenris, if two warriors from different clans had spoken to each other the way he and Sven did, there would have been a duel moments later. Aenar did not seem to realise that bickering could be just as much a way of passing the time as playing chess.

'Maybe you should concentrate on the game,' Ragnar suggested. 'You are already a keep and a thrall down.'

Ragnar turned his attention back to Sven, who was looking as pleased as a cat that had swallowed a sailor bird. 'So, who have you been talking to?'

'Tremont, the Navigator's apprentice.'

'He's not her apprentice. For one thing, he's part of our fleet, a man of Fenris. For another thing, he doesn't have a third eye.'

'So what?'

'I sometimes wonder if everything the teaching engines put into your head leaked out again, then I remember they need a brain to work on in the first place.'

'Ha bloody ha! If you had bothered to wait for me to finish, you would have heard me say that whatever he is, he knows what is going on. He's always on the command deck. He hears what the sensor augurs see in the divinatory engines as soon as they give their reports, and he tells me that we've cleared a path through the Chaos fleet and are putting into orbit over Garm within hours. That was why they fired the big engines two hours ago.'

Ragnar considered Sven's words. They sounded suspiciously plausible and they fit the facts. Or maybe it was just that he wanted to believe them.

Like the rest of the company, he was getting a little fed up with being cooped up on the ship. After the excitement of their battle with the mutants, the past few days had been anti-climactic.

'I heard something interesting at breakfast this morning,' said Aenar. His hand was hovering over the dragonship again. Ragnar could not believe he had missed the obvious trap.

'Are you going to jump the thrall?' Sven asked.

'What did you hear?' Ragnar prompted.

'I heard that the Great Wolf sends twenty-four Wolves as thralls to the Navigator's House in return for her services.'

'What?' Ragnar almost laughed. The tale sounded ludicrous. No Great Wolf could do such a thing. There would be a rebellion if he even hinted at it. Sven did laugh.

'Sounds like Strybjorn or one of the others was having you on again,' said Ragnar.

Aenar looked up at him.

'Again?' he asked.

'Like the time he told you that all new Blood Claws had to polish the armour of a Wolf who had been initiated at least a year before them.'

'You mean we don't have to?'

Sven groaned. 'And Ragnar says I'm dumb.'

'No – I know you are. But where did you hear this nonsense about thralls and Navigators?'

'From Sven's friend, Tremont.'

'I never said he was my friend.'

'What did he tell you exactly?'

'That every time a new Great Wolf is chosen he must send two dozen Wolves to Belisarius in repayment of some ancient debt.'

'That can't be true,' said Ragnar.

'It is true,' said Sergeant Hakon striding across the room. 'At least in part.'

'How can that be?'

'Like everybody else, our Chapter needs Navigators to guide our ships through the immaterium. If we did not have them we would be reduced to jumping blind.'

He paused to let his words sink in. All of them knew exactly what that meant. Jumping blind into the immaterium meant a good chance of never coming out again. Only Navigators had the skill to guide ships through the void and bring them safely out the other end. And even they made mistakes sometimes. Ragnar had known this since the tutelary engines had placed the knowledge in his brain, but he could see now that he had never fully assimilated it or thought out the consequences. He had simply assumed that the Navigators were sworn to the Chapter's service down through the generations just like the ships' crews. Thinking it through he could see the error in his thinking.

He reviewed the facts the teaching machines had placed at his disposal. Like Space Marines, Navigators were unique, their origins dating back to a time before the Imperium. They were gifted with unusual powers – their psychic talents – available only to themselves. The Emperor and his primarchs had possessed that gift too, but the primarchs had vanished long ago and the Emperor was entombed within his life-giving throne. In effect, the Navigators controlled all commercial and military travel within the Imperium. Were it not for the fact that they were divided into a number of mutually antagonistic houses, they would have a stranglehold on the human realm.

The thought deeply worried Ragnar. It was all very well having Space Marines, but it would all stand for nothing if the Chapters could not reach the worlds to which they were assigned or travel where they pleased, and when. Ragnar realised that it was possible to wield power without wielding a gun.

The control the Navis Nobilitae had over space travel had made them rich and powerful beyond the dreams of most planetary governments. They had ensured that without them, the Imperium and possibly even the Adeptus Astartes, the Space Marines, would be helpless.

'Does the Great Wolf really send human tribute to the Navigators,' Ragnar asked.

'Of course not,' said Hakon contemptuously. 'Such foolish words are unworthy of a Wolf. The tale is an old and complicated one, reaching back to before even the founding of the Empire. We have an alliance with House Belisarius of the Navigators that was forged by Russ himself…'

'An alliance,' said Sven, his tone showing that he, like Ragnar, found this far more acceptable and understandable.

'Aye. There is a pact between us. They provide us with the means to sail our ships between the stars. In return, we provide the Celestarch of Belisarius with a bodyguard.'

This too sounded only fair. For priceless as the service of a Navigator might be, surely the service of a Space Marine must balance it in the scales.

'The Navigators swear to obey the Great Wolf as they would obey their own ruler. The Wolves, for the duration of their service, obey the Celestarch as they would their own leader, and protect him with their lives if need be.'

'No one has ever told us any bloody such thing,' grumbled Sven.

'Doubtless, when Logan Grimnar feels the need to discuss every aspect of the Chapter's business with a Blood Claw, he will call upon you,' said Hakon tartly.

'I think what Sven meant was that the tutelary engines never taught us this,' said Ragnar, attempting to drag his friend out of hot water. Sven's expression told Ragnar that he had meant no such thing, but he kept his mouth firmly shut. Hakon looked at him.

'The machines are ancient and no one, not even the Iron Priests, entirely understands their workings. They are intended to teach what it is needful for a Marine to know. They cannot fill your head with every detail of our Chapter's history. Not even Sven's skull is empty enough to hold all of that. And sometimes there are gaps; the transfer of knowledge is imperfect. That is why people like me are here, to teach what the machines leave out.'

Ragnar considered this for a moment. He could see that there was sense in the sergeant's words. Moreover, he could see a problem he had never considered before. He would never know if the machines had missed out important knowledge until it was too late. He did not have the ability to know if anything was not there. How could he? Most of what he knew came from the engines themselves.

Hakon's nostrils flared. Once more he seemed to be able to read Ragnar's thoughts.

Ragnar wondered whether, if he lived to be as old as the sergeant, he too would be able to read his comrades' moods and thoughts and feelings so accurately by scent alone? Perhaps Hakon's ability was a product of age and wisdom more than of his senses.

'Sometimes the learning is there,' said Hakon, 'but it is like a scroll left on a shelf in a library, rather than an epic learned by a skald. If you do not read a scroll, how will you know its contents? And sometimes there are problems with the transfer of knowledge and it lies dormant for many years before it is fully assimilated. The brain is a peculiar thing.'

'Sven's certainly is,' said Ragnar and seeing the sergeant's expression, wished he had not been so facetious. Hakon seemed unusually communicative today, not his usual taciturn self.

'Forget my brain, and this talk about machines. How are these heroes who go to the Navigators selected?'

'Doubtless you will find out if you ever need to know,' said Hakon.

'You mean you don't know?'

Hakon shrugged. 'Who said they were heroes?'

Sven fell silent for a moment while he considered this. Ragnar wanted to ask another question, but Aenar chose this moment to put the chess piece down and ask a question of his own.

'When will we be landing on Garm?'

'We are in orbit over the world now, as you would see if you chose to look out one of the portholes,' said the sergeant. 'My guess is that we will be on the surface within hours. The Great Wolf will not want to waste any time in recovering the Spear of Russ or freeing the shrine from malefactors. And we must collect the gene-seed of our brethren.'

'The gene-seed of our brethren?' spluttered Sven.

'Aye, you do not think we would leave our most sacred shrine outside Fenris undefended?'

'I would have thought that there are few enough Wolves,' said Ragnar sharply. 'The Emperor must have more important things for us to do than guarding shrines.'

'There is a base here, Ragnar. A transit camp. A way station. Garm is an important crossroads and trade route. We have a presence here to repair our ships, to let our troops rest and recuperate. The place was commanded by an old comrade of mine, Jurgen Whitemane.'

Ragnar could tell from the sergeant's tone that he did not believe his old friend was still alive.

'If he is dead, we will bloody well avenge him,' said Sven.

'Aye, that we will,' said the sergeant grimly. Ragnar looked at the sergeant. There was something strange about him. He was in a fell mood. Ragnar was reminded of all the tales he had heard of men whose wyrd had come upon them, who had walked out to their inevitable doom. He shivered, hoping that this was not a premonition.

The doorway opened. Morgrim Silvertongue stood there. He spoke quietly and with authority. 'Ragnar, you are to come with me. The Wolf Lord would have words with you.'

As HE FOLLOWED the skald through the metal corridors of the starship, Ragnar wondered what was going on. Morgrim's face was expressionless and gave him no clue. When he tried to speak, the singer brushed him off, not rudely, but like a man who has other things on his mind. Had he been a fellow Blood Claw, Ragnar might have persisted, but the man was one of the Wolf Guard, and you did not intrude on their thoughts unless asked.

He hoped that nothing bad was about to befall him. Perhaps Berek Thunderfist's vanity could not stand the tone Ragnar had used when he had been cut off back on the Chaos ship. Perhaps he meant to call him out and have vengeance. Ragnar tried to dismiss these thoughts as fool-ish. There was no honour for a warrior as renowned as Berek in fighting with a Blood Claw, and Wolf Lords brawled with their followers only on the rarest of occasions. The thought was simply ridiculous.

And yet, he was nervous. It was not every day a Blood Claw was singled out for the attention of the Wolf Lord. Per-haps he intended to reward Ragnar. Perhaps he intended to promote him to Grey Hunter at last. Ragnar's heart leapt at the prospect. If that were so, as far as he could tell, he would be the youngest Blood Claw in generations to be elevated so swiftly.

Immediately he tried to throttle the hope. It was his youth that made just such a promotion unlikely. Who did he think he was, to be singled out so?

They passed two officers of the ship's company, resplen-dent in their grey tunics with the wolf's head emblazoned above the sign of the thunder fist on their breasts. They returned the men's salutes absentmindedly and strode on. Ragnar realised he was in part of the ship he had never vis-ited before, the chambers assigned to the company's leader and his Wolf Guard.

A terrible thought occurred to him – perhaps his cow-ardice had been noticed? Perhaps his fear at entering the corridor of collapsed metal back on the Chaos ship had come to the attention of the Wolf Lord. Perhaps he was about to be punished for this flaw, or ridiculed or... he told himself that this too was a ludicrous concept. He took a deep breath and schooled himself to calmness. Whatever Berek Thunderfist wanted would be clear soon enough. He would just have to wait a few more moments to find out.

They strode into a long, narrow chamber in which war-riors of the Wolf Guard worked on their suits of Terminator armour. Ragnar wished that Morgrim would pause for a moment, so that he could inspect these ancient revered arte-facts. This was the first time he had ever come so close to one. Like all young Space Wolves, he aspired to wear this armour one day. Only the best of the best, the most trusted and most able of a Wolf Lord's retinue, ever achieved such heights.

As it was, all he managed was a quick glimpse of a suit of armour, far larger than a normal Marine's carapace, powered by the most potent of hydraulic systems, emblazoned with attachments for the heaviest of weapons.

Ragnar caught the smell of ancient ceramite and the overlay of ten thousand years of technical unguents. He felt a sense of near overwhelming power. A feeling of simple reverence filled his heart.

Even as it did so it occurred to him that perhaps the bard had been instructed to lead him this way. By all accounts, Berek was something of a showman and quite capable of arranging something like this to create the right impression. Again, Ragnar told himself he was being ridiculous. Berek was Wolf Lord; he did not need to do anything to impress a lowly Blood Claw. Ragnar considered this. Perhaps that was true, but Berek was also a great leader, and went to great lengths to secure the loyalty and respect of his troops. Perhaps this only showed his attention to detail.

Ragnar forced himself to relax. He wondered why he had been selected and not Sven or any of the others. Perhaps he was not unique. Perhaps Berek would see them all separately. He was at once disappointed and relieved by this thought. Part of him wanted to be singled out, to stand apart from his companions in the pack. Part of him felt guilty about this, as if he were somehow being disloyal to his friends and companions. Well, whatever it was there was nothing he could do about it now. Matters were out of his hands.

They strode into another larger chamber. A great deal of expense had gone into fitting this one out. The walls were covered in wooden panels; massive wooden beams gave the illusion of supporting the ceiling. In one corner burned a fire, or rather a flickering holospherical illusion. A great trestle table sat in the middle of the floor, surrounded by carved chairs of real wood. A barrel of ale stood ready in one corner. On the walls were various tattered banners, battle honours taken on a hundred fields on a hundred worlds. It was these alone that kept the place from being a near perfect counterfeit of some rich lord's hall, back on the islands of Fenris.

Sitting on a great throne, on a raised dais at the end of the room, was Berek Thunderfist. He was flanked by Mikal Stenmark and another Wolf Guard. Berek's leonine head rested on his massive metal hand. He looked up as Ragnar entered.

'Welcome, Ragnar Blackmane,' he said. 'It's past time that you and I had words.'

TEN

'WHAT DO YOU want of me, Lord Berek?' Ragnar asked.

'First I want to thank you for saving my hide back on the Chaos ship, lad. That was quick thinking and it got me out of a tight spot. If it weren't for you I might not be sitting here, quaffing ale and toasting my victory.'

'I am sure you would have fought your way clear anyway, lord,' said Ragnar. Berek's answering smile told him that this was exactly what the Wolf Lord thought.

'Perhaps. Perhaps not. Thanks to you I did not have to try my luck. Just as well. It's best not to test the fates too often.'

Ragnar waited to see what Berek would say next.

'It seems to me that you should be rewarded,' said the Wolf Lord.

'Doing my duty was reward enough.'

'I see old Ranek taught you well. That was the sort of answer I would have expected from one of his pupils.'

Once again Ragnar was silent. No words seemed expected of him. The Wolf Lord appeared quite capable of speaking for two. He took one of the golden arm-rings from his bicep. He gestured for Ragnar to stretch out his arm and then clamped it into place himself. Ragnar could see that the torque coiled like a serpent. Its spring-like tension held it exactly in place. He smiled. This was exactly the gesture a Fenrisian chieftain would use to reward a faithful follower. In the old tongue another word for jarl was 'ring-giver'.

'Thank you, Lord Berek. I am honoured.'

'By accepting it, you do me as much honour as I do you,' said Berek ritually. It was obvious that he was merely mouthing the ancient form of words, but still, it was a princely gift.

Ragnar did not know quite what to say.

'I am honoured, lord.' Ragnar said.

'Of course you are. And rightly so. And now, you will accompany me to the Great Wolf's ship. The Wolf Lord's gather. There we will make our final dispositions for the drop on Garm. I mean to see Berek's company has the place of honour.'

Ragnar was a little shocked. Why was he being singled out for this honour? He felt out of his depth. Was this some sort of test? Did the Wolf Lord want to see how he behaved in front of other great captains, if so why? 'Surely that is the Great Wolf's decision, Lord Berek.'

For a moment only, he felt like he had said the wrong thing. Berek was obviously not a man to admit that anyone was his superior. His face grew frosty for a second, then a moment later he grinned and laughed. 'I am sure even Logan Grimnar can be persuaded, young Ragnar.'

Ragnar realised that he had passed some sort of test. He had been spoken to by name. He was no longer just a lad. He was glad that Berek felt this way, for it was the right and duty of every Fenrisian warrior to speak his mind to his chieftain, and Ragnar intended to preserve that privilege, no matter how intimidating his liege lord was. Fortunately Berek had responded like the clan chieftain he styled himself to be. Despite his initial misgivings, Ragnar found himself warming to the Wolf Lord.

Morgrim grinned. It seemed that the skald thought he had done the right thing. Mikal Stenmark's cold glance told him a different story. It said, you got away with it this time, lad, but don't make a habit of it.

The shuttle sped closer to the *Pride of Fenris*, the Great Wolf's massive flagship. Berek stood at the massive armour-glass window, gazing covetously at the old warcraft. It was a Retribution-class battleship of ancient design, its hull pitted and scarred by a hundred battles. It dwarfed the shuttle like a sea dragon would dwarf a sprat. From where Ragnar stood it looked like the maw of one of its weapons could swallow their whole craft. Obviously this ship would not have had any trouble defeating the Chaos cruiser, one to one. He voiced his thought to Morgrim Silvertongue. Quietly as he spoke, the Wolf Lord still overheard him.

'Aye, lad, true enough, but then we would have missed out on that glorious boarding action.'

The ten men of the Wolf Guard accompanying them laughed agreement. Ragnar turned his glance back to the *Pride of Fenris*. He did not necessarily agree – if they had not boarded the ship many Space Wolf lives would not have been lost, and Aenar would not have been wounded.

Thrilling as the fight had been, and glorious as the destruction of the Chaos craft was, Ragnar was not convinced it was worth the price. He was enough of a man of Fenris to relish the glory of what they had done, and to be glad he had earned a place in the legend-maker's chants, but at the same time, another part of him counted the cost. It was an unnatural thought for a Space Wolf, he knew, but he could not help entertaining it.

The shuttle moved closer to the flagship. Ragnar felt someone watching him and turned to see the Navigator. She was a tall woman, pale, slender and exotically beautiful, with long silver hair and eyes like chips of ice. A scarf was draped around her forehead covering the disturbing pineal eye. He smiled at her. She nodded back calmly. He shrugged and looked away.

'Why is the Navigator with us?' Ragnar asked Morgrim.

'Shayara is with us because Lord Berek wants her to be,' replied the skald. There was an undertone of amusement in his voice. 'Her insights are often useful.'

'Is that so?'

'Navigators don't think like we do. They do not see reality the same way either. It is surprising how often they see things we don't. And sometimes Shayara has the gift of foretelling, powerful as any Rune Priest.'

'That could be a useful gift,' said Ragnar.

'And a terrifying one,' Morgrim replied and said no more.

THE COUNCIL HALL on the *Pride of Fenris* was like Logan Grimnar's chambers back in the Fang, a little smaller, a little less ornate, but nonetheless they belonged to the Great Wolf just as recognisably as Berek's belonged to him.

As Berek and his men entered they were greeted by a great roar of approval from the assembled Wolf Lords and their guards. Even Logan Grimnar and his entourage of priests banged their chestplates with their fists in warriors' applause. It was obvious that all had heard and greatly approved of Berek's destruction of the Chaos warship. All that is, except Sigrid Trollbane. He applauded but his face was twisted, his expression that of one who has swallowed a lemon.

This was Ragnar's first opportunity to study his liege lord's great rival and he took advantage of it. Sigrid was a tall man, spare and thin. All excess flesh seemed to have been burned from his face. His hair was dark and straight, his features sallow, his lips thin and unsmiling. His eyes were large and cold and glittered with a chilly introverted intelligence. The overwhelming impression he gave was of concentration. He looked like a racing hound straining at a leash. For a moment his eyes met Ragnar's and there was a shock of contact. Ragnar felt he was the focus of all the Wolf Lord's attention. It was like feeling a searchlight play over him, or suddenly knowing that he was in the sights of a sniper's rifle.

Sigrid tilted his head to one side, and considered Ragnar as if he was an interesting new form of insect life. A faint frown of puzzlement graved itself on his brow. He was obviously trying to work out who the newcomer was and why he was here.

Ragnar refused to be the first to look away. A cold smile played across Sigrid's lips and he turned and said something to the chieftain of his bodyguards, a huge bear of a man with a bristling beard and a shiny bald head. The giant laughed loudly at whatever his lord said. Ragnar could not help but feel he was being made the butt of some joke, but here, under the eyes of the Great Wolf and his retinue, was not the time or place to do anything about it.

'Welcome, Berek Thunderfist,' boomed Logan Grimnar. 'Your presence gives us honour.'

'And we always appreciate the drama of your entrances,' said Sigrid. His voice was deep, resonant and surprisingly powerful. There was a sadness to it, and an ironic mockery as well as a touch of hatred. 'Last to arrive, as always.'

Logan Grimnar cast a warning look at Sigrid. He obviously did not appreciate having his speech of welcome interrupted. Was the Trollbane's dislike really so intense that he would risk the lord of the Chapter's ire, Ragnar wondered?

'You know what they say: first in battle, last in council,' said Berek, smiling amiably. Ragnar studied his chieftain closely. There was a change in his manner again, doubtless for this new audience of influential lords. Now he was the picture of the bluff Fenrisian warrior, his natural intelligence hidden behind an ingenuous manner. If he was deliberately contrasting himself with Sigrid's sneering intelligence he could not have done a better job. Ragnar saw the room respond. Many of the other Wolf Lords looked at Berek approvingly, and at Sigrid with something like disdain.

'Well spoken,' said Logan Grimnar, smoothing over the obvious rift. 'And now that we are all here it is time to discuss the drop on Garm.'

Ragnar felt a thrill of excitement pass through him. The drop was going to go ahead soon. He stood now at the hub of things. This was where the decisions would be taken that would affect the lives of himself and his comrades, and he would be among the first to know of them. It was a heady feeling.

'I have had a request from the Imperial field commander for our Chapter to spearhead the drop…'

A roar of approval greeted this news. It was after all only appropriate that Space Marines be called upon to lead the Imperial attack. Surprisingly Logan Grimnar raised his hand for silence. At once, the Wolf Lords went quiet. The Great Wolf gestured again. Some technical adept was obviously working his wizardry for at once a glowing sphere, recognisable as Garm, appeared in the air above them. It was twice as tall as a man. Ragnar could see the blue-black of the seas, the white of the clouds, and snow-fields, the multi-coloured blisters that were the cities.

'Lord High General Durant has suggested that we attack here, at point alpha-four-omega.'

As Logan Grimnar spoke their point of view dropped towards the planet. It swelled in their field of vision to become a topographic map of a huge hive city. Parts of it were colour coded – blue was loyalist, angry red was enemy. At this point, there was far more red than blue. A shimmering circle pulsed at the point where the general wanted them to drop.

'I have regretfully declined his request,' said the Great Wolf. 'I have told him it is our first duty to free the sacred shrine of Russ from the clutches of the heretics and to recover the Spear. Only then can we move to cleanse this world of the filth who are the Emperor's enemies.'

Once again the assembled Wolf Lords roared their approval. Ragnar understood the Great Wolf's decision. At one and the same time the Great Wolf had put the Imperial general in his place and established their real priorities. He had let Durant know that the Space Wolves were with his command, not part of it. They were outside the normal

Imperial power structure and would act as the supreme lord saw fit. Ragnar had been taught how the rest of the Imperium worked. Doubtless General Durant thought in terms of his own plans and priorities, and would like nothing better than to see the Space Wolves subordinated to his aims. Logan Grimnar had let him know this was not the way it was going to be.

The Great Wolf gestured again and the view in the holosphere changed once more. It showed the ruins of an enormous pyramid-shaped building. A statue of a rampant wolf had stood on the top of the roof; now it lay smashed in three pieces. In the side of the building, a monstrous set of metallic double doors had been blown open. The skeletons of dead warriors lying amid the rubble put them into scale. They were near five times as high as a man. The whole building was riddled with shots. Thousands and thousands of bullet holes pockmarked the walls. Massive craters had been ripped out of the wall. Here and there enormous duralloy girders jutted from the plascrete like broken ribs sticking through skin.

Ragnar heard gasps from some of those present, men who obviously recognised the building. It did not take much guesswork to tell him that this was the Shrine of Garm's Skull. As far as he could tell someone had done a pretty good job of storming it. As Grimnar continued to speak the view panned backwards and outwards.

Ragnar could see the structure of fortifications surrounding the shrine. The flatness of the plascrete plain was broken only by turrets, emplacements and bunkers with interlocking zones of fire. Enormous fortified walls, bristling with turrets, enclosed the plain forming a killing ground almost a kilometre square.

Now the whole area was full of wreckage and dead bodies. The twisted remains of tanks filled the ground. Corpses lay bloating in water-filled craters, their weapons still close at hand. Huge chunks of plascrete had been ripped out of the earth by artillery fire. Amid the flotsam and jetsam of war, patrols of men moved, scavenging from the dead. Amid the burned out remains of the bunkers, war-weary men huddled around trash-fires and warmed their hands at gas braziers. The air had a hazy, polluted look. A blanket of strangely discoloured snow covered most of the ground.

'We can't get an internal view of the shrine's inner sanctum,' said the Great Wolf. 'The shielding is still effective.'

'It's fair to assume that in so short a time there can have been no internal modifications,' said Berek. 'We can use the architectural schematics we already have.'

'We can assume nothing,' Sigrid contradicted. 'It is merely wishful thinking to believe that nothing has changed.'

Logan Grimnar looked at his two bickering captains like a parent regarding two squabbling children. 'The schematics are the only things we have to go on currently. Nothing from the orbital divinatory engines suggests anything has been changed. When we seize the shrine we will proceed as always within hostile terrain until the Iron Priests have time to perform cleansing and purification rituals.'

'How are we going to do it?' asked a voice from the back that Ragnar did not recognise.

'The same way as always,' said Logan Grimnar. 'With bolter in one hand and chainsword in the other.'

That got a laugh from everyone except Sigrid, though even he gave a sour smile.

'To give the tale a true telling, we shall begin with a short orbital bombardment at these points.'

The map returned. Red skulls appeared at each corner of the building until the whole shrine was cordoned off.

'How brief?' asked Sigrid.

'Thirty seconds. No more. We go down thirty seconds later. The bombardment should detonate any mines or other nasty surprises the tech-augurs have missed and give us a clear landing site. I want five companies on the ground in drop pods. There will be Thunderhawks for air support. Three transport shuttles will bring the armour in once the perimeter is secure. I am allowing two minutes for that.'

'What about the shrine's defences?' asked Sigrid. 'Is there any possibility they have been subverted?'

'All our divinations tell us that most of the defences were destroyed in the initial attack. The last signal broadcast before the shrine was overrun tells us that Brother Jurgen managed to purge the datacores and self-destruct the major weapon-systems.'

'My company stands ready to enter the shrine and begin purification of the heretics,' said Berek. Ragnar looked at his chieftain, sensing the tension. Berek wanted very badly to be first into the shrine, he wanted the glory of reclaiming it for the Chapter. 'We have recent experience of such action on Xecutor.'

'All our companies have such experience,' said Sigrid. 'I too volunteer my company.'

Immediately a chorus of voices made it clear that all present were keen to have their companies perform this duty. Logan Grimnar spread his arms wide for silence.

'Berek and Sigrid, you both make the assumption that you are going in the first wave.'

Both of the Wolf Lords openly stared at the Great Wolf. At that moment it looked like they were both considering challenging him. Grimnar's steely glance quelled them. Once he was sure they were not going to say anything stupid, he smiled. 'Fortunately, you are both correct in your assumptions. You will be going in with Grimblood, Redmaw and Stormforge. I don't want to hear any challenges from those in the second wave either, before anybody speaks. Time is short and we need to get the wheels in motion.'

'Who will begin cleansing the shrine?' asked Stormforge.

'Given their recent spectacular performance on the Chaos ship, Berek's company will have the honour.'

Ragnar looked over and saw a look of pure hatred written on Sigrid's face. This did not bode well for the future, he thought.

ELEVEN

RAGNAR LEANED BACK inside the drop pod and surveyed the rest of the squad. For the duration of the landing, it seemed, he was back with the Blood Claws, and he was glad. When it came to fighting, he would rather be alongside Sven and Hakon and Strybjorn – who he knew well and had fought alongside many times.

They were all strapped into the cramped interior of the pod. Space was so tight that they were pressed up against each other in the dark. The familiar smell of his pack filled the recycled air reassuringly. He glanced around at faces old and new, and was glad he trusted everyone present. All it would take was one tiny error, for one bolter to go off accidentally within the confines of the pod, and the results would be catastrophic.

Sergeant Hakon caught his glance and nodded grimly. Ragnar found the gesture strangely reassuring. He had followed Hakon into many tight spots before and had always come out. He saw no reason why this time should be any different. Then he too smiled grimly. Not unless something went wrong...

The drop pod could malfunction in a hundred different ways. The heat shields could fail and they could burn up on atmospheric entry. They could be caught by defensive fire as they made the drop. The reverse thrusters could malfunction and they could be flattened like crushed bugs by impact with the planetary surface. They could…

Hastily he concentrated on the Litany of Acceptance, using the ancient words to drown out all the niggling little voices that worried away at the back of his mind. He concentrated on breathing, on regulating the beat of his double heart, on preparing himself for arrival.

The orbital bombardment could fail to clear the minefields. They might land on a killing ground between defensive bunkers. They might go too soon and be caught by their own orbital support weapons. They…

'What's the matter, Ragnar?' asked Sven. 'You look like you just remembered you left all your ammo back in your cell.'

Ragnar glanced across at his friend. Sven read him all too easily, just like he could read Sven. Despite his pose of ferocious indifference, Ragnar could smell Sven's own uneasy fear. It might simply be a natural response to being confined in this small space or…

Ragnar smiled suddenly. It was obvious now why his mind was racing more than normal: it was being in the drop pod. He did not like it at all.

Once more he was hemmed in on all sides, but this time it felt worse. Now that the purity seals on the pod were fastened, there was no way out until they hit the surface of Garm. The pod was their only protection against heat and altitude and the dangers of enemy fire. It was a tiny island of security in a deadly ocean of peril. The operative word was 'tiny'. Now more than ever Ragnar was aware of his dislike for being enclosed. It was too much like being entombed. At least now he was aware of the source of most of his fear and unease and could resist it.

'It's just the smell of your breath, Sven. You've been at the curdled goat cheese again, haven't you?'

Sven grimaced. 'A man has to eat. Best to go into battle on a full stomach. Who knows when we'll see decent rations again.'

'I'm sure there's plenty to eat down there,' said Aenar, his face glowing with a mixture of good cheer and apprehension. He looked very young, Ragnar thought.

'We'll soon find out,' said Torvald. 'If I am killed in the first minute, don't anybody forget to say the rites over me. It would be just my luck to go down to hell unblessed and have the old hag who cursed me waiting there.'

Ragnar glanced around the inside of the pod. Overhead was the gargoyle encrusted control panel, familiar from a hundred practice drops. The internal walls were all inscribed with murals depicting familiar scenes from the Chapter's legends. Behind Sven, Ragnar could just make out some details of Hengist Torvaldsson's battle with the great serpent of Doomflare. Doubtless the product of some Wolf's long leisure hours between combat practice and the meditation cell.

'Synchronise,' said Sergeant Hakon. A low bell-like chiming sounded in Ragnar's ears as the ancient technical systems checked that the chronometers of his armour were perfectly synchronised with those of the sergeant and his battle-brothers.

'Aye,' Ragnar responded, and listened to the familiar litany of replies from his comrades. 'Russ be praised.'

'One minute,' said Hakon. Immediately the chronometer countdown was superimposed on Ragnar's field of vision. He closed his eyes and the clock remained there, its gothic lettering ticking away the time until the pod was expelled from the *Fist of Russ* and began its atmospheric entry. He reviewed his pre-battle preparations one last time.

All of his equipment was primed and ready. He would break left when they hit the ground and give supporting fire as the others advanced. In his mind's eye he could picture the pattern of the drop that Berek had outlined to them. They would be slightly closer to the entrance to the shrine than the Wolf Guard and were to advance immediately into it, securing the company's way into the depths.

He checked his physical responses. His heartbeats were perfectly relaxed now. His mind was clear. His anxieties were under control. Glands in his implanted lymphatic systems manufactured hormones to enhance healing and trace chemicals to speed his reflexes and dull pain. All familiar programmed changes before battle. In the past, he had not had enough experience to even be really aware of them, he had just known he felt better, faster, stronger. Now, he was capable of distinguishing each small new response.

He was aware that Hakon had begun the Prayer to Russ, and found that he had joined in, mouthing the words without really realising it. 'Lend us the strength to smite the Emperor's foes. Grant us the grace of an honourable death if our hour is come,' he muttered. 'The Emperor be praised.'

Even as the old sergeant spoke, there was a loud clang, and a juddering sense of movement. 'Drop pod away,' murmured Sven. 'Garm here we come.'

At first, there was the immense pressure of continuing acceleration as the drop pod arced downwards on its approach trajectory. Hakon reached up and touched one of the controls on the board above. Suddenly in the air in front of them a holospheric image appeared.

Ragnar saw the fleet retreating behind them, and all of the other drop pods leaving the blast-tubes of the fleet and rushing downwards like so many burning flakes of thistledown. Ahead of them loomed the great glowing shield of the planet. Great oceans of white cloud drifted over the face of the continents.

Hundreds of tiny runes glittered below the image, giving out myriad bits of information to those who could understand them. Some of their meanings had been lost in the dim mists of time in the days when such systems had first been devised, but Ragnar knew enough of the symbols to be able to pick out those which displayed their speed, altitude and ambient temperature. Outside now it was cold, the chill of interplanetary space.

They were away. It would take long minutes for them to reach the insertion point for atmospheric entry and many more minutes after that for them to penetrate the atmosphere. In that time, the fleet would have moved on to to a position over their drop point, and if the Navigators had got their calculations right, would begin the support barrage, stopping mere seconds before the course of the falling drop pods intersected with the blast of their mighty weapons.

Ragnar told himself that this was all a long-established ritual, that the Chapter fleet and its warriors had done this thousands upon thousands of times, but this was his first long drop in anger, and the thought of mistakes being made troubled him deeply. As the drop pod reached its final angle of attack, the sensation of acceleration and of its associated weight vanished, leaving him drifting upwards from his seat, free of gravity, restrained only by the tug of his harness.

Within the drop pod all was silent now, save for the muffled breathing of the men. There was no turning back now; they had passed the point of no return.

The first faint tremor in his seat drew Ragnar out of his brief reverie. The whole pod vibrated slightly. His training told him that it was merely the first tickling touch of the atmosphere on the pod's shell, but for a moment a deep primordial fear reached up from the depths of his being and screamed that the pod was malfunctioning and they were all going to die.

'The breath of the wind,' said Sergeant Hakon, in his calmest and most reassuring tone of voice. From the sudden relaxation of the tension all around him, Ragnar knew that he had not been the only nervous battle-brother. The sergeant's next words were less than reassuring. 'Best brace yourselves. Things could get rough.'

Ragnar glanced around him to see how the others were taking this. The sergeant looked calm, and as stone faced as ever. Sven grinned like a lunatic, fangs glinting in the light of the holosphere. Aenar looked pale and nervous. Torvald kept a small cynical smile on his face. Strybjorn looked as grim and calm as Hakon. A glance up at the holosphere showed Ragnar that the planet was no longer visible as a disk. They were now racing down into the atmosphere and the wind demons of the upper air had them firmly in their grip.

The whole pod shuddered and shook. A faint creaking sound fretted at Ragnar's nerves. It sounded as if any moment the whole ceramite and duralloy structure might crumple inwards and crush them all. Much as he knew how unlikely this was, the thought still haunted him. He also found it all too easy to imagine the blazing beams of defensive lasers reaching up to burn them from the sky. At least such an end, if it came, would be quick. Once more the sense of being trapped in a confined space returned, redoubled. Ragnar fought down the urge to rip at the restraining straps and lash out about him.

Now flames licked all around the hulls of the drop pods above them. The heat shields on the bottom of the drop pods were starting to glow cherry red. Streamers of superheated hair flickered all around them. This was no normal atmospheric entry such as a shuttle or a Thunderhawk would make. This was a swift insertion, designed to get them on the ground as quickly as possible and with little fuss. They were flying on minimum power, easy to mistake at this altitude for a shower of meteorites.

Even as Ragnar watched, bits of the pods above them burst away. The whole pod shook as if hit by a gigantic hammer, and something hot and metallic fell away from them too, its contrail visible on the viewscreen. For a moment it looked as if they were disintegrating, but he knew this was not the case. This was merely the pod shedding its outer skin, creating decoys that would show up as multiple images on any sensor system that might be observing them. The theory was that this proliferation of targets would make it difficult for the defenders to pick them off as they came in to land. At this altitude it would also increase their resemblance to a meteor shower breaking up under atmospheric impact.

Ragnar hoped that it would work. For the first time, in all of the times he had ridden groundwards in a drop pod, his life might depend on the success of this stratagem.

Now the view in the holosphere flickered alarmingly. Either there was some problem with the power circuit or it was simply being obscured by the plasma trail of the pod itself. The shaking of the pod increased. The runes orbiting the holosphere told Ragnar that their velocity was increasing at an alarming rate as they plummeted through the thin upper atmosphere of Garm. An eerie high-pitched whine rose to audibility, swiftly followed by small thumping noises as if rain were pattering against the outside of the capsule. Ragnar knew it was not rain, merely the turbulent air.

The thumping noise grew and along with it so did the shaking. It sounded now as if the fists of thousands of air daemons were pummelling the drop pod's side. The whole craft shook and echoed. Ragnar felt the craft veer and swerve minutely as it dropped. He clutched the seat with both fingers to give himself some sense of stability. The flickering light of the holosphere illuminated the faces of his companions. Their features all seemed frozen in expressions of excitement, dismay or exaltation.

Sven opened his mouth and let out a long wolf howl. It echoed around the confined space like the wail of some demented spirit, drowning out for a moment even the whining of the wind and the pounding of the turbulence. Aenar joined in and, within moments, the whole pack was howling save the sergeant.

Hakon was busy making minute adjustments to the control panel above them. Ragnar watched him. The drop pod was moving through the thin air at a far greater speed than a human body would fall normally. The resistance of the air was too small to slow it much at this height.

The turbulence became much worse. Now it seemed like the pod was caught in the fist of a giant who was determined to shake the life out of the tiny people trapped within it. Without their restraining harnesses the Blood Claws would have been tossed helplessly around within the pod from floor to ceiling. As it was, Ragnar could see the flesh on the faces of his companions wobble like jellies.

They continued to howl now, maddened by excitement and the prospect of imminent action.

Ragnar knew the massive orbital bombardment would begin soon. It had been carefully timed to start just before their drop, so as to not give the enemy too much advance warning. By the time the heretics realised it was over, the Space Wolves would be on the ground and swarming over them. That, at least, was the theory.

In his mind's eye, he pictured the titanic wave of las- and projectile fire blazing down from orbit, cratering the ground, smashing their foes' defences, clearing the way for them. He tried not to imagine an error that would result in this fragile pod being caught in the deluge of destruction.

'One minute,' said Sergeant Hakon. The words came over the comm-net and were audible even over the thunder of the turbulence. The howling stopped abruptly. Ragnar felt a tension in the pit of his stomach and a deep-seated excitement surge through him. Another glance at the runes told him that the drop pod had decelerated enormously. The turbulence must have come from increased air resistance. The view in the holosphere was becoming clear again. Wisps of red and grey and yellow marred by inky stains of black were all around them.

Clouds, he thought. Clouds mingled with pollution. We're almost down. Relief warred with tension. This was the point of maximum crisis. If the defenders had spotted them, this was when they would be shot down. Destruction could take them unawares; they would be removed from existence instantly and there was absolutely nothing they could do about it. Such a sense of helplessness was not something Space Marines were used to. The only protection now was prayer; the only shield was faith.

An enormous wash of yellow light blazed through the holosphere. For a moment Ragnar was disoriented, then he realised that he had just caught the final blaze of the barrage before it cut out, as they passed through the lowest band of the polluted clouds. Beneath them he could see the astonishingly large towers of Garm. In a glance he got some idea of the geography of this part of the world.

The land beneath them was divided into hundreds of small islands, separated by channels of water and industrial run-off. Massive metal and plascrete structures – factories, hab-units, power cores and industrial temples – covered each island. Some were mere blackened hulks, plasteel skeletons lying amid the rubble that had once clothed them. Others showed huge gaping holes, the result of artillery fire or internal explosion.

At one point, around their drop-zone, it looked like the barrage had set the whole polluted river alight. Flames danced unnaturally along the surface of a fluid that bore little resemblance to water. Arcing into view he could see the blasted craters of the place where they would land. Far, far off in the distance he thought he saw massive war machines moving. It appeared that loyalist ground forces were mounting a diversionary attack to cover their landing. No. That had not been mentioned in the planning session. Perhaps it was simply some opportunistic warlord taking advantage of the distraction provided by the barrage. Perhaps it was merely coincidence.

Sporadic fire from building-mounted defence lasers leapt into the sky around them. None came close to their drop pod. Had they been spotted or was this merely some form of automated point defence system, designed to fire on anything that dropped into this particular airspace? If so, Ragnar was glad that the barrage had done its work. Normally such networks covered the entire sky over a city. This seemed to be functioning only sporadically.

Sporadic or no, he thought, offering up a prayer to Russ, all it would take would be one shot and this world would be rid of them. There was no way the armour of a drop pod could withstand the impact of a blast from a defence laser.

'Suspensor failure,' said Hakon over the comm-net. 'Brace yourselves.'

Looking at the runes on the holosphere Ragnar suddenly realised they were not slowing down. The gravitic suspensors which were supposed to slow the final stage of their descent had not automatically cut in. In moments they would be smashed to bloody pulp against the ground. This was not looking good, Ragnar thought.

TWELVE

PANIC BRIEFLY THREATENED to overwhelm Ragnar. His worst fears all seemed to have come true. He was trapped in this tiny pod with no way out, about to smash into the earth after dropping from a great height. Then the moment passed; self-control returned. If he had only moments of life remaining then he would not give way to fear. He would meet death like a man, even if it was not the death he would have chosen.

Sergeant Hakon had other ideas. He reached up and flipped the emergency handles on the panels above his head, manually activating the suspensor drive. For a moment, nothing happened, then Ragnar felt as if a giant hand were crushing him into his seat as the suspensors wrestled with the planet's gravity. A smell of ozone filled the air, and Ragnar thought he heard a high pitched scream as the ancient machine's overloaded generator quit. Acceleration returned sickeningly. The sensation of dropping twisted Ragnar's gut. The hope that had flared briefly died, only to return a moment later as the secondary power system cut in.

'Brace yourselves!' Hakon bellowed again. 'This is going to be touch and go.'

The altimeter runes told Ragnar that impact was imminent. He held himself in the crash position, thinking they were still going too fast. Seconds later he was thrown tight against the restraining straps with enormous force. He felt the harness flex but hold. His neck muscles strained to prevent whiplash. The force of the impact was enormous.

Any moment, he expected to feel a tidal wave of agony rip through his body. It did not come. Instead, the drop pod began to roll end over end, finally coming to rest with a jarring bump. After a few seconds, the sides groaned open, like a metal flower unfolding its petals to greet the sun.

'Disperse,' said Hakon in a cold commanding voice. Ragnar hit the buckle of the restrainer harness and sprang clear, drawing his weapons and readying them. A wave of steam greeted him as his feet touched the plascrete covered surface of Garm, the snow boiled away by the heat of the drop pod's impact. Ragnar thought it was the heat shield cooling, but a quick glance told him a different story. Part of the side of the capsule glowed cherry red. It looked like one of the enemy las bursts had come a lot closer than he had thought, hitting the drop pod a brief glancing blow.

Probably why the automatic systems failed, Ragnar thought, as his eyes searched for a target. He knew just how lucky they had been. If that ravening energy beam had kissed the cupola of the drop pod for more than a microsecond, they would have been vaporised.

The stutter of small-arms fire from nearby told him that some enemies at least were still battle ready.

He stood knee-deep in snow and took a breath of the cold air of Garm. It was chill as Fenris in winter, but smelled of rotten eggs, sulphur, and all manner of pollution. A faint wave of nausea told Ragnar that his body had already started the process of adapting to it, of filtering and purifying. Strange, he thought, what small things attract the attention after moments of crisis.

Despite the danger, exaltation filled him. The cause was not merely the chemicals his altered glands were pumping into his bloodstream. He was on the ground. He had survived the rough passage through the high atmosphere and he was here with a foe in front of him and a weapon in his hand. Dangerous the situation might still be, but at least here was a danger he could so something about. It felt like his destiny was once more within his own hands.

With another quick glance, he took in the situation around him. The other drop pods were on the ground. The Wolves were out, weapons spitting death in all directions.

Small groups formed up to assault the Shrine of the Spear. At this range it looked more like a fortress than a shrine, and one that had recently been taken. The burned out remains of automatic defence systems dotted its sides. Ragnar could see uniformed heretics on fortifed balconies. The snouts of las-rifles poked out through windows.

Here and there runes, the signs of Chaos and heresy, polluted the sacred walls. Ragnar snarled a curse and prepared to advance.

As far as he could tell there had been no casualties among Berek's company. The only slight problem was that due to their drop pod's malfunction, they had fallen far out of the cluster pattern, and they were much closer to the massive doorway than they were supposed to be. Behind them, craters and rubble rose from the plain. Here they were on a level killing ground, the only cover being the remains of their drop pod.

A stream of shells hit the plascrete in front of him, sending rock-hard chips clattering against his armour, raising small fountains of snow. Ragnar raised his head and spotted the shooter, mounted on the high battlements above the door. With one fluid motion, he raised his bolt pistol and fired. His single shot smashed through the sniper's skull and decorated the carved wall behind him with brains.

'Nice shot,' he heard Sven murmur. 'Now all we need is twenty more like it.'

A hail of fire sent Sven scurrying behind the still glowing pod. Ragnar leapt to join him. He could see that Hakon and the others were pinned down on the open ground in front of them. Unless they could take out their attackers it looked like life was going to be short for the rest of their squad.

Suddenly there was a roar of rockets and streaks of fire smashed into the enemy emplacements on the walls. Briefly the guns fell silent. Clouds of smoke billowed.

'Looks like the Long Fangs finally decided to unpack their rocket launchers,' said Sven, grinning cheerfully. He glanced towards the remains of the massive shrine doors. 'You thinking what I am thinking?'

Ragnar nodded. He vaulted over the side of the pod and raced towards the steps, Sven right beside him. Seconds later the rest of the squad had joined them, taking advantage of the confusion the Long Fangs' heavy weapons had wreaked among the defenders.

Within moments they were on the stairs. Suddenly a hail of fire erupted all around them. He saw the sandbags in the doorway and the nest of heavy guns within it. Acting instantly he threw himself flat on the massive steps, and lobbed a grenade towards the foe. A chain of explosions told him he was not the only one who had had this idea. Moments later he was back on his feet again, running forward towards the emplacement.

Bullets churned the ground around his feet. One clattered off the shoulderpad of his armour with enough force to spin him around and send him to the ground. Sven raced past, blazing away with his pistol at the surviving heretics, chainsword already keening in his hand. As he picked himself up, Ragnar watched his fellow Blood Claws vault the half-demolished wall of sandbags and go ravening through the shocked enemy. Obviously the defenders had not expected an assault of this speed and ferocity.

Ragnar got his first real glimpse of them now. They were normal enough looking men, garbed in white and grey camouflage uniforms, padded against the cold. Thick dark goggles protected their eyes, and filter masks covered their mouths giving them a sinister insectile look. In their hands most of them clutched well-used autorifles tipped with serrated edged bayonets. Many of them shrieked and wailed and tried to run as the Wolves smashed through them, but one or two had the presence of mind to keep fighting.

As Ragnar watched, one man who had obviously been feigning death – quite convincingly judging by the amount of blood covering his tattered uniform – leapt to his feet and aimed a bayonet at Sven's back. Calmly Ragnar took aim and put several bolter shells into him. The force of their impact crumpled the man like a ration carton crushed in a Marine's fist.

Ragnar raced forward to join the fray, diving into the midst of the struggling bodies, lashing out at the men around him with his howling chainsword. Within seconds the machine gun nest was clear and the Blood Claws were fanning out towards the others behind the makeshift sandbag emplacement.

With a disgusted look on his face, Sven examined his chainsword. A stray shot must have hit the power source for the blades no longer rotated. Black smoke belched forth from the hilt and the mechanism wobbled and came apart in his hand. It had taken more damage than was apparent. Sven looked around for a moment, and then an evil grin appeared on his face. Nearby lay a heavy autogun. Somewhat miraculously, it did not appear to have taken any damage from the grenade explosions. What were the chances of that, Ragnar wondered, then dismissed the thought. In war, given enough time, most events, no matter how improbable, could happen.

Sven raised the heavy automatic weapon one handed, and smiled, looking very pleased with himself. It appeared that he had not picked up the weapon a moment too soon. Deeper within the shrine the defenders had rallied and now a wave of them, hundreds strong, was surging across the chipped marble flooring back towards the gateway. Despite the natural feeling of superiority drummed into him by his training, Ragnar suddenly felt very outnumbered. There were five Space Wolves in the remains of the machine gun nest, versus several hundred foes.

'I make the odds about five to one,' said Sven.

'Nice to see your arithmetic is as good as ever,' said Ragnar deciding that Sven had the right idea. Perhaps he too could find another functioning heavy weapon in the rubble.

'Let's just cut those odds a little,' said Sven. He raised the machine gun one handed and opened fire into the oncoming mass of infantry. It cut through them like a scythe, chopping bodies in two, punching bullets right through the chests of oncoming men to bury shells deep in the bodies of the warriors behind. Sven let out a long howl of pleasure. The muzzle flare of the machine gun underlit his face, making him look daemonic. He stood in the middle of a storm of bullets, completely unfazed by the death whizzing all around him. Amazingly he began striding forward, ignoring the bullets, blasting away at their foes, causing unbelievable amounts of destruction.

It was like watching a hero from the ancient sagas. There was something terrifying about the mechanical way in which Sven walked forward mowing the foe down as he went. For a moment, the sight halted even that enormous mass of men. It seemed for a few seconds that Sven might rout them single-handed.

Then from the back came a shout and the sound of firing. Ragnar made out a man in a white winter uniform who resembled an Imperial commissar, bellowing instructions to his followers and they began to come on again, firing away. Now the weight of lead hurling past him was too much even for one of Sven's insane bravery. He began to step backwards towards the emplacement, firing as he went, until he tumbled backward into the pit alongside Ragnar.

Looking down, Ragnar could see his friend was not entirely unscathed. His armour was cracked in a dozen places and blood leaked from the gaps. A bloody slash marred Sven's cheek, another had torn away a whole chunk of his crested hair. Still his eyes blazed with feverish battle lust. He reached forward to pick up the machine gun again, and pulled the trigger. For a few seconds it roared and spat out a hail of death, but then it stuttered and died.

'What in the name of Russ…' muttered Sven.

'It's overheated,' said Ragnar. 'The barrels have fused. You kept firing too long.'

Sven lobbed it viciously in the direction of the enemy. 'Bloody useless thing!' he shouted. From the distance came a crunch of bone and a shriek of pain. Ragnar guessed that Sven's throw had been accurate.

'Congratulations,' he said. 'You've invented a new way of fighting. Instead of shooting enemies with heavy weapons, we'll throw them instead.'

'Wouldn't you be better off fighting than bloody talking?' asked Sven with surprising mildness. He was already scouring their position for some new means of offence.

'Your mastery of tactics astonishes me,' said Ragnar, poking his head over the wall of sandbags and letting fly into the tightly packed mass of bodies. As he did so, a blast of fire surged all around him, forcing him to pull his head back into cover. It looked like someone on the other side possessed the sense to set up more heavy weapons to cover the enemy's push forward. They were pinned down until the infantry swept over their position. Things were not looking good.

Well, more than one way to skin a dragon, Ragnar thought, setting down his pistol and tapping his grenade dispenser. He was a Space Wolf. He was more than capable of judging the position of the onrushing enemy by their footfalls and their scent. He lobbed a handful of grenades over the sandbags out towards the enemy. Moments later a wave of screams and explosions filled his ears.

'I think you might have got one,' said Sven. 'Lucky throw.'

Sven lobbed a grenade over his shoulder too. Another explosion. Another scream of agony. 'That's how it's done,' he said.

Ragnar looked at him. 'Things would go a lot better if we could take out their supporting fire.'

'Really. I would never have thought of that,' said Sven sardonically. He lobbed another grenade. Another explosion ripped through the inside of the building. Ragnar could tell that their foes were close.

'They'll have to stop firing soon or they'll hit their own men,' said Ragnar.

'And when they do–'

'This!' said Ragnar. As soon as the support fire stopped, he leapt up and began blasting away with his bolt pistol. The heretics were so close that he could see his own distorted reflection in their goggles: a twisted grey-clad figure splattered with blood. The muzzle flash of his gun was dazzling. Almost as soon as he had popped up he saw the oncoming infantrymen ready their autorifles to blast him. They were obviously just as prepared for the moment when the support fire stopped as he was; what they lacked were his superhuman reflexes.

He was hunkered down again before any of them could pull the trigger. A tidal wave of bullets passed over him, and thunked into the sandbags behind his back. He could feel the structure shudder under the impact.

'That was smart,' said Sven sarcastically, lobbing another grenade. 'I hope the others are doing better.'

The grenade blast was so close behind them that it was near deafening. 'Best get ready for hand-to-hand combat,' said Ragnar.

'With what? My fists?'

Ragnar tossed him his bolt pistol, and activated his chainsword.

'Even you ought to be able to do something with two pistols, Sven.'

'I imagine something will come to me,' said Sven with a crooked grin.

'It had better. They are just about on top of us.'

THIRTEEN

'LET'S GIVE THEM a warm welcome then,' said Sven, springing up just as the shadow of a man with a bayonet loomed over him. He began blasting away, bolt pistol in each hand. Shells blazed out at close range burying themselves in human flesh before exploding. Sven stepped sideways, still shooting, spraying their foes with both pistols. Ragnar took one more moment to watch him then twisted and sprang out over the sandbags, landing in the middle of the oncoming wave of infantry.

Holding the chainsword with both hands, he cut right and left, shearing limbs and breaking bones, splattering himself and everything around him with bright red blood. A howled battlecry erupted from his lips as he surrendered himself to the fury of close combat. All of his pent up aggression, all of his earlier worries and fears during the descent, powered his rage. He struck with tigerish swiftness, moving through the mass of foes like an unleashed daemon. For a few brief instants he was unstoppable, but then the sheer mass of onrushing troops bogged him down. The enemy were all around him, stabbing with bayonets, pumping out bullets at close range, too intent on preserving their own lives against this unleashed berserker in their midst to worry about hitting their own comrades.

Ragnar ducked and weaved, but the ground was slick underfoot with blood, and it was hard to keep his balance, avoid his enemies and get power behind his blows. He tried his best though. Even as he felt a bayonet find the gap between shoulder-plate and upper armguard, he hacked down one man and smashed in another's face with a punch. Teeth sprayed everywhere under the impact of his gauntleted fist.

A stab of pain behind his knee told him that another of his foes had managed to find a weak spot in his armour. A backhanded slash with the chainsword ensured the man would never do anything else again. Already he could feel the wounds beginning to clot but the healing process was slowing him. He lashed out again and again and with every stroke a foe died. But for every man who fell there were two to take his place. There were just too many of the heretics for one small squad of Blood Claws to hold back.

A bullet from out of nowhere grazed Ragnar's temple. It felt like someone had just hit him with a sledgehammer. He shook his head to clear the falling blood from his eyes, and in that moment, a crowd of men seized him, trying to immobilise his limbs and still his deadly blade. With a roar, he lifted two of them and dashed their heads together with a sickening thump. As he did so he felt an arm go round his neck, as someone tried to drive a knife into his throat.

Ragnar threw himself forward, hoping the momentum would toss his assailant from his back but the man held on for grim death, and drove the knife home once more. Blood slicked Ragnar's chestplate – and it was his own.

Now a real killing fury settled on Ragnar. He was no longer fighting to preserve his life but to take as many of his foes down to hell with him as he could. He shook his head and rolled his shoulders trying to throw off his attacker, and as he did so he lashed out with his chainsword, catching another man in the belly. Ropes of entrails slid from the man's gut but Ragnar advanced anyway.

In his fury he lost his footing on the slick intestines and tumbled over backwards. There was a crunch as something cushioned his fall, and Ragnar realised it was his dagger wielding assailant. The man's arm now dangled limply around Ragnar's neck.

Above him loomed a huge man with a rifle. Before Ragnar could react, he smashed the butt of the gun into Ragnar's skull. The blow would have caved in the head of any normal man, and even his reinforced bone structure could not entirely protect Ragnar. Sparks flickered before his eyes, and for a moment all he could see was blackness. He sensed rather than saw the man draw back his rifle for another blow and stabbed forward and upward blindly with his blade. He felt it connect with something, and pass through the moist sack of the man's flesh and cleave through his innards. The man screamed, and voided his bowels and bladder.

At that moment, Ragnar's sight returned and he rose to his feet. His fist smashed into the man's face and sent him toppling over backward. Ragnar reeled forward, howling with anger, chopping at any foe within reach. Still they came on, an endless tidal wave of enemies. He could see none of his battle-brothers, and their smell was lost among the scent of heretics and cordite. Perhaps they had already fallen. Perhaps he was the last of his squad still left alive. If so, he resolved, he was going to make the traitorous heretics of Garm pay dearly for the lives of himself and his comrades.

Ahead of him, he could see the man in the commissar's uniform. It no longer looked white and clean. It was stained with blood and blackened with smoke. Somehow he had lost his mask. The man's cold face paled a little as he saw Ragnar staggering towards him but he raised his chainsword defiantly, and advanced to meet the Blood Claw with the powerful confident step of a skilled warrior.

As their blades crossed Ragnar realised that he faced a worthy foe. The man's skill was tremendous. Normally, he

would not have physically have been a match for a Space
Marine, but Ragnar was bruised and battered from his earlier battles, and the Garmite was fresh and hungry for glory.

Sparks clashed and chainswords screamed as they met.
The commissar ducked below the sweep of Ragnar's return
stroke and lashed out, catching the young Wolf on the arm.
The vambrace of his armour smoked as the friction of the
chainsword bite heated it unbearably. Ragnar stepped forward, grabbing the man's sword arm with his free hand and
closing his grip tight. With a sickening crunch bones gave
way. The commissar did not utter a sound although his face
went pale and sweat beaded his brow. Ragnar thrust his own
head forward in a swift butt to the bridge of the man's nose,
breaking it. As the Garmite fell backwards, blood leaking
from his nostrils, lips tight with self control, Ragnar lashed
out with a kick that broke the man's hip. As the man fell,
Ragnar's stamping foot crushed his skull.

One or two of the Garmite soldiers looked upon their
dead leader in horror, but they were filled with confidence
and their morale held. It did not matter how strong Ragnar
or any individual Marine was, there were just too many foes.
Like angry ants swarming over an armoured beetle, they
came on, stabbing, hacking, pumping bullets at Ragnar with
startling disregard for their own lives and the lives of their
comrades. The sheer mass of flesh moving inexorably as a
sea pushed Ragnar back towards the emplacement. He felt
like a swimmer caught in a riptide, but still he fought on,
blood and sweat threatening to blind him.

From out of nowhere something caught Ragnar behind
his weakened knee, and he collapsed into a half crouch.
Something heavy crashed into his skull again. Stars novaed
across his field of vision. He felt suddenly weak and nau-
seous, barely able to keep upright. In all his time as a Space
Marine he did not think he had ever felt like this. The
knowledge that he was about to die sparked fury within him
but pinned by the press of bodies, weakened by wounds
and loss of blood, he could not summon the energy to turn
his bloodlust into action. Instead he kept chopping and

hacking, lashing out with fist and foot and head as well as blade. He knew it was a hopeless struggle. His limbs felt heavy as lead. His opponents seemed as numerous now as when he had started.

Still a grin came to his lips, and a howl erupted from his throat. This was a warrior's death, better by far than being charred to a crisp within a super-heated drop pod. No Space Wolf could ask for more.

His howl was answered by a war-cry from close by. 'For Russ and Berek!' he heard someone shout and was surprised to see the man in front of him cloven in two by the blow of a chainsword. Sergeant Hakon stood there, looking like some daemon of slaughter. Blood covered him from head to foot, his armour was painted almost totally red by it, and his grey hair was the colour of rust. He picked up another Garmite and tossed him back among his fellows, bowling them with the sheer force of impact, then he charged among them, lashing right and left and leaving Ragnar a clear space among the carnage in which to catch his breath.

Ragnar stood panting for a moment, watching as the sergeant slew every infantryman within reach, before tossing his head back and emitting a monstrous howl of triumph. Even as he did so, a lash of tracer fire whipped in from somewhere to the left and took the sergeant in the skull. The whole side of Hakon's head was blown away, leaving exposed fragments of brain. Like a mighty tree toppling the sergeant fell forward and was still.

For a moment, shock paralysed Ragnar. It seemed impossible that the sergeant was dead. He had been there, invincible and indestructible from the first day Ragnar had arrived at Russvik. He had trained and fought alongside the Blood Claws until they knew his face almost as well as they knew their own. He was part of the squad, its leader, and guiding light... and now he was gone.

Ragnar stood frozen as the tidal wave of Garmite infantry surged back in his direction. Part of him had lost heart at the sight of Hakon's fall. Part of him simply wanted to stand still and let the oncoming soldiers slay him as they had slain the sergeant. What was the point of fighting? He was just going to die like the squad leader.

Even as these thoughts flickered briefly across his mind, he savagely suppressed them. The fury he had felt earlier returned, his rage felt boundless. From deep within himself he drew on reservoirs of strength he had not known he possessed. The weakness fell from his limbs. Hakon had bought him a respite that had allowed him to recover. It was time now to repay his debt to the old man.

He leapt forward, bullets clattering off his armour with a sound like a blacksmith's hammer falling on metal. Seeing his face contorted with rage, a few of the Garmites panicked but most of them were brave men. They kept firing and braced their bayonets, readying themselves for the colossal impact of Ragnar's charge. Even as he sprang forward, praying to Russ that no bullet would wound him mortally before he could kill more foes, Ragnar heard more Space Wolf war-cries from close at hand.

Suddenly he was aware of mighty figures nearby, crashing through his enemies with weapons blazing and chainswords shrieking. Dozens of Wolves had closed with the foe, emerging from the haze of gunsmoke and dust to smite the enemy. They swept into the melee alongside Ragnar, smashing through the Garmite line like a thunderbolt through rotten timber.

In a heartbeat, the whole complexion of the fight around the shrine's entrance changed, as the Garmites' initial success turned into a rout. Tough, battle-hardened warriors the natives might be, dedicated to the cause of wickedness beyond sanity, but the sight of a mass of Space Marines surging through them was enough to break even their morale. The great mass of them turned tail and tried to flee, and then they were dead.

'We bloody well won,' said Sven, looking at once pleased and angry. It was a typical response. He still glared around him, sensitive to the slightest movement, reacting to the smallest noise or change of scent. An hour after Logan

Grimnar had declared the shrine cleared, he was ready for combat in a heartbeat. Even the re-shaped metabolisms of Space Marines took time to calm down after the fury of battle had passed. There was an aftershock, Ragnar realised. He felt that way himself.

'At what cost?' Ragnar asked.

'You're still bloody well here aren't you? So am I.'

'How about the others?'

'Aenar was wounded again. Torvald is fine. Strybjorn took a couple of knocks, but he'll be all right once the healers look at him.'

Ragnar shifted his weight. There was pain there, far worse than anything he had experienced during the battle. Then, it was as if his mind had shut out anything that would not help keep him alive. Now it was more difficult to ignore. He had removed his greaves and sprayed the wound with synthetic flesh. The skin was already starting to knit as his body healed itself. There was a dull ache in his stomach that he realised was hunger. He removed a ration-tube from his belt and began to suck on it. The taste was bland, and it did not feel like he could get any sustenance from a mere paste, but he knew it contained all the nutrients he needed. More than that, it contained the alchemical ingredients that would help him heal. He recognised that hunger; his body craved the raw materials with which to repair itself.

'Good idea,' said Sven and began to slurp loudly at a tube of the food-paste. 'Some beer would be even better.'

Ragnar glanced around. They were on the outskirts of the field hospital. In airtight tents, the Wolf Priests worked their rituals on wounded Marines. Dozens of the less badly wounded sat around. A priest moved among them, deploying medical augurs. His examinations were quick but thorough, more in the nature of simple checks to make sure his patients were all right. While it was true that a Space Marine would heal naturally and swiftly from almost any injury that did not cripple him, there was no sense in taking chances. It was not unknown for men who had taken blows to the head to walk around normally for hours afterwards then keel over and die.

'What about Hakon?' Sven asked.

'He's still in there,' said Ragnar. 'The priests would not let me stay while they performed the rituals. One of them told me he is most likely going to join his ancestor spirits.'

'Look over there,' said Sven. Ragnar glanced in the direction of Sven's pointing finger. He saw Berek Thunderfist and Morgrim Silvertongue stride forward. The Wolf Lord paused here and there to exchange smiles, jokes and words of encouragement with the wounded. Every time he did so, the man's spirits would perceptibly rise. As if sensing Ragnar's eyes upon him, he looked up and gave Ragnar a cheerful wave. Ragnar waved back and the Wolf Lord strode over towards him.

'No, don't get up,' said Berek as Ragnar and Sven made to rise. 'You have both taken honourable wounds in battle. You deserve to rest.'

They stayed in place. 'Sergeant Hakon is in a bad way,' said Berek. 'He is in a coma. His spirit hovers over his body.'

'Will he recover?' asked Ragnar.

Berek shook his head. 'No.'

'Will he die?'

'We do not know. Even if he lives there has been too much damage to his brain. He will not be fit for war ever again.'

'It is not the end he would have wished,' said Ragnar.

'Nor any of us,' said Berek. 'But these things happen. It is not Sergeant Hakon's fate that I wished to talk with you about, Ragnar.'

'No?'

'Now that Hakon is gone, your pack needs a new leader. Things are in a very fluid state at the moment, and we are expecting the Garmites to counter-attack at any hour. Until I have time to assign someone, you are in charge of the squad, Ragnar. I will make the announcement after the evening rituals.'

Ragnar simply stared at Berek. This was not the way things were usually done, but then again, it was the Wolf Lord's choice. Ragnar was sure that there must be better, more experienced men for the task available, but it seemed that for reasons of his own, Berek had chosen him, for the moment. Perhaps this was why he had been asked to accompany him to the *Pride of Fenris*. Perhaps Berek already had him in mind for command. Who could tell?

'Thank you, lord,' said Ragnar.

Berek clapped him on the back. 'I am sure you will do well. You fought bravely today. And this is an auspicious place to get your first promotion.'

Sven gave Ragnar a sour look but kept his mouth clamped firmly shut. Ragnar was surprised by his restraint. Berek turned and strode away, bellowing greetings and jokes to the men. It did not surprise Ragnar that he seemed to know all of their names. Morgrim followed.

Ragnar looked at Sven; Sven looked back at him. 'I fought as well as you bloody did. Why did he not pick me?'

'Maybe he wanted someone with half a brain,' said Ragnar.

'He could have picked Hakon then,' said Sven and grimaced. Even he seemed to realise that the joke was not funny under the circumstances. Ragnar stared at him for a moment, feeling like a gap was opening up between himself and his friend. Sven met his faze levelly for a second and then grinned.

'I can think of worse men to follow,' he said.

'Who?' asked Ragnar.

'Give me an hour or two and I am sure someone will come to mind. Or maybe a day.'

'If you have any stray thoughts give them a warm welcome. They will be in a strange place.'

'Ha bloody ha. I can see that becoming a leader of men hasn't improved your sense of humour.'

FOURTEEN

RAGNAR STARED IN wonder at the inner sanctum of the
shrine. Ahead lay the avenue of heroes, its wall niches
filled with statues of famous leaders of the Space Wolves,
and tapestries depicting scenes of their most famous victo-
ries. He was glad the place did not seem to have been
much touched by the heretics. It had been stasis sealed
when the complex was invaded, and it had taken the
attackers time to burn their way through into the massive
fortified vault. And they had got what they came for too.
The Spear of Russ was missing! Even now, the Great Wolf
and his captains and the priests discussed what to do next.
They had freed the shrine but its most precious treasure
was gone. It was a calculated insult to the honour of the
Chapter.

How would the primarch feel on his return to discover his
weapon in the hands of enemies? Could he return at all, if
the prophesy could not be fulfilled? Ragnar was suddenly
glad that such questions were not for him to debate, or
answer. He had a more personal mission here. This was a

pilgrimage and a time to consider his place in the Chapter
and in the world.

Ragnar limped forward. His leg still ached a little from his
wounds although they were healing fast. It was a walk, not
so much as through distance as through time. Every step
took him deeper into the past. At the beginning of the walk,
near the entrance hall, he passed the most recent heroes of
the Chapter. He recognised the figure of Anakron Silvermane, who had directly preceded Logan Grimnar as Great
Wolf, and looked in wonder at the tapestry depicting his last
stand, fighting grimly against the eldar host that had surprised his command position on Melkior. Stranger yet was
the realisation that he recognised some of the other figures
depicted in that near legendary event. There was Grimnar
himself, bloodied but unbowed, fighting some gaudily clad
eldar assassin. There was even Sergeant Hakon, garbed as a
Grey Hunter, battling with an eldar guardian. The death of
Silvermane had taken place nearly four centuries before. It
was strange to think that some of the men in the shrine
today had been there. It was one thing knowing that the
process that turned a man into a Space Wolf could vastly
extend the span of his years. It was another encountering
evidence of the fact.

Ragnar smiled. He was glad he had chosen to make this
pilgrimage alone and in the darkest watches of the night,
while most of his battle-brothers slept. He felt the need to
make this journey, for the weight of responsibility that had
fallen on his shoulders wearied him. It was reassuring to
stand in the presence of these ancient artefacts and feel himself part of a long procession of men who had walked this
way in the past. He had something in common with the
generations of fearsome warriors that had preceded him. It
made him feel as if he were connected to something
greater than himself. He needed something to bolster his
self-confidence. From now on, until he failed or was
replaced, his decisions would affect the lives of his comrades
and friends. If he made a wrong choice, Sven or Aenar or any
of the others might die. Once he would not have minded,

indeed would have exulted at being in a position to engineer the death of Strybjorn, but he did not feel that way now.

If anything, he knew he would feel worse if his former enemy died because of his orders, for he would never be able to tell whether he had secretly wanted the man's death and caused it. That would be a great dishonour.

He strode past several more statues of Wolf Lords, looking for faces he recognised but found none. Hardly surprising, for a man had to be dead to get his likeness sculpted from stone in this part of the shrine. He asked himself if he should have turned Berek down and refused the promotion no matter how temporary. He knew that, despite his doubts, he would not have. Although part of him was near paralysed by the thought of his new responsibilities, another part of him revelled in the fact that he had been picked out from among so many worthy warriors and given this opportunity. It was a great honour to be singled out in such a way by Berek Thunderfist. He knew that he was being tested in the field, and that if he did well here, he could expect further recognition, perhaps one day even become part of the Wolf Guard. Did Berek see that potential in him? Would that not be a great thing?

He paused for a second to consider it. Once there had been a time when it had seemed a great enough honour merely to have been selected to be one of the Wolves. Now, he wanted more. Was his whole life destined to be like this? Would it always be a case of climbing one mountain, only to discover a greater peak lay beyond, and that he must climb that too? Where would it end – when he was a Wolf Lord, when he was Great Wolf? He smiled at the thought, even though he knew that part of his mind was seriously considering it. And why not? Someone had to be Great Wolf. Even Logan Grimnar had been a Blood Claw once, difficult as that was to imagine now.

He allowed himself to consider it for a while. He pictured himself on Logan's throne, issuing orders to the Wolf Lords, listened to respectfully by the warriors of the whole company, commanding a fleet, standing as an

equal to any of the great lords of the million worlds of
the Imperium of Man. He pictured himself not as he was
now, but grown old and grey and rugged, with features
hewn from stone, and a voice that sounded like granite
cracking. He pictured himself giving orders that affected
the fate of worlds, striding heroically through desperate
battles on a hundred planets, writing his name in the
annals of Chapter history. He saw himself immortalised
here in statue and tapestry and painting. There was a
thought that thrilled his young heart, and not his alone.
He knew that every Wolf, even Sven, must think these
things sometimes.

He strode on for a dozen paces wrapped in his dreams of
glory, but as he did so, other thoughts filtered into his mind,
less bold, less bright, more chilling. He turned and looked
up at the massive oil painting of the Battle of Balinor, a can-
vas depicting one of the most famous fights of the 38th
millennium. Beneath it stood the statue of Great Wolf Fenrik Grimheart. The statue held a battered old helmet under
one arm, and a notched chainsword in the other. It was the
same sword that the painter had depicted covered in blood
in the picture.

Where was Fenrik now, wondered Ragnar? Gone, along
with all the others whose statues lined this corridor. They
had found glory and they had found greatness, but in the
end the grave had claimed them too. No matter how
famous, men had still sung their funeral songs, and toasted
them with the burial cup. Their gene-seed had been
returned to the Chapter just like the gene-seed of the common warriors who had followed them. Yes, they were
remembered in song and saga and the annals of the Chapter, but they were gone. Their thrones were occupied by a
different man. In the end, what had all their striving got
them but the same reward as everyone else?

Even as the thought occurred to him, Ragnar knew that it
was not so. Those men were remembered. They had written
their names in history in blood and fire. They had shown
themselves to be worthy companions of Russ on the day of

the Final Battle. But had not the warriors who followed them done that too? It would not just be the Great Wolves remembered here who would fight on the Last Day. Others whose names had not been remembered, who had perhaps been even more worthy would be there too.

Ragnar looked on down the corridor, to the almost endless parade of statues, to the hundreds of works of art and battle honours that lined the way. Strange, he thought, he had expected to find glory here, but he had not expected to discover melancholy at the same time. Perhaps the two were inextricable. He was contemplating the greatness of elder days, but in doing so he was also being made aware that such days had passed. It was at once a depressing and a reassuring thought.

The old days were gone. The future was a palimpsest on which nothing had yet been written. He found his mood had come full circle. Men always passed on, always had, always would. Only the Emperor was eternal. One day, Logan Grimnar would be gone, and someone else, maybe Berek, maybe Sigrid, would sit in his place. And they in turn would be gone, and a new man would stand where they had stood. Why should that man not be Ragnar?

Still there was a kernel of sadness in the thought now that had not been there when thoughts of future glory had entered his mind. In order for him to reach that distant goal, good men would have to pass away. Men he liked, or at least respected. It was one thing to tell yourself that such was the way of the universe. It was another to think about what it really meant.

He tried to bring back his earlier bright dreams in all of their radiance. He tried to feel as he had felt but a few short minutes ago that this first promotion was but one first step on the long march that would lead him to the Great Wolf's throne. He brought them back but now he found them grimmer and darker. For he knew that command was not simply going to be an endless series of heroic deeds committed with the eye of history upon him. It also involved great responsibility and great weariness.

Logan Grimnar looked old. Not feeble, for he was as hale as a gnarled and weather-beaten old oak, but still old. There were other men in the Chapter as old as he and they did not seem so obviously ancient. Command had weighed Grimnar down, and carved some of those lines on his face, and even from his own limited experience of it, Ragnar was beginning to understand why. By his own decisions, Ragnar might bring death to himself and his comrades, but the Great Wolf could conceivably bring ruin to the entire Chapter, and end the existence of something that had endured for ten millennia. The thought of it made Ragnar shiver. It was not a good thing, on this dark night, to contemplate such things, particularly not in this place. Perhaps the loss of the Spear was an omen. Perhaps far worse things were yet to come.

He paused for a moment, about half way along the great approach, for he could see figures coming towards him. It seemed he was not the only one who had chosen this late hour to make his devotions. As the figures approached he could see that it was Sigrid Trollsbane and his hulking bodyguard.

Ragnar was not surprised. Sigrid had a reputation for piety. As he stalked closer, he noticed Ragnar and the company markings on his armour and his face froze. His scent acquired a slight acrid under-taste of hostility. He swept past Ragnar without a greeting, not even appearing to notice him. Ragnar shrugged. If a Wolf Lord deemed him beneath his notice, it was none of his business.

Perhaps though there was more to it than that. It seemed all too possible that the man was hostile because of the company to which Ragnar belonged. If so, that was madness. They were in a war here, and they were all on the same side. Internal dissension could easily prove fatal.

Ragnar knew he was being unrealistic. Such tension was common, perhaps even normal, given the structure of the Chapter. All of the companies competed with each other in many ways, as did their Wolf Lords. There were many competitions and tournaments between companies, and much good-natured banter too. Within companies, the various claws and packs would often develop rivalries as they attempted to prove their superiority. And, of course, it was not unknown for there to be long-standing rivalries between individual soldiers. All warriors wanted glory: for themselves, for their squads, for their company, for their Chapter, and probably in that order, unless they were very unusual men.

Ragnar found himself remembering an old saying among his people: 'When a man seeks the hand of a woman, he may have at most a dozen rivals. When a man seeks glory, the whole world is his rival.' And Ragnar supposed, all of history too, for the Wolves constantly measured themselves against the mighty deeds of their ancestors. In this place, with the footsteps of Berek's great rival fading behind him, such thoughts came easily.

Ragnar wondered exactly why Berek and Sigrid had so great a dislike for each other. It seemed more than they were simply rivals for the position of next Great Wolf, or at least, they perceived themselves to be. Perhaps it was just their wildly varying personalities. The two seemed polar opposites, as different as night from day. There were rumours that once, long ago they had even been friends, and that a rift had sprung up among them. Ragnar decided that, when he had the time, he would investigate.

He strode on, passing figures of men from the dawn ages of the Chapter, and scenes from the first two millennia after its founding. He hurried his footsteps, keen now to see the inner sanctum itself, resolving that he would return to look upon these ancient artefacts later, when he had more time.

Ahead of him, he could see a blue glow, flickering through the mighty archway. The arch was surmounted by the head of a wolf, and each massive stone was marked with the runic writing of his Chapter. The stones themselves radiated an aura of awesome age. Ragnar knew he was approaching the very heart of this mighty temple complex.

He stepped into one of the most ancient shrines of his brotherhood. It was a vast chamber with a vaulted ceiling and odd crystalline slits in the ceiling through which lights descended in mighty beams. The way to the sarcophagus of Garm was worn smooth by the feet of all the Wolves who had approached this sacred site over the preceding centuries. The enormous coffin was also a shrine. It dominated the northern part of the sanctum. The rest of the vault was plain and undecorated save for the tiled floor which depicted a scene of the heads of four mighty, fearsome wolves, opening their mouths to swallow a gigantic moon.

The sacred flame leapt almost ten times the height of a man above him, and it glowed with a chill blue light that illumined the fane. He stood before a sarcophagus carved from the tusk of a gigantic, long extinct sea monster, the notorious dragon whale of Garm which it was said Russ had slain with a single cast of the Spear.

A sculptor of genius had turned the tusk into an amazing work of art. Its entire surface was carved with an incredible level of detail. Ragnar looked closely and saw scene after scene of battle and conflict in which thousands upon thousands of Space Wolves in the antique style of armour favoured during the Great Crusade fought with hordes of monsters, aliens and daemons. Ragnar knew from his studies that each and every warrior who had still been alive when Russ had strode this world was represented here. Every suit of armour bore its own individual markings. Every visible face was different. If you looked closely you could see character and emotion expressed on their miniscule features.

Here was a Wolf Lord, his mouth open in a bellow of rage as he slew the mutated worshippers of Chaos. There was a sergeant smiting the monstrous tyranids. There was Russ himself, larger than any mortal, wrestling with Magnus the Red, the wicked cyclopean primarch of the Thousand Sons. The intricate sculpture made it obvious how little some things had changed in ten thousand years.

Here were Rhino armoured personnel carriers, looking exactly the same as the ones stationed outside the shrine now. There were Thunderhawk gunships that might have been the craft that Ragnar himself had ridden in recently. The products of the great templates of the ancients represented a peak of engineering perfection that had never been surpassed, and most likely never would.

The top of the sarcophagus was a representation of Garm as he had been in life. His image lay like an ivory giant atop the casket that held his bones. Its open hands were held on its breast in such a way to be obviously clasping something. Ragnar knew without being told that they had held the Spear of Russ.

Standing on this spot, Ragnar could feel its holiness. Russ himself was said to have had some part in the creation of the sarcophagus, imbuing it with a portion of his power, granting his blessing to the master sculptor Corianis. A flickering flame of light burned in the air above the shrine, illuminating it, and by the casting of shadows lending the battle scenes an illusion of life, making the figure on it seem almost alive.

But there was definitely something missing. This was the place where the Spear of Russ had rested. If something could make you aware of itself merely by its absence, it was the Spear. This whole shrine was meant to be its resting place, and with the sacred weapon gone, it seemed somehow meaningless. No, that was not true. It just did not feel whole. Even Ragnar, who had never been here before, could tell something was missing, and could have done so even if he had not known the significance of the place.

Ragnar reached out and touched the shrine. He thought he felt a faint tingling pass through the tips of his gauntlet. It was amazing to think he was touching something that Russ himself had touched, that he was in the presence of something the primarch had created. He closed his eyes and felt renewed. Energy flowed into him from the shrine. The ache of his wounds dulled. He had no doubt whatsoever that he was in the presence of holiness.

He closed his eyes and breathed in the cool air of the shrine. The flame gave no warmth, merely light. The tingling in his fingertips increased and he made to draw his hand away but could not. Strangely, he felt no sense of panic. The warmth continued to flow from the tomb. He tried to open his eyes, but they felt as if the lids had been glued shut.

Strange patterns flickered across his darkened field of vision. The silence intensified till his own heartbeat felt like a drum. The smell of ambergris from the censers drowned out all of the scents around him. Perhaps he was having some sort of delayed reaction to his wounds. Perhaps he should try and break away and seek help. He dismissed the thought. He did not feel as if anything were wrong. In fact, he felt a growing sense of wellness, of rightness, of benison.

The glow increased. The warmth deepened and flowed through him. He knew that in some strange way he was reaching out and touching the spirit of Russ, that all of the years intervening between the Primarch's time and his own meant nothing. In some timeless time and spaceless space, a spirit still hovered and looked out on his followers. He knew that he was touching the divine directly, and the feeling awed him. The ground on which he stood, and the shrine which he touched, were both holy. He knew that for as long as he lived he would not forget this moment.

His eyes opened. His grip was freed. He turned to depart the sacred place, renewed. They would find the Spear, he knew. They had to.

FIFTEEN

'WHY ARE YOU looking so bloody happy, Ragnar?' asked Sven. He waited only a moment for a reply and returned to squeezing the tube of field rations into his mouth.

Ragnar leaned on the fortified parapet of the outer wall and looked out into the distance. He was troubled and Sven knew it. He just did not quite know how to express himself.

Bluish snow, tainted by alchemical pigments, fell in chill cold flakes. Ragnar stuck out his tongue and tasted one. It tingled in his mouth as he swallowed. He studied their surroundings. Enormous buildings disappeared into the monstrous, low-hanging purple and black clouds that filled the sky, roofing the city. In the distance he could hear the crackle of a firefight.

Ragnar felt strangely reluctant to answer his friend's question. There had been something personal and sacred about his experience at the shrine and he did not want to share it with anyone else at the moment. He wanted time to think about what had happened.

Ragnar glanced around. The rest of the Blood Claws were huddled along the wall, staring into the distance. Aenar raised brass field magnoculars to his eyes and looked out for a moment, before handing the viewing instruments to Torvald. It was obvious they were looking for some sign of the battle going on out there. Strybjorn held his weapon at the ready, looking relaxed yet alert. The rest of the pack lay sprawled along the wall, taking their rest while they could. It was a trick they had learned from the Grey Hunters – sleep when you can.

Behind them the previously empty space around the shrine was filled with the massive bulk of Imperial spacecraft, each disgorging its cargo of men and machines. Now the Wolves had established a safe beachhead, General Trask, the Imperial field commander, was prepared to reinforce it. Tens of thousands of Imperial Guard, hundreds of massive battle tanks and dozens of heavy artillery pieces were being deployed on the plain around the shrine. Not nearly as many as were holding the spaceport twenty kilometres away, but enough to make the shrine all but impregnable.

From up here Ragnar could make out the standards of the 12th Maravian Guard regiment, the twin-headed eagle holding a solar disk in its claws. The Maravians themselves lined the emplacements in the walls nearby. Tall, broad shouldered men in light blue winter combat uniforms, they held their lasrifles as if they knew how to use them. A veteran regiment according to camp rumour, they held themselves apart from the Space Wolves, seemingly a little in awe of them.

One of them, obviously a green recruit, had actually asked Ragnar whether the Wolves really had cleared the shrine in the teeth of ten times their number. Ragnar had told them it was only five times, but that had been enough to silence the lad. Lad! Ragnar smiled. The man was probably older than he was.

Another glance showed Imperial Guard officers in braided uniforms and commissars in thick, black coats moving among along the battlements, come to inspect the position for themselves. The officers smiled and talked, at least until they got close to the Wolves; the commissars looked stern and forbidding. One of them caught Ragnar's glance and gave him a tight-lipped smile. Ragnar grinned, showing his fangs, and the commissar looked away. He was not sure whether it was because the man was intimidated, or he thought Ragnar might be some sort of mutant to be cleansed. Ragnar would not have bet against it being the latter. Not all servants of the Imperium regarded the Space Marine Chapters with awe, or even liking.

Not that it mattered under the circumstances. Ragnar felt sure that if it came to fighting, the Wolves could take out this entire regiment, no matter how badly they were outnumbered. He pushed the thought from his mind. Everyone was on the same side here. Out beyond the walls were hordes of heretics and daemon-worshippers. There were enemies enough to go around without looking for any closer to hand.

Sven had had enough of being ignored. 'Are you just going to stand there with your mouth open and wait for a Thunderhawk to fly in or are you going to answer my bloody question?'

'I was thinking about what to say.'

'Are you ill? You don't usually take so long to answer.'

Ragnar looked back at Sven for a moment, and wondered whether he should tell him. He looked significantly at the Moravians for a moment and Sven nodded, and gave them time to pass way off along the parapet, then slowly, in halting stumbling words, Ragnar tried to explain what he had felt in the shrine the previous evening. Sven belched loudly but said nothing. When Ragnar finished speaking, he looked up at him searchingly.

'I've heard that others have had the same experience. Some of the Wolf Lords, some of the Long Fangs, one or two Grey Hunters. Never heard of it happening to a Blood Claw. Maybe you should talk about it with Ranek or one of the Rune Priests. Maybe it means you'll be the one to find the Spear.'

Sven's tone suggested that for once he was not joking. Ragnar considered this for a minute. Sven was only echoing what he himself had thought in the minutes after he had left the shrine. Then he had felt like running to find Ranek and tell him what had happened. Some instinct had stopped him, and he had gone to sleep instead.

'The priests are all in the sanctum with the Great Wolf and his retinue, working divinations, trying to find out where the Spear is. Who knows when that will be done?'

'When you get the chance, talk to them,' said Sven.

'I will,' said Ragnar.

'Maybe I should go and look at the old pile of bones,' said Sven stifling a yawn. 'Maybe Russ will appear and promote me to Grey Hunter.'

Ragnar shook his head. Sven did not seem capable of taking anything seriously for more than a few minutes. No, Ragnar corrected himself, maybe he just hid what he took seriously behind a screen of levity.

'Think they will find the Spear?' Sven asked eventually.

'They have to.'

Slowly a thought seemed to work its way from Sven's brain to his tongue. He looked almost embarrassed to voice it. 'Would it not be terrible if we were the ones, our generation, this Chapter, I mean, who lost the Spear of Russ.'

So, despite appearances, some things did weigh heavily on Sven's soul.

'We will find it, and when we do, the ones who took it will pay.'

'Why did they take it, do you think?'

'Because it's ancient and sacred.'

'To us. To the folk of Garm, yes. But to heretics?'

Apparently, thoughts also found their way into Sven's head sometimes.

'Maybe they will use it as a rallying point. Claim that they are the ones blessed by Russ. Chaos worshippers have done such things before. Their holy one, Sergius, is claiming that the Emperor has forsaken Garm and that only Chaos can save the world.'

'He's probably praying for Chaos to save him, now that I am here.' Ragnar could almost see the thought return to trouble Sven's mind.

'Wasn't the Spear supposed to be magical? Garm did wound Magnus with it, after all, and Russ used it to kill a heap of monsters. Could it not protect itself? And why couldn't old Leman Russ leave it at the Fang like any sensible Space Wolf would have done?'

'I am not Leman Russ, Sven, I can't answer that. Maybe he left it here for some purpose. Was it not as a mark of his respect for Garm?'

'I mean, the locals did not exactly make a good job of protecting it, did they?'

'They did for ten thousand years.'

'Aye, I suppose so.'

Silence fell again. Ragnar considered Sven's words. What could the heretics be doing with the Spear? Ragnar had at first thought they had taken it merely to spite the Wolves, but Sven did have a point. If the Spear was a mystic weapon in some way, then what other things could they be up to? He shook his head. He was neither a mystic nor a scholar. It was not for him to answer such questions.

Ragnar returned to studying the distant cityscape. The buildings were huge, larger even than many of those he had seen on Aerius. They also looked much older, as if they had been hewn from enormous chunks of granite eroded over the millennia. Their exteriors were soot blackened and scarred by acid rain. The ancient gargoyles clinging to their sides were mere blank outlines. Everywhere black clouds puffed from enormous high chimneys. Even though war raged all around, the forges of Garm continued to work.

That was another part of their current problem. Garm was a major centre of weapons production, and had been since the time of Russ. As long as those factories kept working they would churn out an endless supply of munitions that would keep the war going, perhaps even allow it to be taken to other worlds. There was no shortage of armaments here. No shortage of men to use them either, judging from what he had seen. Then his mind returned to the question of the Spear.

Rumour had it that interrogation of the surviving heretics revealed they were little more than bandits, a horde made up from the local militias who had been driven from their destroyed factory keep. There had been tens of thousands of them in the initial attack, spurred on by this Father Sergius, who had since vanished along with his acolytes and the holy relic. All that Ragnar could gather was that Sergius had once been an Imperial priest, high in the temple hierarchy. He had been a well-respected scholar too. It just went to show, anybody who was not a Wolf could be a heretic. You just never knew.

Looking through the magnoculars, Ragnar could see the evil sign of the Eye of Horus blazoned across the sides of one of those cloud-piercing keeps. Just the sight of it made him feel sick with hatred and anger.

Focusing on the building showed him the fighting that was under way. Shots blazed from the slit-like windows at the tiny figures advancing across the cratered concrete plain below. Heavy weapons lashed out at Predator tanks. It was hard to judge whether those men there were loyalist or rebel. The banners told no story. They bore a white bear on a blue background. From the briefing he had received before they made the drop, Ragnar knew that these were supposed to be a faction loyal to the Imperium, but that meant nothing. The situation here on the ground was fluid.

Another complication was that every factory keep was an independent kingdom ruled by its own Merchant House, in theory owing allegiance to the Imperial governor, in practice contributing only tithes and conscripts to the planetary levies. Each Merchant House had its own private army, its own weapons, and its own legacy of grudges and hatreds with rival Houses. It seemed that the assassination of the governor and the breakdown of planetary order had given everyone the excuse they needed to start paying off those grudges. This was civil war on a scale that almost defied comprehension. Alliances shifted daily.

From reports they had received it seemed that it mattered less whether a House was loyal or rebel than whether it was prepared to help you smash your hereditary enemies. Treachery was the rule; savagery the law. So far the fighting had been contained on the western continent, and even here there were still large pockets of stability, but as the fighting wore on, it was spreading across the map like a stain of spilled blood. Soon, the whole world would burn, if steps were not taken to prevent it.

'Looks like they've got themselves a nice little fight going on over there,' said Sven. 'Wish the Great Wolf would let us go and join in.'

'I'll be sure to mention that the next time I see him,' said Ragnar. 'I'm sure he will give you leave to go and sort out the Garmites.'

'Bet he won't,' said Sven. 'We'll need to stay here and play nursemaid to the Guards.'

Another glance backwards showed him massive cloth-metal pavilions erecting themselves automatically. Mess halls, administrative centres, field temples to the Machine God. Among them he could see inquisitors, spacefarers and soldiers of all ranks.

It looked like the entire paraphernalia of the Imperial war machine was being dropped onto Garm. Rumour even had it that a Titan legion would join them soon. Ragnar hoped so. He had long wanted to see one of these mighty man-machines from up close.

Overhead, Thunderhawks flashed across the sky, striking at distant positions. The action seemed more like a vast tiger unsheathing its claws, a swipe in the air to test its strength rather than a considered attack on the enemy. In time the Imperial tiger would roar and strike. At the moment it lay quiescent, surveying its prey.

'I think I have seen enough bloody snow for one day,' said Sven. 'I think I'll go to the shrine and see if Russ will talk to me. Most likely he will, I reckon. He will say: "Sven, you're a bloody hero. Go out and show this world what Space Wolves are made of."'

Ragnar was beginning to wish he had never told his friend of his experience back in the holy of holies. He could see he was going to take a lot of joshing about it.

'He'll say: "Sven, if you had a brain you would be dangerous."'

'I am bloody dangerous, Ragnar. So are you. So is everybody in this stronghold. I just want to know when we'll get a chance to prove it to the enemy.'

Ragnar looked into the medical sarcophagi, wondering why Hakon had sent for him. The old sergeant lay stiff and unmoving. Gurgling tubes, filled with greenish fluid, snaked from the walls of the ancient bio-magical machine into the sergeant's flesh. His carapace had been peeled away, giving him a strange vulnerable look. His skin was pallid, like that of a corpse. A metal mask covered one half of his head, hiding the great hole in his skull. The scars on the remaining side of his face stood out even more strongly. Only his eyes looked alive. They burned with fury.

The Wolf Priest nodded to Ragnar, telling him it was all right to speak, and then retired to his duties. A few moments later, Ragnar could hear him muttering medicinal incantations over some of the other patients.

'How are you?' Ragnar asked. Hakon's lips quirked into a tight smile, but the fury never left his eyes.

'I have been better,' he said.

'You will be so again.'

Hakon gave a near imperceptible shake of the head. 'I do not think so, Ragnar. I have heard the healers speaking; there is too much damage for my body to heal. Parts of my brain were blown away. My spine is damaged. I will never fight again. Or walk for that matter.'

There was no self-pity in Hakon's manner, only truth. Ragnar did not know what to say. Confronted by the magnitude of the sergeant's loss, he suddenly felt very young and inexperienced.

'I heard you were field promoted,' said Hakon. 'That is why I asked to see you.'

'I would have come anyway.'

'No matter. I think you will do well, Ragnar, if you live and learn to control that fury of yours. It's a great thing in a warrior to be a berserker; it is not such a good thing in a leader. A leader needs to be able to see clearly at all times. It's one thing to throw your own life away in combat, even if it's not a very clever thing; it's another thing to throw away the life of your pack.'

'I know, sergeant. I do not think I am ready for this...'

'No one ever does, no matter what age they are. Do not think that way. I can see you have it in you to be a great leader one day, Ragnar. You are a thinker, perhaps too much of one, and the Chapter has need of men who can think as well as fight.'

Ragnar did not know what to say, so he kept quiet.

'I would have recommended you for Grey Hunter soon. You and your packmates Sven and Strybjorn are about ready for it. It seems Berek Thunderfist has already seen that.'

'What do you mean?'

The sergeant's voice was soft and rasping, and Ragnar realised there was a certain underlying sadness in it. Hakon was speaking like a man who knows he is going to die soon, he realised.

'I had some doubts, but I do not think Lord Berek has any. I think you are just about ready for Grey Hunter, but I am not totally sure. Because of your fury; it can be a terrible weakness in a man. Berek seems to think differently, but then he always lacked a certain prudent caution.'

Ragnar opened his mouth to say something, feeling that he should defend the Wolf Lord, but Hakon interrupted. 'Don't misunderstand me. The Wolf Lord is hungry for greatness, but he has other virtues that make up for it. He is a great leader whatever flaws he may have and you can learn from him, if you watch him. You'll learn from his flaws too, if you are as smart as I think you are.'

'Why are you telling me this?'

'Because I am an old man, Ragnar, and I do not have much more time in the flesh. I can see something in you,

Ragnar, Ranek could as well. I am not sure that it is something good, but good or no, I believe you will have a great impact on the Chapter – if you survive. I am trying to make sure that you do more good than harm.'

'I will always do my best.'

'Aye, and that might be your undoing, Ragnar. For you are headstrong and have very distinctive views of what the best is. It's a failing that most Wolves have, until we get some grey hair and a little sense.'

Ragnar wondered whether the healing potions were making Hakon's mind wander. They sometimes did that even to men with constitutions as strong as a Space Marine's. Under the strain of injury even their bodies' ability to metabolise poisons and drugs sometimes behaved strangely.

'Is that all you have to say?' Ragnar asked.

'No. Despite what I just said, I wanted to tell you that I was proud of you. You were the best batch of aspirants I ever trained at Russvik. Maybe the best I ever saw. See that you live up to that.'

Pride filled Ragnar at the old man's words. Hakon had always been a rough-tongued man, and never spared a word of praise for anybody. Apparently, he had hidden his true feelings.

At this moment, two Iron Priests entered. Something about their attitude told Ragnar that they had come to take Hakon away. They gestured for him to leave. Hakon saw this and nodded.

'That's all. Go now, and may Russ watch over you.'

Ragnar nodded and made the sign of the wolf. He could see Hakon flinch as he tried to do the same and his body would not respond. Ragnar halted for a moment then turned to go. As he left the medical bunker, he knew for certain that he would never see the old man again, and that left him greatly saddened.

SIXTEEN

'WHOSE BLOODY BRILLIANT idea was this?' muttered Sven, as they slid quietly over the lip of the crater and into the night.

'Yours,' said Ragnar. The Thunderhawk had dropped them off kilometres from their target to give them a chance of surprise. The darkness was nearly total. The red glare from the chimneys of the distant factory keeps underlit the clouds, but here in the vast space between the buildings all was shadow. Ragnar tasted the air, hunting for the scent of enemies; he found none. He cocked his head and heard only the scuttling of the giant rats moving between the buildings.

'What?'

'You did say you wanted action so I asked the Great Wolf–'

'Is that right? Did you also suggest this bloody stupid mission?'

'Quiet!' Ragnar held up his hand for silence.

'Yes, your majesty,' muttered Sven.

A glare told him that Ragnar meant it. 'There's something over there. Next crater,' he sub-vocalised into the comm-net.

'Bearing north, north-west. Distance about two hundred metres. Looks like the augurs were right.'

Ragnar looked back at his small squad. He knew they had all been listening in on the sealed link. Ragnar gestured for them to keep moving. He was certain now that he had heard something. He was not sure what, but he was certain it was not rats. He picked his way forward carefully, alert for the booby traps and landmines that dotted this cold, empty no-man's-land. He considered how the crater might have come to be occupied without orbital surveillance spotting anyone moving into it. Suddenly someone had just been there.

Old maintenance tunnels and subway systems ran under the plascrete plains. Most had been sealed off, some had been flooded with toxic waste, but a few were still in operation. Some of them had even been exposed to the surface by the blast craters. Ragnar could remember seeing gaping tunnel mouths and masses of twisted girders in some of the aerial holoprints of the terrain. Anyone trying to make a night approach to the shrine would probably use them. Or there was always the possibility of magic, he supposed. The Chaos worshippers might have used sorcery to teleport themselves in. But why?

Ragnar dismissed the thought. That was what he and his squad were here to find out. All they needed to do was investigate and report back their findings. If it was a problem they could deal with, they would. If it wasn't, the Chapter would. All nice and simple, which made a change. Little seemed to be straightforward here on Garm. The place was a seething hotbed of intrigue, treachery, betrayal and shifting alliances.

So far the Rune Priests' divinations still had not been able to locate the Spear. To all intents and purposes, Father Sergius and his minions had disappeared from the face of the planet. All the priests had been able to work out was that something terrible and evil would happen if the Spear was not returned. Such portents were hardly surprising under the circumstances.

Of course, there were hundreds of rumours flickering over the comm-net, but so far none of them had checked out and many had been set-ups for ambushes. Ragnar smiled savagely. The would-be ambushers had learned to their cost how unwise such attacks were.

Ragnar held his weapons ready and tasted the air. The wind had changed and brought new odours to his nostrils. Yes, there it was. Amid the chemical tang he could pick out the faint odour of unwashed bodies, the pheromone traces of fear and anger. There were men out there, in the nearest crater. Not many, but enough to spring an ambush.

Ragnar's flesh crawled. The hairs on the back of his neck rose. At this very moment, an enemy might be sighting a bolter at him. In a heartbeat, its shell might pass through his head and send him to greet his ancestors in hell. The rest of the pack sensed the change in him, and crouched down, making their silhouettes smaller. A moment later they too caught the scent. He could tell by the tiny pack noises they made, and the change in their own scent.

Who was out there, he wondered, easing his weight down gently, making less noise than a cat. Another patrol? This no-man's-land was full of them at night, the orbital augurs spotted the heat trails of many groups of men. All of them had learned to avoid the killing ground around the shrine, but that still left this whole vast industrial wasteland to fight over.

Judging by the signs of firefights they had witnessed, they often encountered each other as well. Or it might just be refugees fleeing some broken factory keep, seeking shelter amid the debris of a world shattered by war. Or it might be something else.

Ahead of them the lip of the crater loomed. Whoever was inside it had not spotted them yet. Hardly surprising for they lacked the night sight and the enhanced senses of the Space Wolves. Ragnar told himself not to be overconfident. He did not know this was the case. They might have night vision magnoculars. They might have all manner of divinatory sensors. They might be mutants with night-adapted eyes. They might have the aid of evil magic. They might just be waiting until he reached point blank range before opening up with every weapon they had. He recalled the words of Ranek: 'In war, you cannot afford to make the easy assumptions, to see only what you want to see. You need to engage with the world as it actually is, not as you think it should be. Anything else, and you will find yourself quite quickly dead.'

The lip of another crater rose above them now. He could see it was made up of packed rubble and interspersed with torn and twisted girders, and the thick steel mesh that had once reinforced the surface. Among the broken stonework bones gleamed brightly, and the burned out remains of a few groundcars lay like the carapaces of monstrous metal beetles. Ragnar paid close attention to them, for they provided good cover for any potential ambushers.

Quickly he advanced onto the slope, testing the rubble carefully with his foot, knowing that if he displaced any, if it gave way beneath him, he might as well light a flare to give away his position. Cautiously he moved up the slope in a half crouch, until he came to the crater's rim.

So far, so good.

Nothing had gone wrong. No one had opened fire. An ambush now seemed unlikely. Still, the hardest part was yet to come. He needed to get over the rim without being spotted, and without silhouetting himself against the skyline for anyone taking refuge in the crater to spot. Here the night's blackness should help him.

He eased himself down until he was flat and then slowly, gradually, raised his head above the rim. He could see the dim shapes of men below him. A gentle snoring told him that most of them were asleep. Not exactly an alert patrol, but the smell of gunmetal told him that they were armed. There were at least a dozen men down there too. Under the circumstances it would be easy enough to take them out. A group of sleeping men with one or two dozy sentries would hardly be any challenge for a group of Blood Claws. All he need do was give the signal and those men down there would be sent straight to hell. But...

There was something about these men. They smelled scared and weary, but there was no taint of Chaos to them. Of course, this did not mean anything. There were plenty of heretics who showed no outer stigmata of their evil and there were an equal number of perfectly human dupes who believed in the cause of Chaos. At the same time, there was the possibility that these men were allies. Again, that presented a problem, for a man could die just as easily from a friend's bullet as a foe's. Those men down there were scared and armed and might just start blazing away if a stranger spoke to them out of the night.

Briefly, Ragnar considered his options. What should he do? He could order the squad to open fire and wipe the strangers out. Had he been certain they were heretics, he would have done so without a qualm. Considerations of honour did not enter into account when you were dealing with daemon worshippers: you squashed them as reflexively as a man would squash a venomous spider. But he was not entirely certain, and that being the case, he could not bring himself to order their deaths.

'Keep me covered, I am going in for a closer look,' he sub-vocalised silently into the comm-net. Affirmatives rang in his earbead. Keeping himself low, he slid over the rim of the crater, and down into the bowl. These men were careless, he thought, to have left no sentries on guard, and no sentinel devices. Tired or no, under war conditions there was no excuse for it. Silent as a shadow, he moved closer to the group, taking advantage of every bit of cover. A stalking wolf could have been no quieter.

His every nerve was stretched to the sticking point. Every sense was ratcheted up to the keenest. Even as he moved, he realised he had made an elementary mistake. He was the squad leader now. He should not be risking himself. He should have sent one of the others forward. It was too late to worry about it now.

Instead he pushed all such thoughts from his mind and concentrated simply on keeping quiet and alive. The men who were awake were huddled around something. His nose told him it was a small smokeless stove, powered by some chemical oil. The strange acrid tang of it made his nostrils twitch. They were cooking something: meat of some sort. As he moved closer, he picked out more details. All of them were wearing thick insulated uniforms, covered in fur lined greatcoats, and their breath steamed into the cold night air.

Since Ragnar's body had adapted to it, he had never given the cold here a second thought, but he could see these men were wrapped and muffled like tribesmen for winter back on Fenris. Several of them wore two greatcoats, and had their hands muffled in great furry gloves. All of them wore filter masks over their faces to protect against the heavily polluted air.

One of the men was an officer. He wore a high fur hat with earflaps to cover his face, and epaulettes of rank showed on the shoulders of his tattered coat. A cloak of thick fur was draped on one shoulder. Ragnar assumed this was another emblem of rank, for it would have been far more practical for the man to have wrapped it around himself.

Ragnar was so close now he could almost reach out and touch the officer, and still no one had noticed him. These men almost deserved to die for their carelessness alone, he thought. Then again, few of them possessed the superhuman senses and reflexes of Space Marines either, and none of them had learned the craft of stealth hunting the wild beasts of Fenris.

'Cold tonight!' said one of the men. The accent was so thick and guttural as to be almost incomprehensible, but it was still recognisably Imperial Gothic. 'Cold enough to freeze the nadgers off a snow dog.'

Ragnar froze in place, keeping low, wondering if one of the men would spot him. It seemed unlikely; most of them had been huddled around their stove staring at its small purple flame. Their night vision would not be good. 'We should never have left Ironfang Keep,' said another.

'We did not have much choice,' said the officer. His voice was higher and his accent clearer than those of the common soldiers who had spoken. Ragnar had studied enough of the ethnography of the Imperium to know that he most likely belonged to the ruling class here. At the very least he was of a higher social strata than the first two. 'Not with Sergius's dogs running the show now.'

Ragnar felt a surge of excitement. Perhaps this man knew the location of Sergius? He tried to think calmly. Maybe not. Every loyalist on the planet talked about the heretics as Sergius's dogs.

'Begging your pardon, sir, but we should have stayed on and fought.'

'Stayed on and been killed is what you mean,' said the officer. 'Like Lord Koruna and the rest of the clan.'

His tone said that he wanted no argument, and so did the way his hand played with the flap of his pistol's holster, but his men were tired and scared and obviously a long way from home. Discipline was fraying fast.

'Some of our people are still holding out. We could have stayed with them.'

'If we are successful we can fetch help. There's no way we can hold out against the heretics now that the priest and his infernal minions are there.'

'How do you know those ships we saw coming down were not more heretics? The Emperor knows we've seen enough of them come out of the Eye of Terror. Those comm-net broadcasts could be a trick. It could all be a trap by the Chaos lovers to lure us to our doom. We don't know the Wolves have come back to take their shrine.'

'We don't know for certain. That's what we're here to find out. If those ships are loyal to the Emperor, we might be able to get aid.'

'And if they are not, sir?'

'Then we go back to Ironfang and die alongside our people.'

Ragnar had heard enough to tell him what he wanted to know. These men did not talk like heretics, and he doubted they were play-acting for his benefit. There was no way they could even have spotted him. And any attempt to get closer to the shrine would be suicidal now. He decided it was time to intervene. The officer strode away from the fire to urinate. Ragnar followed him into the darkness and waited for the man to complete his business.

The Space Wolf rose slowly and placed his bolt pistol against the officer's neck while clamping his hand firmly over his mouth. The man briefly tried to struggle but it was as futile as a mouse struggling in the mouth of a wolf; the Space Marine's strength was simply too great. Ragnar carried the man deeper into the darkness at the crater's edge, then spoke quietly and rapidly into the man's ear.

'I have a bolt pistol at the base of your skull. If I pull the trigger your eyes will have a second looking at your brains before you die.'

Ragnar could smell the man's fear now. He controlled it well but it was there. He tried kicking at a rock to make a scuffing sound, but Ragnar lifted him clean off his feet.

'Your troops are covered and my men are on a hair-trigger. If you make any noise, or try and alert them, they will die. Do not do anything foolish again.'

Ragnar felt the man relax. The tension went out of him. He could also see that the man was now trying to work out what was happening. He was thinking that if things were as Ragnar had said, why were he and his warriors still alive? Ragnar allowed him a moment's silence to give the thought time to sink in, then spoke again: 'You are loyal to the Emperor?'

Again the man hesitated for a second. Ragnar did not think it was because he was a heretic; the officer was trying to decide what would happen if he said yes. He obviously felt his life was in the balance. A wrong answer would most likely prove fatal. Ragnar decided not to give him any help with his response. The reply would be an interesting indicator of his character. He could feel the man's neck muscles move as he tried to nod. Ragnar let him move his head.

'That is very fortunate,' said Ragnar, 'since I am too. However, the situation here is tense, and it would be unfortunate if two forces loyal to the Emperor were to come to blows because of a misunderstanding. I am going to let you go, but don't do anything stupid. If you do it will be fatal… for you and your men. Do you understand me?'

The man nodded once more. Ragnar let him go, and he whirled to confront him. Even in the gloom Ragnar saw the look of shock on the man's face and smelled his bewilderment. Ragnar was at least a head taller than he was and much broader and heavier. His captive was doubtless wondering how such a presence could have possibly snuck up on him. Realisation dawned slowly, and the man's confusion was replaced by wonder.

'You are a Space Marine,' he said.

'I am a Space Wolf,' Ragnar corrected him. The officer's knees threatened to give way so great was his relief. At the last second he regained control of himself, and Ragnar did not have to catch him.

'The Emperor be praised,' the man muttered. 'The Emperor be praised.'

'Are you all right, sir?' came a voice from around the fire.

'I am fine,' the officer replied. There was a burst of laughter from the nearby soldiers. It was just as well the officer did not have ears as keen as Ragnar's, otherwise he would have caught the coarse jokes his men were making about how long he was taking. Sven was probably enjoying them though, Ragnar thought.

'You're from the shrine,' murmured the officer. 'It was your ships that we saw landing.'

Ragnar nodded.

'The Emperor be praised indeed. Some of the rebel scum claimed it was reinforcements for their own side. Maybe now we have a chance.'

'Tell your men that we are coming into the camp. Tell them not to shoot. Then we can talk.'

The officer complied, yelling that he was about to come back with an ally, and not to shoot otherwise there would be hell to pay. Ragnar sensed the confusion among the soldiers. They were wondering whether it was some sort of trick or trap. Ragnar decided that he had better take a hand.

Many of the sleepers were rising hastily, reaching for their weapons.

'I am a Space Marine and an ally. We have you surrounded but there is no need to worry. As long as you do not shoot there will be no trouble.'

Again he sensed confusion, anger and fear. The situation could easily turn nasty, so he decided to take a risk in order to keep it under his control. He pushed the officer ahead of him and strode confidently into the group of men. Lasrifles pointed at him, fingers tight on their triggers. Then he saw looks of wonder, fear, even awe on the men's face as they recognised him for what he was. The long links between Garm and Fenris had left all the natives capable of identifying that.

'By the Throne, the Wolves have come,' said one man. He sounded very pleased and relieved.

'Now we can sort out those heretics!' said another. In moments they had swarmed around him, slapping his back, clutching his arm. They seemed utterly relieved, like men who had been lost in a desert and suddenly encountered a guide. Within moments their earlier mutinous attitude had completely disappeared. Ragnar was almost touched by this show of the faith that the people of Garm had in the Wolves. He supposed those ten millennia of history had done something to instil it.

Looking closely at them now, he could see that their faces were pinched and starved; the hands clutching their weapons were painfully thin. Most of them had a slightly feverish look in their eyes. These were men who had obviously endured great hardship, and who were relieved by his presence.

'The Emperor has sent his warriors to save us from the heretics,' said one man.

Ragnar considered this for a moment. He supposed in a way, that it was true. 'Aye,' he said. 'That is true.'

'Just in the nick of time too,' said another. 'The rebels were bad, but those daemon worshippers are the worst of all.'

'Daemon worshippers?'

'Aye. Sergius and his men. They have a temple in Ironfang Keep. How they kept it secret so long I will never know. They are down there performing some evil ritual night and day. The Gods of Darkness alone know what they are up to. Some say they are opening a way through the warp storms to the Eye of Terror. Others say they are summoning a legion of daemons.'

'A temple to Chaos?' Ragnar asked. The men all spoke in affirmatives.

'Then it shall be cleansed,' he said.

SEVENTEEN

RAGNAR'S BLOOD CLAWS took up position among the local militiamen, positioning themselves as sentries so they could watch all the approaches. Ragnar could see Aenar and Torvald talking to the men reassuringly. Sven and the others kept watch on the crater's rim.

Like children in the presence of protective parents, most of the Garmites lay down to sleep, possibly their first decent night's rest in many days. Ragnar sat down near the oil stove, careful not to look directly at the flames. The officer sat opposite him. He fumbled inside his greatcoat, then removed a flask that smelled of strong alcohol and politely offered it to Ragnar.

Ragnar considered for a moment. He could smell no poisons, other than the usual toxins that filled the air and water here. It was still possible, he reckoned, for there to be some subtler narcotic within the flask, but the officer's scent gave no hint of treachery. More important was winning the man's trust and finding out what he knew. Ragnar realised that he was not doing this for purely military reasons. This was the first approximately friendly Garmite he had had any contact with, and he wanted to get the man's views on what was happening here. He took the proffered flask and swigged away. The alcohol burned against the back of his throat, and he felt the usual flush of heat and faint wave of nausea as his body compensated for it. The officer took his flask back and helped himself to a generous mouthful before stoppering it and putting it back inside his coat.

'The real stuff,' he said. 'Not made from brake fluid or vat alcohol.'

'Good,' Ragnar said, more because it was expected than because he agreed. He had tasted much better booze on his travels. If truth be told, he preferred Fenrisian beer.

'Jan Trainor, captain of the Iron Fang Industrial Militia,' he said, placing his hand over his heart in a gesture of greeting.

'Ragnar of the Space Wolves.'

'I am very glad to have met you, Ragnar of the Space Wolves. You do not know how glad.'

Even over the thick cloud of fuel fumes and alcohol, Ragnar could smell the man's fear. He did not judge Trainor a coward. The man's bearing suggested toughness and courage. His scent spoke of weariness, and his bearing of a man who had been living with his nerves stretched to the breaking point for too long.

'Why?' Ragnar asked.

Trainor looked around to make sure they were not being overheard, and lowered his voice as he replied. 'These past few weeks have not been easy. There have been times when I thought we were all going to die.'

'We are all going to die,' said Ragnar. 'Nothing in life is certain save death. It is how we choose to meet it that matters.'

Trainor gave him a bitter smile. 'You are a Space Marine, and I would expect you to feel that way.' The Garmite raised his hand in a gesture of appeasement. 'I mean no harm by that. It's just that I am no more than half a soldier. I put in my time in the keep militia, and because I was born into one of the high clans I am an officer, but if truth be told, I am really a forge-machine supervisor who has been given a gun and sent out to fight.'

Ragnar considered this. He had enough schooling now to understand most of what the man meant. He realised how much he had changed over the past few years. The unlettered barbarian who had grown up amid the islands of the world sea of Fenris would not have been able to grasp the concepts, even if he could have spoken this man's language.

'It looks like you have been doing your share of fighting,' he said, to encourage the man.

'There has been enough to go around.'

'Tell me about it.' Ragnar wanted to ask about Sergius but he also wanted a chance to judge this man and the worth of his words, so he moved towards his goal slowly.

'Even during the best of times there is always tension among the high clans who rule the keeps. Trade disputes, infractions of mining claims, arguments over transit tithes on merchant caravans, the usual thing.'

Perhaps for you, thought Ragnar. It all sounded outlandish enough to him. He tilted his head and considered for a moment. Perhaps not. Where resources were scarce, men always fought. He understood this well enough; even on Fenris it was the case, although there it was for possession of islands and fishing grounds. This place did not sound too different, in its own way.

'And there are always bandits, cultists and mutants. When I put in my basic two years in the militia we were forever hunting them down. Sometimes it was hard to tell where banditry started and politics began. Sometimes the bandits were financed by other keeps, or even disgruntled factions within our own, but you just try proving it...'

Ragnar realised the man was talking because he needed to talk. He had kept this to himself for too long, and could not share it with his troops, and now he was with someone he considered at least an equal, he wanted to get it off his chest. Ragnar nodded encouragingly and let him speak. He was learning more from the way this man spoke, from his attitude and his bearing, than he could ever learn from a hundred intelligence auguries, no matter how detailed.

'From time to time, the cartels, the tower leagues, would go to war to settle their differences. I fought in one. I saw thousands of men killed. I thought it was war. I had no idea. I had no idea...'

'Go on.'

'There have always been tensions among the keeps... Always. There have even been wars before that have ended up with Imperial intervention. Sometimes by your Chapter. I have studied these things; I know. It was that devil Sergius and his acolytes, always stirring things up behind the scenes while preaching peace and loyalty on the surface... When this all started I thought it was just going to be another one of those, bad enough in its way, but understandable. I was wrong. I don't think anything could have prepared me for the ferocity of it.'

So far Ragnar had seen nothing that matched the ferocity of any of the engagements he had fought in during his career, but this young man was doubtless judging things by a different standard.

'It started with a trade dispute between those Bronzehelm bastards, and Ambershield. The two big regional cartels were drawn in. The League of the White Bear for Bronzehelm. The Fists of Garm for Ambershield. Then they called on their allies, and we all waited for war. That's when we first started to hear the rumours.'

'Rumours?'

'Human sacrifice. Daemon worship. Cannibalism. Both sides were accusing the other. No one knew what to believe. Incidents grew worse. There were massacres of merchants, raids on outlying communities. People would be found with their hearts torn out and horrified looks on their faces. The old governor, Coriolanus, sent in his own men to investigate. They vanished. He announced he was sending off-world for the Inquisition, shortly afterwards he was assassinated. That was when the real trouble started.'

'Real trouble?'

'Father Sergius began preaching that the last days were here, that soon Chaos would come. At first, he told people merely to make peace with their souls, that the end was nigh. I heard the man speak on the comm-channels and his sermons were awesome. There is something in his voice that compels you to believe him, that dispels doubt. His charisma is incredible. And his cult had grown very strong amid all the anarchy. His preachers were everywhere, ministering to the wounded, aiding the poor and the sick. In the beginning we thought they were just another splinter sect of the Imperial cult – there are hundreds here, and they have always been tolerated…'

'But?'

'But we were wrong. Sergius's words spread more despair than you could imagine. Everyone believed that the final battle was nigh. Soon the Wolves would come, and Russ to lead them, and the last days would be on hand. Russ is not with you, is he?'

Ragnar laughed and shook his head but then studied Trainor intently. Obviously Sergius had made a very deep impression on him. He was quite a preacher indeed. Ragnar wanted to know more.

'No – the primarch has not returned,' said Ragnar.

'But the Wolves are here?' There was a feverish intensity about the man now.

'We came to free our shrine and aid the people of Garm. Sergius did not need immense powers of prophesy to foretell we would do that.'

Trainor looked relieved, although what Ragnar was saying was only common sense. It was a testimony to the compelling nature of this heresiarch's words that he had not considered that fact for himself. Perhaps there was sorcery at work here. Or perhaps, in the atmosphere of mass hysteria surrounding this unholy civil war, all sight of common sense had been lost.

'Sergius's followers changed their tune after that. Little by little, day by day, the message changed. Soon, it was inevitable that Chaos would win. After that it was folly to oppose Chaos. Then it was suicide. Then it was only sound common sense to side with the victor.

'The strangest thing of all was that so many believed him. There was power in his voice. Even if your faith in the Emperor was strong, it somehow compelled belief. There was such sincerity and passion and belief there. It was almost magical.'

'Perhaps it was magic, evil magic.'

'Aye, perhaps. Sergius's followers went from aiding the poor to fighting their enemies, and they seemed invincible. It was said that bullets could not harm them, and that their cloaks turned blades, and when they were wounded they healed almost instantly. If I had not seen that myself I would not have believed it...'

'Tell me more,' Ragnar prompted. 'You said Sergius is based in your home keep.'

'Aye, and has been for days. It's supposed to be a big secret but he's there.'

'That's not just another rumour.'

'No – I saw him with my own eyes.'

Ragnar held his breath. Perhaps he was closer to finding the location of the Spear than he could have hoped. 'When?' he asked, keeping his voice flat, calm, slightly disbelieving.

'Lord Koruna massed all the loyalist forces to drive the heretics out of Ironfang, nearly ten thousand men, all loyal to the Emperor.

'We drove downward from the upper halls, clearing them as we went. We would have succeeded too had it not been for Sergius. We drove them all the way back to the temple doors. The heretics were all but beaten when Sergius and his bodyguard appeared – and the things they had brought with them.'

'Things?'

'Daemons, monsters, mutants from the lowest depths, in their thousands. They used sorcery, they were unstoppable. I shot at Sergius myself but some evil spell turned my las-beam, just as it turned the bullets aimed at him. He killed Lord Koruna himself in hand-to-hand combat and that broke our morale and we turned and fled the field. No one wanted to face an invulnerable man in close combat.'

'After that?'

'The heretics hunted us through our own keep. We fought back, but it was hopeless. For every heretic we killed, two more took his place. They even laughed at us as they died. One prisoner spat in my face and told me that soon we would all regret choosing the wrong side. That Lord Sergius was performing a ritual that would bring Chaos to Garm and make all his followers immortal. That was when…'

Ragnar could smell Trainor's shame. 'That was when you killed him?' he asked gently.

'Aye, I killed a prisoner, an unarmed man. It was a dis-honourable thing to do.'

'You did the right thing. The man was a heretic. Death was his inevitable fate.'

'I wish I could believe that. He seemed to think immor-tality was. The Emperor preserve us, what if he was right?'

'He was *wrong*.'

Trainor looked at him doubtfully and then spoke. 'After that we fought from tunnel to tunnel and hab unit to hab unit, until eventually we managed to get into the old transit network and make our way here. We encountered some patrols but I don't think we were followed.'

'Could you get us back in?'

'Aye – I worked in the tunnels for years, doing mainte-nance. There are dozens of entrances if you know them, for transit and repairs on the geothermal power routes. I have the maps in my satchel. It's how we got out.'

'Good – we will need them.' Trainor did not look too happy about the prospect of going right back to the place he had just fought his way out of. Silence fell between them. Ragnar knew that he had to get this man back to the shrine. The Rune Priests would want to talk to him and probe his mind, to verify the truth of what he had said. By Russ, if it was true. Suddenly a voice spoke over the comm-net.

+Sven here, your lordship. It looks like we've got trouble.+

EIGHTEEN

RAGNAR THREW HIMSELF belly down beside Sven. Looking out from the crater's edge, he could see what had his battle-brother worried. There appeared to be several hundred warriors approaching. They were accompanied by huge hounds, enormous mutated mastiffs with sharp teeth and long, lean bodies. The dogs sniffed at some sort of trail, and proceeded quietly.

'We're downwind of them,' said Sven. 'Take a sniff.'

Ragnar already had. His senses were keener than Sven's. There was a corrupt stench to both the dogs and their masters that went beyond the basic pollution saturation common to everything on this world.

Ragnar knew the stink, he had smelled it before in other places and other times.

'Chaos,' he said.

'Nothing gets past you,' said Sven. 'Looks like they came out of the big hole to the under-paths over there.'

'They might not be following our lads.'

'And I might take to drinking milk rather than beer,' said Sven. His expression showed exactly how likely he considered both eventualities. 'That's the way our militia friends came – no doubt about it.'

'What are we going to do?' Sven asked. 'There's too many of them for even me to fight with any hope of victory.'

'A realistic assessment of the situation,' said Ragnar dryly.

'There's no need to be so bloody sarcastic.'

'I think it's time to summon a Thunderhawk,' said Ragnar. 'Maybe more than one.'

Sven nodded. Under the circumstances a hasty retreat, either on the gunship or under cover of its weapons, seemed like a good idea to him too. Ragnar patched himself into the comm-net.

'This is Squad Ragnar calling Castra Fenris. Position alpha-twelve-gamma-two. Requesting Thunderhawk cover. Position under pressure from approaching hostiles. Am accompanied by some locals with important information. Praise the Emperor.'

There was a delay of only a few seconds as he was patched into the company's command core. The people at the other end knew that no Space Wolf would be making such a request frivolously.

+Castra Fenris. This is Brother Gundar. A Thunderhawk is on its way. Hold your position. Activate your beacons. Praise Russ.+

'Ragnar acknowledging. Out.' Ragnar switched channels, dropping to the squad level. 'Ragnar to battle-brothers. Prepare for Thunderhawk pick-up. Switch on your beacons.'

A line of icons flashed on his field of vision letting him know that all of the squad had activated their beacons. The Thunderhawk would now be able to locate them. 'Sven, get the Garmites back up here, weapons ready. We may have to fight our way out of here, and I want every gun on those mutants.'

Sven made no comment. All humour had disappeared. He moved to carry out his orders. As he did so Ragnar focused his magnoculars on the hunters.

In the bluish light of the ancient viewing lenses he could make out their pursuers now. They were garbed in a manner similar to Trainor and his men, although they looked better fed and equipped.

The leaders wore ornate metal masks, moulded to resemble slightly distorted human faces. Instead of mouths they had grilles that indicated filtration systems. Ragnar had seen pictures of those masks before; these men were followers of Sergius. The men the cultists commanded were unmasked and their features were blotchy, as if they were suffering from the early symptoms of some hideous pox. Ragnar had seen that look before, on the faces of the followers of Chaos: the men were in the early stages of mutation. The hounds too carried the mark of the mutant.

He could see they did not quite resemble the hounds of his homeworld, for they looked more rat-like. Their tails were hairless, their features rodent-like. Hideous boils erupted through their mangy fur. Sores wept on exposed patches of skin. In spite of this, they appeared strong and hungry.

It was obvious that they were following Trainor's trail for now they were moving directly towards the crater in which Ragnar and his companions were concealed. Mutants or not, the men were well armed and well equipped, and there were far too many of them for Ragnar's liking. He glanced back over his shoulder in the direction of the shrine, wondering how long it would be before the Thunderhawk arrived. Not too long, he prayed.

The scuff of boots and the scent of soldiers told him that Trainor and his squad were moving into position near him. Some shouldered las-rifles. Two men wheeled a heavy autogun into position. The weapon looked battered and badly maintained. Ragnar hoped it was in better condition than it looked. Such a weapon could wreak awful havoc on a large body of men approaching over relatively open ground. If it worked.

Ragnar looked over at Trainor. 'Tell your men not to fire until the heretics are well within range. That way we'll get more of them.'

Trainor nodded acknowledgement and gave the orders. Ragnar was already making calculations. It did not look as

if the Thunderhawk was going to arrive in time. If that was
the case, he wanted to make sure they killed as many
heretics as possible. Their position was not a bad one. They
held the higher ground, and they possessed a heavy
weapon. The lip of the crater provided a natural parapet.
The real problem was that there were so many of their
opponents and so few of them. Ragnar had only his own
small squad, and Trainor had about two dozen men, at
maximum.

They were outnumbered by perhaps ten to one, and he
could see that their enemies had heavy weapons too. Plus it
was always possible that they possessed some of those
uncanny powers with which Chaos gifted its followers. Ragnar had seen those in action before, and knew that they had
better be ready for anything.

Even as these thoughts raced through his head, the wind
changed. The mutant hounds caught their scent and sent
out an odd chittering sound. One of the masked men
immediately gave orders. The heretics began to fan out,
units moving in both directions to encircle the crater. They
intended to attack from both sides at once, perhaps even
encircle the position. Ragnar let out a long breath. There
was not much he could do about that. He only had enough
warriors to hold a small section of the line. The best they
could do was sit and wait for the Thunderhawk to arrive – if
it did.

No. There had to be something more. At the very least, he
could set men to watch the flanks and give warning. A
glance told him that Sven and Aenar were already doing just
that.

'Strybjorn and Torvald – keep an eye out and make sure
no one gets behind us without you seeing them.'

+Affirmative. Praise Russ. Out+ the two Blood Claws
responded in near unison.

The heretics moved upslope now, slowly. They were being
cautious, taking advantage of all the cover provided by the
rubble, but there was something else. They moved like men
who were more than a little nervous. Every now and again

one or two of them would glance fearfully at the sky. Were they expecting the Thunderhawk too, he wondered? Had they somehow broken the encryption on the comm-link?

No. Ragnar had seen Trainor and his men do the same thing when they moved. After a moment, he realised what it was. They were simply nervous because of the night and being in the open. Ragnar supposed that for people who had grown up within the walls of the great factory keeps, and only gone abroad in armoured vehicles, moving across an open plain, even one made of concrete, must be a strange and unfamiliar experience. And the unfamiliar often made men nervous. He patched himself into the Chapter level comm-link and spoke again: 'Squad Ragnar to Castra Fenris. Can you tell me when that Thunderhawk will be here?'

+Castra Fenris to Squad Ragnar. Estimated time of arrival: two minutes and thirty seconds standard.+

Ragnar let out his breath in a long sigh and checked the time on the chronometer superimposed on his field of vision. There was enough time, he thought – just, if only the heretics would continue the slow pace of their advance. Of course, once the gunship arrived there would be trouble. He could not imagine the heretics letting them board and get away without a fight.

He turned to Trainor. 'When the Thunderhawk arrives. I want you and your men to board first. We will cover you.'

The soldier nodded and moved off to tell his men. They seemed a little relieved, although the smell of their tension continued to increase. Ragnar spoke into the comm-net once more on the squad channel.

'Brothers – be ready to cover the militia when the Thunderhawk arrives. They board first. Sven: after your performance back in the shrine I want you at that heavy autogun. When the militia start to climb aboard the Thunderhawk, I want you to cover them. The gunship will be here in two minutes.'

+Bloody affirmative, praise bloody Russ+ said Sven. More affirmatives arrived over the link.

Far off in the distance Ragnar could hear the howl of mighty engines. He recognised the sound, it was a Thunderhawk, coming closer at speed. He glanced backwards and saw nothing. Not surprising, the gunship would be coming in low, using all available cover and showing no running lights.

The sound of shouting from down below told him that he was not the only one who had noticed the sound. The heretics had paused in confusion, wondering what the noise was. Ragnar tried to put himself in the position of the enemy commander. What must that metal-masked man down there be thinking?

He was probably wondering what was approaching. He could work out it was an aircraft, and the chances were it would not be friendly.

What would I do, Ragnar asked himself? Unless the objective was very important, I would order my men to take cover and wait, to see what happens. That seemed to be the heretic's response. He bellowed something to his men, and they hunkered down in small potholes and behind large boulders, using every available scrap of cover. Ragnar could see some were unlimbering their heavy weapons, rocket launchers and heavy autoguns. The rocket launcher might certainly be able to take down a gunship. There was a small chance the autoguns might be able to do the same despite the vehicle's armour.

+Squad Ragnar, this is the *Hawk of Asaheim*. We are on your beam. Expect to be there in one minute. Honour to Russ.+

Quickly Ragnar came to a decision. 'We are in a large crater. The traitors have heavy weapons. Pick us up in the centre of the crater. Target on beacon five. Praise the Emperor.'

'Affirmative. Glory to the Wolves.'

'Everybody except Aenar, switch off your beacons. Aenar, get back there into the centre of the crater.'

In a heartbeat the Blood Claws had responded. Ragnar bellowed, 'Trainor – take your company to the middle of the crater. My brothers will cover you!'

Trainor looked confused. Doubtless he was wondering what company Ragnar was talking about. There did not seem any point in telling him that that had been for the benefit of any enemy listening. 'Go now, man!'

Trainor did not need a second telling. He set off in the direction in which Aenar was already loping. Almost panicking, his men did the same. Their withdrawal sent rocks clattering down the sides of the crater.

'Sven, get that heavy gun!' said Ragnar but the Wolf was already moving towards it. Behind them the roar of the Thunderhawk was louder. It must be almost on top of them now. Looking back Ragnar could just make out a black shadow dimming part of the sky. It skimmed up over the crater's far edge, and with a blast of its landing jets, gave away its position.

A fiery contrail marked the rocket that erupted from the heretics' position. Ragnar prayed that the firer had not had time to draw a proper bead. Now would not be a good time for the gunship to go down. He raced over and slid into position alongside Sven. 'The rocket launcher – take it out now!' he shouted, pointing to the enemy heavy weapon.

Sven grinned evilly and pulled the trigger. A stream of tracer blasted across the night, just as an enormous explosion ripped the sky behind them. Ragnar risked a look back. The Thunderhawk was still there. It had dropped below the level of the crater as the rocket blast cut through the sky above it. Even so, the shock wave had unbalanced the craft, and as Ragnar watched it, dropped like a stone towards the ground. Ragnar ground his teeth in frustration. Inside the cockpit, he could see the Wolf pilots wrestling with the controls. At the last second, a lateral jet flared into life, and the gunship righted itself before settling none too steadily on the ground.

Beside him Sven kept blasting away, howling challenges and threats at the Chaos worshippers. For a few heartbeats it looked like he might be able to hold back the enemy all by himself, then answering streams of tracer ripped the night, and the hard plascrete of the crater lip began to disintegrate under the weight of enemy fire. Ragnar hauled Sven back with one hand as fountains of flame flashed above his head.

'Time to go,' he said into the comm-net and loud enough for Sven to hear him. 'The Thunderhawk is waiting.'

Acknowledgements filled the earbead. Sven looked up at him and snarled. The madness of battle shone in his eyes. His lips were open and saliva gleamed on his fangs. He did not want to go, Ragnar could tell, he wanted to stay and fight. Ragnar could understand, part of him felt the same way. There was no joy like the joy of battle. Even as the thought crossed his mind, an odd smell, reminiscent of garlic and curdled milk, reached his nostrils. He felt a tingling within his skull and the hairs on the back of his neck started to lift.

'Sorcery,' he said, wondering what evil the heretics were about unleash upon them. He did not have long to wait. The evil odour intensified. There was more than a hint of rotting meat to it now. Unbidden the image of hordes of maggots gnawing through his dead flesh sprang into his mind, so vividly that he knew that it could only be the product of evil magic. The gleam faded from Sven's eyes to be replaced by nervousness.

'Time to go,' said Ragnar and they both turned to race towards the gunship's landing point. Half way there, Ragnar risked a glance back over his shoulder. Tendrils of oddly glowing mist, strangely reminiscent of the tentacles of some massive beast, swept along the lip of the crater. Moments later clouds of glittering yellow and green boiled up from the depths in a choking nauseating fog.

'They might just as easily have used bloody smoke,' muttered Sven. 'Bastard bloody show-offs.'

Ragnar was not quite so sure. Certainly the roiling mist would cover any advance the heretics were making but it might easily have some other purpose. He did not like the look of it all, and did not fancy the idea of being plunged into it in the least.

'Well, one thing's for sure,' he said. 'We know now that Trainor was not lying when he talked about the Chaos cults.'

Sven looked at him as if he had just said something particularly idiotic. As the words left his lips, the mist boiled towards them, one mighty tentacle sweeping out faster even than a Space Marine could run. It sought them with uncanny intelligence, for all the world like the limb of some monstrous kraken. Ragnar took a last glance to fix the direction of the gunship in his mind and raced on, as the mist swept over him.

It was like being plunged into a murky sea. Suddenly his sight was obscured. He could just make out the shadowy figure of Sven running beside him, then he became aware of a burning in his lungs and a stinging sensation in his eyes. There was some sort of poison at work here. His head swam as his system attempted to adjust to the presence of the toxins. Without thinking, he rammed his helmet on his head, and sealed the systems of his armour. He wanted to take no chances with being slowed down now. Every second might prove vital. There was a click as the vents in the helmet shut and his armour's sealed systems kicked in.

At once, his senses became less keen. His sense of scent was completely cut off, and his hearing was muffled. For a Space Wolf this was like being blinded twice. He relied as much on his ears and nose as upon his eyes. Now he was no more gifted in this area than Trainor or any of his men. Swiftly he spoke orders into the comm-net, warning of the mist, telling his brethren to be prepared. Hopefully they had spotted what was happening as swiftly as he had, but he was taking no chances.

Behind him he heard the baying of those enormous hounds, and the sound of pawed feet crunching forward on loose plascrete. He glanced backwards, hoping not to trip, and thought he made out a long loping form racing towards him. Whatever it was, it did not seem to have any trouble tracking him in the gloom. He raised his pistol for a snapshot but then a burst of heavy autogun fire chopped it in half. Its death cry was answered by the howls of massive beasts all around. Somehow the helmet did not seem to make these any quieter. If anything they had become louder. Perhaps it was just another trick of the mist.

Sven raised himself from one knee and raced along beside him again. 'You're getting good with those things,' said Ragnar.

'Must be all the practice I am getting. I'll make Long Fang before I make Grey Hunter at this rate.'

Ahead of them, the Thunderhawk bulked large in the gloom. Ragnar sprang in through the open hatch and glanced around. Things looked bad. Many of Trainor's militiamen were down. A few of them were coughing up blood or an awful greenish slime. Most of the Wolves present had their helmets on, and stood by the door, weapons pointed outwards, ready to shoot at any threat revealing itself in the gloom. The Thunderhawk shivered under his feet, like some mighty beast readying itself to leap into the sky. From beneath them came the roar of the autogun, audible even above the howl of the engines.

'Sven! Get in!' Ragnar bellowed, as the other Blood Claw stood below them, blasting out into the gloom with the heavy weapon. Near the vents of the gunship's jets the mist was thinning and Ragnar could see the beasts closing on him.

Even as Ragnar watched something sprang from the darkness and locked its jaws around Sven's throat.

NINETEEN

THE HUGE BEAST's fangs had barely closed on his neckguard when Sven bludgeoned it with the butt of the autogun. The monster's head broke open, spouting blood, but it still would not let go. Ragnar jumped from the gunship, chainsword ready, and swung it downwards. The weapon sliced through the beast's chest sending gore streaming everywhere.

'I told you to get in!' he shouted to Sven.

Sven rolled to his feet. 'The hound had other ideas.'

'The hound is in no position to argue.'

'True,' said Sven. His eyes widened and he raised the gun to fire. It sputtered a few rounds of tracer then began to make an awful grinding noise. It sounded like the mechanism had jammed. 'Bloody shoddy thing,' said Sven. Ragnar turned his head and saw what he was looking at. More of the great hounds raced closer, their long lean shapes visible in the mist only as shadows.

Sven leapt through the open hatch of the gunship. Ragnar decided he had better join him quick. As he did so the

Thunderhawk lurched skyward. What was wrong, wondered Ragnar? Were they caught in an updraft? Had the rocket explosion damaged the steering mechanisms more than he had thought? Were they engaged in some sort of evasive action?

He sprang upwards, clutching the bottom of the doorway with his left hand. It clamped into place as the Thunderhawk rose still further. Ragnar felt a heavy weight impact on his lower leg, almost pulling him free.

He saw one of the hellish hounds had leapt up, gaining purchase on his ankle with its teeth. More of them sprang below but could not quite reach. The Thunderhawk started to drift downwards again. Something needed to be done about that, Ragnar decided. First things first, though.

He lashed out with his free boot and caught the hellhound in the ribcage. There was a sickening crunch and the creature dropped. Ragnar pulled himself up one handed and flopped over the lip of the open hatchway. As he did so Sven finished fiddling with the mechanism of the autogun and leaned out of the doorway, blasting away at the hounds beneath. Quickly Ragnar patched himself into the commnet.

'We are all aboard, *Hawk of Asaheim*. Time to go. Russ be praised.'

+Acknowledged. The Emperor is good.+

The Thunderhawk gained speed. The acceleration rolled the off-balance Ragnar back towards the door, as the gunship pulled into a tight turn. Sven stood there, legs braced and continued to blaze away. Ragnar caught sight of the mist churning like a storm-tossed sea below him. It filled the crater now and swirled unnaturally round its edge, leaving the ground clear below. Certainly there was proof, if he needed any, that it was in no way natural. All around in the distance he could see the hulking shape of the keeps.

'Get away from the door, Sven!' Ragnar ordered. His battle-brother stepped back and Ragnar slammed his hand onto the pressure pad that slid it closed. He glanced around the inner cabin.

'Any casualties?' A chorus of negatives sounded from the Blood Claws. The militia did not look so lucky. More than half of them were bleeding from several orifices; more were vomiting on the floor. Ragnar did not feel so good himself. Nausea churned in his stomach, and he felt feverishly dizzy. Sven looked about as bad as he felt. His face was pale, and sweat beaded his brow. Whatever had been in that mist must have been potent to cause such distress to a Space Wolf.

He moved over towards the militiamen. Trainor and a few others looked alright. Ragnar noticed that the breather masks on their faces looked different from the others, obviously of better quality. 'Have you encountered that killing fog before?' Ragnar asked.

'We have heard of it,' said Trainor. 'I thought the heretics were using poison gas, but I have never seen any sort of fumes act like those.'

'Nor I,' said Ragnar. 'It was evil magic.'

'Nothing our enemy could do now surprises me,' said Trainor. 'Their wickedness knows no bounds. Sergius is a daemon in human form.'

The hull reverberated to the sound of an enormous explosion, and the Thunderhawk lurched to one side. That was rather too close for comfort, thought Ragnar, wondering whether the missile had come from the heretics they had left below or from some other source. Not that it mattered much – it would only take one direct hit with a sufficiently powerful weapon, and they would be done for. Still, there was nothing he could do about it. Their fates lay in the hands of the crew. At least there was something he could do for the poor devils in front of him.

Ragnar reached into his utility belt and pulled out his medipack. There were broad spectrum anti-toxins inside it, for use by Wolves whose poison processing glands failed. He hoped they might be of some use to the men dying in front of his eyes.

The Thunderhawk dropped and swerved once more, and Ragnar was thrown to one side as it pulled into a high-gee turn. Another explosion echoed through the night. The gunship skittered over the shockwave like a man running on the shore of an earthquake-tossed island.

'You'd think they would have bloody well learned to fly properly by now,' complained Sven, as he was thrown backwards into the metal wall. 'I could do a better job myself. Oi! You lot up front there! If you're not more careful I'll come up and show you how it's bloody well done!'

'That's a threat I would take seriously,' said Strybjorn dourly.

'Then I really would know my curse was at work,' added Torvald.

'I never knew you could fly a Thunderhawk, Sven,' said Aenar, all innocence.

If the pilots heard they gave no sign. Instead the gunship banked left and dropped like a stone. Ragnar clutched at the restrainer bar, and wondered whether they had been hit, or whether the engines had failed and they were even now making the long drop to the ground. There came the sound of another explosion nearby.

Ragnar glanced out of the porthole. He could see how low they were now, skimming along close to the ground, flashing between the craters, jinking around the piled wreckage and other obstructions. Surely they must be clear of their attackers by now, he thought.

He waited for long moments, and the Thunderhawk raced onwards. Ahead of them, he could see the shrine and the vast armed camp surrounding it. The gunship decelerated and then dropped rapidly to the landing circle. Ragnar looked around at his battle-brothers.

'We made it,' he said.

'They didn't,' said Sven pointing to the corpses of some of the militiamen lying on the deck.

As he let himself out of the hatch, Ragnar saw a number of Imperial vehicles speeding towards them. There was a Rhino APC with the sign of the Imperial medical service, a ground-car bearing the sigil of the Inquisition and, thundering in from the distance, a land speeder from his own Chapter. Ragnar removed his helmet and sniffed the air. The night smells

of the camp greeted him. There was a faint residue of the
poison mist on his armour but that was only to be expected.

'Looks like someone's been listening in on the comm-net,'
murmured Sven.

Trainor was supervising as his surviving men were carried
down from the Thunderhawk. Ragnar walked over and
clasped his shoulder. 'Stick close to me for the moment,' he
murmured.

The Inquisitorial car arrived first and a tall man, cowled
and masked, emerged from it. Several soldiers of the Maravian regiment accompanied him. He strode confidently
towards Ragnar, his men following close behind like well-
trained dogs. Medics jumped out of the Rhino and raced
forward to begin examining the sick militiamen.

'Well done, Space Wolf,' he said. 'I will take charge of the
prisoners now.'

Ragnar smelled Trainor's shock. This was not the reception he had expected. Ragnar looked at the inquisitor. He
immediately disliked the man's arrogance and his easy
assumption that his commands would be obeyed.

'These men are not prisoners, they are allies.'

'That has yet to be determined by competent persons,'
said the inquisitor.

'Meaning you?' asked Sven. His tone bordered on the
insulting.

'Meaning me. Meaning my Order. Meaning the representatives of the Imperium on this planet. You would do well
not to get in our way.'

'The Emperor picked you personally to speak for him?'
asked Sven truculently. Ragnar saw the inquisitor's hand flex
and come to rest on the butt of his holstered pistol. The soldiers behind him smelled a little nervous.

'Who are you?' asked Ragnar.

'I am Inquisitor Gideon.'

'Well, Inquisitor Gideon, I am Ragnar of the Space
Wolves, and these men are with me. If they wish to go with
you, they may, otherwise they are staying with me until the
Great Wolf tells me differently.'

Gideon turned to Trainor. 'You will come with me,' he said.

Trainor rubbed his head with his gauntleted hand. Ragnar could not help but notice that his hands were shaking. Obviously Trainor feared the inquisitor. It was hardly surprising – the Inquisition did not have a reputation for either gentleness or discrimination when it came to those in its charge. No sensible man would willingly give himself up into its clutches. On the other hand, no sensible man refused an inquisitor unless he had a very good reason to. Or the protection of some equally powerful ally.

'I will stay with Ragnar for the moment, as will my men.'

'You are making a mistake,' said Gideon. There was a definite note of threat in his voice. Ragnar heard the militia officer gulp audibly. He guessed that the inquisitor was smiling beneath his mask. 'Obstructing the Inquisition is always a mistake.' He turned his cold gaze meaningfully on Ragnar.

'Threatening the Adeptus Astartes is always a mistake too,' said Ragnar. This bickering was stupid, they were all on the same side.

Perhaps he should have given Trainor up, but he had not liked the inquisitor's manner, and he sensed something else going on here. He was not sure exactly what, but he was not about to surrender any Space Wolf prize to an outsider, until he was ordered to by his commanders, and he guessed the information locked in the militamen's heads was valuable. And if Trainor had information that would lead to their finding the Spear of Russ his battle-brothers would skin him alive for giving it up.

Behind him, the pilots of the Thunderhawk had pulled themselves out of the hatches on top of their cockpit and were listening with interest. Although technically speaking they were Grey Hunters and both of them must outrank Ragnar, neither had chosen to take part in the discussion which meant either they approved of what he was saying or they were allowing him to make a complete fool of himself for reasons of their own.

'The medical Rhino is ours,' said Gideon.

'We have our own healers,' countered Ragnar.

'While you debate this, those men are dying,' said the inquisitor.

'It takes two to make a bloody quarrel,' said Sven.

At that point the land speeder dropped to the earth and Ragnar was surprised and not a little relieved to see Berek Thunderfist and his personal skald Morgrim climb out.

'What is going on here?' boomed Berek. Ragnar told him.

'You are quite correct, young Ragnar,' said Berek. 'These men are allies and guests of our Chapter, and they will tell their tale to the Great Wolf. If Inquisitor Gideon wishes to come along, also as our guest, he may. We are of course requisitioning the use of the Rhino to bear off the needy.'

Inquisitor Gideon stared hard at Berek but said nothing. Obviously giving commands to a young Blood Claw pack leader was different from arguing with a Wolf Lord, and a famous one at that. He transferred his gaze to Ragnar and the meaning was clear. Ragnar had made himself an enemy this day. More fool you, thought the Wolf.

Berek strode over and clapped him resoundingly on the shoulder pad with his gigantic metal hand. The impact almost sent the Blood Claw flying. Berek spoke in the tongue of Fenris, so low only he could hear it. 'Well done, youth. Give these vultures nothing that belongs to the Wolves.'

Ragnar was not sure Trainor would like to hear who he now belonged to, but he kept the thought to himself. 'Let us be away!' boomed Berek. He gestured for Ragnar and his brothers to accompany him, as they loaded the sick and unwounded militiamen into the Rhino and headed off towards the shrine.

Inquisitor Gideon and his men accompanied them.

As HE CLAMBERED out of the Rhino, Ragnar saw more large ships had descended from orbit. They were even more vast than normal transport ships, and it soon became obvious why. The sides of one of them had swung open to reveal the monstrous humanoid figure of a Warlord Titan within. The mighty machine's weapons were stowed parallel to its body for landing.

Like a monstrous insect emerging from its cocoon, the Titan strode forth. As it did so, massive frames extended outwards from within the Adeptus Titanicus ship. Attached to these were trolley-mounted cranes and repair systems. As the Titan moved, the earth shook beneath its massive metal foot. Its carapace weapons raised themselves into the ready position. The huge multi-melta in its right fist swung to bear. Looking on it Ragnar suddenly understood the superstitious reverence so many held the Adeptus in. The Titan might have been some living manifestation of the Machine God himself. Perhaps it was.

Trainor and those of his men still capable of moving were ushered from the Rhino towards the great sheet-metal tent reserved for visitors to the shrine. Inquisitor Gideon followed swiftly on their heels as if afraid his prey would somehow elude him. The others were carted off to the medical bays by half-mechanical thralls, brought down from the Wolf fleet above.

As they approached the entrance to the shrine, two Rune Priests stepped forward. In their hands they held long carved staffs which they used to bar the way of Trainor and his men. A moment later Ragnar sensed the presence of sorcery as the priests used their unusual talents to probe the minds of the newcomers. Such a precaution was only natural before outworlders were allowed into the presence of the Great Wolf.

'You may pass!' announced the senior Rune Priest, before turning his attention to Gideon and his men. The inquisitor submitted to the same inspection as Trainor although with less grace. As he noticed this Berek smiled grimly, then they hurried into the depths of the shrine.

Ragnar immediately noticed the number of people coming and going. They were not just garbed in the armour of the Wolves. Here were commissars, officers of the Imperial Guard and fleet, even a few in the elaborate uniforms of the Adeptus Titanicus. The shrine was now the nerve centre for the whole Imperial force. Everyone around him moved with purposeful strides, and that special excitement and nervousness that told they were in a war zone on an alien world.

Within minutes they had made their way into the great reception area, where Logan Grimnar and his retinue waited. The Great Wolf lounged on his massive floating throne, surveying the crowd like a jarl looking upon a mass of petitioners. His priests flanked him; his Wolf Guard stood ready to defend him. For this occasion they were garbed in massive suits of Terminator armour, the most powerful man-sized combat armour in the Imperium.

As Ragnar and his crew moved forward, a path was made for them through the crowd. No matter how high ranking, they parted to allow Trainor and his escort to pass. A hundred strides brought them to the foot of the dais over which Logan Grimnar hovered.

As he got closer Ragnar could see the others who stood just below the dais. They were powerful men indeed. One wore the uniform of a Princeps Maximus of the Adeptus Titanicus. He was a massive man, who seemed more than half machine. One entire side of his body seemed made of metal. The left half of his face was a metal mask, a long bionic arm protruded from the left sleeve of his uniform. The trousers of his left leg had been cut away just below the knee to reveal a long, slender mechanical limb that ended in a massive claw.

'Lothar Ironheart,' murmured Morgrim from close by. 'And yes, one entire half of him is dedicated to the Machine God. The man has no heart, only a bionic pump.'

Ragnar had heard the name mentioned before. Ironheart and his Titans had fought alongside the Wolves before on several occasions, which was hardly surprising since the Salonus forge world was located close to Garm and his legion owned a supply depot on the planet. The man had made his reputation amid the blazing deserts of Tallarn, and was said to have destroyed three ork Gargants in the battle which had cost him most of his humanity.

Shimmering in the air above the dais was the massive face of Imperial General Balthus Trask, which Ragnar recognised from before. Supervising his troops from his flagship in orbit, he could not be in present in person, but he was making his presence felt over the comm-net. Several lesser Imperial field commanders were present in the flesh. None of them managed to project half the air of command of Trask's image.

Ragnar had not quite realised how much importance was being placed on his prisoners. He had expected Trainor to be interviewed in private by Ranek or another of the Rune Priests. Now all eyes were on them: those of the high commanders and all of the lesser officers. Several of the Wolf Lords stood ready as well, and Ragnar did not doubt that those who were not present would have representatives here who would patch them in over the comm-net.

'Well, Berek,' said Logan Grimnar, 'it appears your cub has done well. Let's hear this Garm man's tale.'

TWENTY

FROM THE HOVERING Thunderhawk, Ragnar watched the massive build-up of troops. It was the first time in his life he had seen an entire Imperial army massed for combat, and the sight stirred his heart. Troops covered most of the plain before the shrine. A dozen Warlord Titans dominated the force, towering over the mass of warriors like men looming over a swarm of insects. The single massive Emperor Titan dwarfed even them. Its long shadow seemed to lie over half the army. The shimmer of its void screens was bright enough to see. Loping swiftly on the edges of the force, lean, wolfish, Warhound Titans took up position for their race towards the enemy.

The Thunderhawk maintained a level altitude, circling over the Imperial army, affording Ragnar a fine view of the action below. A flight of Marauder bombers skimmed past and then were lost in the polluted clouds. Despite their stubby appearance they gave the impression of infinite deadliness.

Already the huge Earthshaker assault guns battered at the enemy position, sending monstrous shells smashing into the walls of the distant keep, not even visible through the snowy mist of the Garmite dawn. The weather diviners on the fleet had prophesied that the mist would clear soon. Ragnar hoped so. The weather here was a two-edged sword. It would slow down most of the vehicles save for the largest tanks and Titans, but at the same time it would help shield their advance. It was not the best of days to try and break into Sergius's stronghold, but it was as good as they were likely to get given the season. And the runes had assured them that time was getting short, whatever the heretic leader was up to, he would do it soon.

Most of the infantry below were in the Rhinos, ready to move into the battle zone. The Imperial Guard might lack the skill and superhuman ferocity of the Space Wolves but it made up for it with numbers. Tens of thousands of men were down there, ready to do battle in the Emperor's name. As Ragnar watched he saw more tanks drive through the snow. They were Baneblades, so large that not even the Titans could dwarf their massively powerful presence. He saw Shadow Swords too, ready to engage any enemy armour that might show. Not that any was expected at the moment. Today they were assaulting a fortress, moving in to liberate Trainor's home keep from the grip of Chaos and reclaim the Spear of Russ.

At least that was the message the Imperial forces intended to send to the enemy.

If the attack was a success and the keep was taken, well and good, but that was not really expected today. The defences were powerful, and the heretics numerous. The real purpose of the exercise was to give the Wolves a chance to infiltrate the fortress, spread fear and terror among their enemies, and locate and reclaim their artefact. After hearing Trainor's tale, the Great Wolf had decided this was what must be done. The Imperial general, seeing that the best chance of crushing the heresy was by striking off its head, had given his support. The death warrant of Sergius had been signed. Now all they had to do was capture the arch-heretic.

Ragnar glanced around the interior of the Thunderhawk. His squad was there along with several others. There was Sergeant Joris, Hakon's replacement and Ragnar's new superior. He was short and squat for a Space Wolf, but his arms were thicker than Ragnar's thighs. He was reputed to be the strongest man in the company and Ragnar saw no reason to doubt it. His head was half bald, leaving only a crescent of hair around the crown of his skull. Joris made up for this by having exceedingly long sideburns and long braided moustaches. His cheeks were ruddy, and his manner was deceptively pleasant and cheerful. He grinned, showing exceedingly long fangs.

Ragnar had been surprised to find the sergeant consulting with him. It seemed he was still regarded as something of a leader for the Blood Claws.

It was the Wolf's way. Once you were in a position, you stayed there until you were promoted or proved yourself unfit for it. If a man can lead, let him lead.

'This is it,' muttered Sven from Ragnar's side. 'This is when I make Grey Hunter. Now is the day, now is the bloody hour.'

'You think so?' asked Strybjorn. Even the prospect of battle did nothing to light his grim visage.

'Yes. Today begins a new chapter in the saga of Sven.'

'Sven the Boastful's saga,' said Ragnar. 'I like the sound of that.'

'You're lucky,' muttered Torvald gloomily. 'There's no chance anyone will make me a Grey Hunter. It must be my curse at work again.'

'It's because you're just out of bloody Russvik,' said Sven.

'Look on the bright side,' said Aenar. 'Our day will come.'

'Yes, when we're old enough to be Long Fangs,' said Torvald. 'If I live that long. Which is not likely.'

Troll loomed over him. 'Don't worry, little man, I will protect you.'

Ragnar closed his eyes and offered up a prayer to Russ. This did not feel right. There was something missing. He glanced over again at Joris. It was odd to see him sitting there. Ragnar half-expected to be looking at Hakon's scarred face. He shoved the thought aside. Never again in this life. Well, he had fought beside other sergeants than Hakon. There was Hengist who had led them into the Chaos temple beneath the Fenrisian mountains for one. There had been Lothar, that time on Xecutor. Doubtless there would be others in the future.

'You're looking pretty bloody cheerful,' said Sven, nudging him in the ribs. 'What's the matter? Missing the thrill of command?'

'Something like that.' Ragnar considered this for a moment. Was that part of his strange mood, he wondered? Did he miss the thrill of command? His initial reaction was to say that he did not. Part of him was glad that someone else was now responsible for the lives of his comrades. Reflecting further, he thought that maybe part of him did. There was something heady about being the leader, about giving orders and having them obeyed, about being master of your own destiny and the destiny of those about you.

Was that why Berek had made him the patrol leader, Ragnar wondered? To give him a taste of command, to see how he reacted, to let him see for himself what it felt like? Had it been some sort of test? It was certainly possible. For all his bluff manner, Berek was a good leader.

Ragnar glanced over at Trainor, glad that the young officer had been assigned to their pack. All of the surviving militiamen had been divided up and assigned to the companies going in. Their knowledge of the inside of Ironfang Keep might prove invaluable.

Trainor did not look well. He seemed to have aged ten years over night. Ragnar guessed that his investigation by the Rune Priests had done that. The ancient sorcerers had deep probed his mind and those of all of his men. They were taking no chances of a traitor leading the Wolf companies into an ambush.

Ragnar felt a surge of sympathy, remembering his own ordeal at the hands of those terrible old men when he had passed through the Gate of Morkai. He doubted that facing Inquisitor Gideon would have been any easier.

Trainor must have passed with flying colours otherwise he would not have been here. One of his men had not been so lucky. Ragnar was not sure he wanted to know what had happened to him. Trainor met Ragnar's gaze levelly with his haunted, suffering eyes. This could not be easy for him, going back to his lifelong home as part of an invasion force, preparing to fight former friends and neighbours who had turned against him. A warrior's lot was rarely easy.

Ragnar thought back to the long hours in Grimnar's throne hall, as the various Imperial commanders had thrashed out their plan of attack. It was an inspiring thought that Trask, who notionally had supreme command of that vast force on the ground down there, had deferred to the Great Wolf's wishes and gone along with the plan to attack the Chaos stronghold and recover the Spear of Russ. It seemed that the worth of the Wolves counter-balanced all of the massive Imperial force.

Of course, Ragnar quickly realised that things were not quite as they seemed. Trask might well be the Imperial Guard commander, but neither the Wolves nor the Titan legion were bound to obey him. Both were proudly independent forces and had let him know it. The Princeps Maximus recognised no authority but the Grand Master of his order. Logan Grimnar recognised none save that of the Emperor. This made Ironheart and the Great Wolf natural allies. It seemed to Ragnar that Trask had gone along as much to keep the peace, and his force concentrated, as to get the sacred artefact back.

In a way, it was a very sensible decision politically as well as militarily. Once the Wolves had recaptured their treasure they would be far more likely to go along with the rest of the general's plans, and if the Wolves went, that made Ironheart more likely to. It seemed that one had to be as much a diplomat as a strategist to lead Imperial armies. Thinking about the rival Wolf Lords in the Chapter, that probably applied to the Great Wolf too. A man would have to be skilful in negotiation as well as war to lead a Space Marine Chapter. It was something that bore thinking about.

Ragnar guessed that Trask too had his own problems. Certainly some of his field commanders had seemed just as keen as Logan Grimnar to attack the Ironfang Keep. Doubtless they wanted the glory, to write their names in Imperial history alongside those of the Chapter. And doubtless they too were as keen to outshine their rivals as Berek and Sigrid. War among the stars was not quite so simple as it was back home in Fenris. There it had simply been a case of the jarl lining up his warriors and ordering the charge. Or perhaps he had simply been too young to understand then. Perhaps all forces of men were like this. Sometimes he felt like he had aged a hundred years since being chosen.

Nearby he saw other Thunderhawks circling. Most of the Chapter's gunships were in the air this day, which was hardly surprising. The plan was a bold one, and it required extreme mobility, the sort that only Thunderhawks could provide. Once they were within the keep then it would be pure infantry work, there would be no room for land speeders, assault bikes or dreadnoughts. There would not even be any use for Terminator armour. This operation required speed, stealth and extreme precision – a series of hit and run attacks on major enemy communication centres, power cores and weapon emplacements, a set of attacks that would demoralise and terrorise the enemy. They would need to locate entrances to the Chaos cult shrine, and then enter it to reclaim the Spear.

To be honest Ragnar was not so sure that the followers of the Dark Ones could be terrorised. He doubted that anything would scare a man who had already given his soul up to the powers of Chaos, not even the righteous wrath of the Emperor's chosen. Fortunately though, they would be in the minority. The deluded fools who had chosen to follow Sergius and his acolytes were not so nerveless. And they still provided the bulk of the enemy's troops. Or so Ragnar hoped.

Once more he ran through the holomaps he had memorised. All of them were stored within the matrix of his armour, but in the heat of battle they could not always be called up, and sometimes armour got damaged. It was better to carry the information in your head. Ragnar visualised the keep as it had first been shown to him. It was a huge structure of the type favoured by humanity on these industrial worlds, basically a cube, a kilometre per side. The cube was joined to the earth by a tangled web of pipes and cables that resembled the root structure of some massive plant. These were power systems drawing thermal heat from Garm's fiery core, and water from underground reservoirs and transit tubes for grav-trains. The tubes clambered up the side of the structure like vines clinging to the walls of some ancient stronghold.

At each corner of the keep's roof, four enormous towers thrust into the sky like spears aimed at the belly of the clouds. These towers were part fortification and part chimney, venting enormous clouds of pollutants into the sky. From the centre of the roof jutted a truncated pyramid, as massive as many islands back home on Fenris. This was the place where the keep's nobility dwelled and where many of the control systems for the entire structure terminated.

He reviewed the access points to the keep that had been overlaid on the holomap. One of them was going to be the entrance for his pack. Below them, the army had started moving forward across the icy plain. In the distance, plumes of smoke, ash and snow rose where the shells impacted. Hell touched Garm there.

The Thunderhawk began moving forward in formation with the rest of the Chapter's gunships, keeping pace with the army, flying so low that the scars on the shoulder carapaces of the Titans were visible. As far as the enemy was concerned, the Wolves would just be part of the attacking force. Looking down, Ragnar got some idea of the scale of the great machines. Close up they seemed even larger than he had imagined.

'Now that is what I call a bloody gun,' said Sven, pointing to the massive cannon clutched in the Titan's enormous metal fist. Ragnar nodded. In all the days since he was chosen he had never wished to be anything but a Wolf, but at that moment, he thought if he had to choose to be something else, it would be the Princeps of a Titan. He tried to imagine what it would be like to control that behemoth of steel and ceramite. It must be the closest thing to being a god that any man could ever experience.

'I don't think you could lift it,' said Torvald gloomily.

'I don't think the entire Chapter put together could lift it.'

Sergeant Joris heard the exchange. 'One Marine in the right place can do ten times the damage one of those things can.'

He spoke with the utter certainty of a man who had experienced the truth of his words. Ragnar supposed it was true.

'Aye, but it's a bloody lot more difficult for us to get to that place,' said Sven.

'And I have a sore foot already,' said Torvald.

'You'll have a sore head as well if you don't stop whining,' said the sergeant.

Torvald grinned to himself. The Thunderhawk juddered and shook as it turned into the wind for a moment, and then slipstreamed the Titans.

'Could they fly any slower?' Torvald asked.

'They could but we would be going backward,' said Sven.

'Like your brain,' said Ragnar. Despite the banter, the tension within the cabin was rising. The words had a brittle quality, and the scent of his pack spoke of excitement and anxiety in equal measures. Aenar had closed his eyes. His lips moved in silent prayer. Trainor had joined him. Strybjorn stared bleakly off into the distance like a man with a premonition of his own death.

Joris moved along the line, checking weapons and armour, making sure the Wolves were ready for battle as soon as they deployed. Ragnar felt a slight surge of resentment. Sergeant Hakon had never done that, at least not so obviously. He had trusted them to look after themselves. With Joris, it was obvious that they were mere Blood Claws, and that he was the veteran. Ragnar found himself looking forward to the day when he became a Grey Hunter, and would be beyond such things.

Suddenly there was the sound of an explosion. To the left a plume of black smoke arose. Ragnar glanced out of the porthole and saw that one of the tanks had been hit. He had no idea by what. As he watched a few tiny crewmen bailed out, and ran for cover. A few seconds later, the tank exploded, sending metal debris fountaining skyward.

'Looks like the heretics finally woke up,' said Sven. 'I was starting to wonder if they were all asleep.'

The other Baneblades started blasting away in response, although Ragnar was not sure what they hoped to achieve. No matter how powerful those guns were, they could do little damage to the walls of the keep.

'Look at that,' said Aenar, pointing out of the right porthole. Ragnar glanced over. He could see that a Warlord Titan was bringing its weapon to bear. The air was filled with an enormous humming sound as the Titan's generators peaked at maximum energy, and then its gun sent a spear of energy lancing at the distant building with a sound like a thunderclap. The sound reverberated like thunder as the rest of the Titans opened up. Ragnar wished he were up in the cockpit now, so that he could get a view looking forward. It would be interesting to see the effects of the Titan's incredible firepower on the enemy.

The battle had begun in earnest now. The Imperial army was firing at will, and their enemy responded in kind. A wave of explosions ripped through the Imperial line as some kind of multiple rocket launcher targeted the onrushing Rhinos. Looking down into the maelstrom of explosions, it seemed impossible that anything could have survived, but when the dust and snow settled Ragnar could see that not a single Rhino had been touched, and all were now far beyond the point of impact. Such were the fortunes of war, he thought.

'My grandmother could bloody well shoot better than that,' said Sven conversationally. 'And she was blind.'

'It would be just my luck to be targeted by the only heretic with a decent aim,' said Torvald. 'I've never been lucky, you know.'

'It's those who know you who are unlucky,' said Strybjorn.

'My mother was cursed by a Bear Clan witch woman before I was born. Have I mentioned that before?'

'About a hundred times,' said Strybjorn.

'What was the curse? That she would have to put up with the gloomiest bastard on the face of Fenris?' asked Sven.

'She would never tell me. She would just look at me and shake her head sadly.'

'I can understand that,' said Sven. 'I do the same myself.'

'Maybe the same witch woman cursed your mother, Sven,' said Ragnar. 'There has to be some reason her son was born so ugly.'

Another explosion sounded. A huge crater appeared in the carapace of the Titan in front of them. Chunks of ceramite flew past the Thunderhawk.

'That was close,' said Aenar.

'It's going to get closer yet,' shouted Joris. 'We're going in.'

TWENTY-ONE

THE THUNDERHAWK ROSE above the shoulder of the Titan, and Ragnar caught sight of the Ironfang rising out of the snow and mist. All along its sides, huge guns blasted away. City defence missile launchers sent payloads of death smashing into the Imperial army. It was an imposing sight.

'Less than half of the turrets are firing,' said Ragnar.

'There must still be fighting going on in the city,' said Trainor.

'Unless it's a trap,' said Torvald with a certain amount of relish. 'That would be just like my luck.'

The Imperial barrage was taking its own toll. Many turrets on the keep had been blasted into smithereens. Flames leapt from their hardpoints. Pools of steaming metal marked where some had been reduced to slag by the Titans' fire-power. Massive explosions carved huge chunks from the sides of the building, exposing twisted girders. Steam poured from broken pipes large enough for Rhinos to drive inside.

Now components of the Imperial force raced ahead, Rhinos and lighter tanks hurtling towards the holes in the lower walls. Land speeders and battle bikes probed even further forward, plumes of snow and ash rising in their wakes. Tens of thousands of autorifles and bolters opened up, as infantry within the building joined the fray. Ragnar saw the contrails of rockets from man-portable launchers as their projectiles tore through the Imperial ranks.

The fury of the Imperial barrage increased. The Titans concentrated all of their firepower on the areas around the weak points in the keep's defences. The tanks added their fire to the weight of hot metal death streaming towards the heretics. The roar of weapons crescendoed, drowning out even the sound of the Thunderhawk's engines. Billowing clouds of smoke and the dazzling glare of explosions hid the keep from sight. It seemed impossible that anything could live amid that storm of death, but it did.

From out of the cloud came an answering hail of fire. Ragnar saw a Titan stumble and crash to the ground, for all the world like a vast wounded soldier. Dozens of Rhinos became blazing coffins for the brave men within. The Warhounds reached the outskirts of the shantytown surrounding the keep, crushing flimsy structures beneath their massive paws, their weapons spitting death towards the enemy.

Hundreds of heretics concealed within the hab bubbles poured out, blasting away at the huge machines with their pitiful weapons, trying to stop them with grenades and weapons intended only to take out tanks and other lesser engines of destruction. They were met by a host of Imperial Guard disgorged by the first wave of Rhinos. The fighting swiftly became close and brutal, fought with bayonets, blades and the butts of guns. All the while, the turrets on the side of Ironfang kept firing indiscriminately into the melee, wreaking havoc on friend and foe alike.

Still the rest of the Imperial army came on, smashing through the shacks and hab bubbles like a drunken man reeling through an insect hive.

Logan Grimnar's calm, clear voice sounded over the comm-net. +Wolves, prepare for battle. Praise Russ.+

The Thunderhawk dropped downwards, lurching slightly as it sent rockets and heavy autogun fire scything into the enemy position. Ragnar grinned at Sven as he made ready to deploy. Already ·the hatch in the gunship's side had slid open. Cold polluted air and strangely discoloured snowflakes drifted in. The ground rose to meet them. The swarm of men battled below. Ragnar clutched his weapons to his chest, readying himself for the leap into the fray.

Moments later the Thunderhawk halted a metre above the ground. Sergeant Joris sprang through the hatchway, followed by half a dozen Blood Claws. Sven joined him, then Ragnar and the rest of his pack. Ragnar flexed his legs slightly to absorb the impact, and glared around seeking a target. His keen eyes spotted a sniper moving along the domed roof of a nearby hab bubble. He raised his bolt pistol and sent a shell hurtling at the man. At the last second his target rolled back out of sight. Ragnar knew it was only temporary. Moments later the long barrel of the man's rifle peeked into view, and then his head followed it. Ragnar did not miss this time.

He glanced around. Dozens of Thunderhawks had landed and were disgorging entire companies onto the ground. So far everything was going according to plan. They were exactly where they supposed to be, close to the manholes covering the access tunnels into the geothermal pipes shown on Trainor's maps. The battle raging around them provided all the cover they needed. Already Marines were lifting the manholes and dropping into the darkness below. Ragnar kept hunting for targets as he prepared to join them.

For the first time he began to get a sense of how big the factory keep really was. It loomed like a mountain above them, its massive shadow falling for kilometres. It had a cold, monumental presence like the Fang back home. Great fountains of industrial slag had gushed down its side, like molten lava. As the slag solidified it became another layer of armour on the keep's side, except where it had been mined by the scavengers who dwelled in the bubble towns. Looking up, Ragnar could see dozens of strange icons painted across its side, and fluttering banners descending from its towers.

This close, the keep looked most unlike a cube. Thousands of lesser structures, turrets, observation points, lift shafts and metallic pipes erupted from its side like a profusion of strange inanimate blossoms. Huge holes gaped here and there. Massive piles of hardened slag rose up the sides like waves frozen in the moment of battering a cliff-side. It seemed almost folly to contemplate attacking such a fortress, but not only were they doing so, they expected to succeed.

Already most of the Wolves had vanished down the holes, and into the darkness below. Ragnar knew it was time to join them.

Below ground it was dark, warm and humid. The air smelled of rotten eggs. Ragnar reached up and with his left hand touched the inside of the massive pipe. It was so hot it would have seared naked flesh; it felt warm even through his ceramite gauntlet.

Ahead of him, he could smell Trainor sweating. The militiaman had removed his greatcoat and jacket and was stripped to the waist. Conditions down here were exactly the opposite of those on the surface. Ahead of them long lines of Wolves disappeared off into the distance. Each man looked ready for battle. In theory, these tunnels were clear, but no Marine ever chanced such a thing. They were ready for combat at any moment.

They followed the main geo-thermal vent for only a few hundred paces, and then ahead of them some of the militiamen moved in to remove another manhole cover. This one was ancient and encrusted with grime. It led into a darker, narrower, lower tunnel that obviously had not been used for a very long time.

Ragnar had to stoop now, for the tunnel was built so that a native of Garm barely had room to stand upright, and the Space Wolf was a head taller than any of them. As he made his way through it, Ragnar felt a growing nervousness and tension within him that he recognised. He did not like being in this enclosed space. He breathed deeply, and offered up a prayer to the Emperor, and his racing heartbeat slowed.

It was not any cooler in this ancient tunnel, and a thick brown noxious-smelling sludge filled the corridor to knee height. Faint wisps of foul smelling smoke rose from it. Beyond any shadow of a doubt, this was toxic.

'What was this place?' Ragnar asked Trainor.

'Who knows? The ancients built these corridors long ago. A web of them extends below the surface of the planet. Most believe they are the relics of ancient mining operations. Certainly some of them lead down into abandoned mineshafts and galleries. We found new ones all the time when we were doing maintenance.'

'You don't believe that? About the mines?'

'I think it's at least as likely as any other explanation. The first keeps predate the Imperium. They were here when Russ walked this world. A lot can be forgotten in ten thousand years.'

'Why are they unwatched?'

'Some of them are monitored. But no one can keep an eye on tens of thousands of leagues of tunnel, not when they are fighting a war on the surface, and with their own people. And most people have forgotten that these tunnels exist. The militias knew of them but up there, right now all is confusion. And anyway, not all of these tunnels are empty.'

That got Sven's attention. 'Really – who would be bloody stupid enough to live down here?'

'Cannibal scavvies, outlaws, forbidden cultists, and it's not just people. There are giant rats, starback spiders, tunnel dragons, all sorts of mutant beasts. Some say they are haunted by the ghosts of the ancients as well.'

'Cheery place,' said Sven glancing around.

'It would be just my luck to be eaten by a tunnel dragon,' said Torvald gloomily. 'Maybe that way the curse will be fulfilled.'

'The curse of Sven's fist will be fulfilled if you don't bloody shut up,' muttered Sven.

'Look up there,' said Trainor.

'What?' Ragnar asked.

The militia officer was pointing to a moving clump of flesh that Ragnar had already scented but not paid too much attention to. When he looked closer, in the light of the pencil beam from his shoulder-pad lamp, he could see the clump was about the size of his fist and moved along on eight legs.

'Starback,' said Trainor. 'One drop of its venom can kill a man.'

He moved extremely cautiously as he went below the spider. Sven raised his pistol as if to shoot it, and then restrained himself. Not even he was crazy enough to send a bolter shell ricocheting around in this confined tunnel. 'Wonder what it tastes like,' he muttered.

'Its flesh is poisonous too.'

'Can't taste any worse than our field rations,' said Sven.

'I bet it would,' said Torvald.

Suddenly the whole tunnel shook. The vibration caused the surface of the sludge to ripple and made the spider drop into the murky liquid. Ragnar imagined it swimming through the sludge close to his leg. The thought was fairly nauseating but did not frighten him. He doubted the beast's fangs could penetrate hardened ceramite. Trainor obviously had the same worry. His face went even paler than usual, and the sweat fairly dripped from him. Hardly surprising really. He was not wearing sealed armour, and he did not possess a Space Marine's immunity to poison.

'What was that?' he asked shakily.

'Big explosion on the surface,' said Ragnar. 'Most likely a Titan got hit, or maybe a power core.'

He wished he had a clearer idea of what was happening above, but they were maintaining comm-silence, determined not to give the heretics within the keep any clue of their approach.

On the surface the forces of the Imperium might be triumphant or they might have fallen. They would have no way of finding out until they were out of these tunnels, and could get a decent view with their own eyes. The plan was for the Imperial forces to hold on to their gains if they could, break through if they could, but, if not, fall back until they got the signal from the Wolves.

'I wish we were out of here,' said Trainor nervously. His eyes kept scanning the sludge, looking for the spider. Sven groped about in the liquid and pulled out the struggling creature. He held the thing in his fist. Its long legs reached out and stroked his forearm. Long polyped feelers extended from its head.

'Is this what you are looking for?' he asked the militia-man. Trainor looked at him as if he were mad.

Sven opened his mouth as if he were considering eating the spider and then closed his fist, crushing it instead. 'Nothing to worry about.'

'Its blood is poisonous too.'

Sven looked at the remains covering his fist, and gave a look of fake horror before reaching out to smear them on the walls. 'Best not touch what's left then.'

They pushed on down the long dark smelly tunnels.

'This is the bloody life,' said Sven. 'This is the true calling of Russ's chosen heroes.'

The sludge was up to their chests now, and there were large and nasty looking centipedal things moving across the surface with a snaky undulating motion. Trainor had assured them these were poisonous too.

'My mother said I was cursed,' said Torvald from the gloom.

'I certainly curse you,' said Sven.

'Look on the bright side,' said Aenar. 'We can't have too much further to go. We've been down here for hours.'

Ragnar studied the rest of the Wolves up ahead. It looked like Aenar was right. The thin probe lights had begun to rise out of the murk, and as Ragnar closed the distance he could see that the Marines ahead of him were clambering up out of the sludge-filled trench onto a long stone platform.

'Looks like our bath is over for the day,' said Sven.

Ragnar climbed up behind the others. The walkway ran off into the distance, and he could see that lights glowed there. Like the others, he automatically cut off his shoulder-lamp. He reached down and helped Trainor up. This last section was not going to be too easy for the militiaman. He did not have the Wolves' keen night sight and heightened senses. Like the rest of the men, he was going to have to be guided. 'Grab hold of my belt,' Ragnar told him.

The last section of the advance took place in eerie silence, considering there were hundreds of armoured men moving through the gloom. There was little doubt they were in the keep now. The walls around them were thick, and crusted with the accretions of centuries of hardened pollution and industrial effluent. The air had taken on the subtle hum of industry. Judging from the smells and the vibrations, massive machines were at work all around. And there were the signs of all the other creatures that shared man's space wherever he went in the universe. Along the bronze pipes overhead, red-eyed rats scuttled. The whine of something suspiciously like a mosquito sounded close to Ragnar's ears.

'Civilisation at last,' muttered Sven with heavy sarcasm.

'Not yet, but we're almost there.'

The section of the keep they had emerged into had seen heavy fighting. The corridors and tunnels here were as wide as the streets of many cities and as high as they were broad. Openings gaped everywhere; shutters lay buckled near the windows they had once protected; metal doors had been torn from their hinges. The remains of small food stalls lay half-melted in pools of congealed slag in the middle of the street. Masses of unburied, unburned corpses lay nearby. A few unbroken glow-globes burned in the ceiling overhead. By their light, Trainor saw his look.

'Not enough people left alive to take them to recycling.'

'Recycling,' said Ragnar with some disgust. He knew customs varied on different worlds, but this was not one he thought he could ever get used to.

'Aye, their bodies have not been sent back to production.'

Ragnar tried hard not to imagine how this worked, but failed. Images of huge dumpsters full of bodies being tipped into pools of recycling fluid to be broken down for their proteins and nutrients filled his mind. On hive worlds everything was considered a raw material, even the flesh of the dead. He must have muttered the words softly for Strybjorn said, 'That's one raw material of which there is no shortage around here.'

'And doubtless we'll be givving them a delivery of even more soon,' said Sven, a cold grin twisting his ugly features. Down the tunnel, moving in single file on each side, spread out in case of booby traps or grenade attack, the Wolves advanced.

Scent told Ragnar that this place was empty. They had chosen the spot for their entrance well. The fighting had spread through these lower tunnels like a forest fire, and having consumed everything in its way had died out, or maybe simply passed on to where there was more fuel.

They were in, thought Ragnar, inside a place where they were outnumbered a thousand to one. Not that it mattered much. They were not expected, and those overwhelming numbers could not be brought against them at one time. Now it was simply a matter of making their way towards their objectives, reclaiming what was theirs and excising the cancer of the Chaos temple from the flesh of the city. Without their leaders, without central control, the heretics would collapse into dispersed undisciplined bands and be easy prey for the Wolves and their allies. If there still were any allies left in this dead, deserted place, he added mentally.

For a moment, the scale of the task seemed daunting. This was just one keep among thousands. Many more would have to be pacified. It was a task that could take a lifetime. Then his training reasserted itself. It might take the lifetime of a normal man, but he had many times that number of years, so what did it matter? And the chances were that it would not take that long.

If the Chaos temple were the source and inspiration of the rebellion, then destroying it would leave the whole heretical organisation headless. Seeing the Imperial victory, those who had sided with the rebels out of opportunism would soon change sides. It would have a snowball effect. The more rebels who repledged their loyalty, the more difficult it would be for the rest to keep fighting with any hope of victory. The whole rebellion was a flimsy structure that could be toppled with one good push.

Or so he hoped.

TWENTY-TWO

ALL AROUND WAS silent. Ragnar felt the emptiness more now that the great companies had dispersed to their objectives. It was an eerie thought that all around him his battle-brothers were moving through the abandoned corridors and ventilation systems of the keep, cutting power lines, blowing up magazines filled with ammunition, destroying comm-centres, assassinating officers, and sowing the seeds of terror amid their enemies. He wished they were closer to their objective, and that he could find release for his tension in battle.

He knew he should be proud. Berek's company had been handed a prime role, taking out the main power-hub for the western wall. Ragnar knew this would cut the energy supply to the great turrets and beam weapons up there, put the supply lifts on manual operation, and force the whole sector to use back-up power batteries for life support functions such as air filtration and circulation, and water pumping.

It was a tactic calculated to strike fear into the heart of any keep citizen. They knew that once the power was off, they had only limited time before the storage batteries ran out, and life support went off-line for good. The time period would get shorter as the Wolves destroyed more of the reserve systems. The awareness of what was going on would be as deadly for morale as the knowledge than an implacable foe was within their defences, destroying their essential systems. And, if worst came to worst, it meant that the enemy would simply die of oxygen starvation, thirst, and all the other ailments that hit hive cities when their life-support failed. Hitting a hive this way was like stabbing a man so that his lungs filled up with blood. He might be able to last for a short while, but eventually he would stumble and fall. It might take weeks but it would work in the end, providing of course, the heretics did not manage to effect repairs. Ragnar doubted they would. When the Wolves destroyed something, it stayed destroyed.

And all the while the heretics were dying, the Wolves would be there – protected by their armour, moving silently and inexorably through the darkness, and killing, killing, killing.

Some aspects of this situation disturbed Ragnar. Any loyalists trapped in the keep would suffer as much as the heretics, as would any civilians. He tried reminding himself that the loyalists would be doomed anyway if the Imperium had not come, and that in war of this sort civilian casualties were inevitable. It did nothing for his peace of mind.

He glanced around as the company jogged along the silent deserted corridors, wondering what this place must have been like when it was occupied. From the residual scents, he could tell that it had teemed with people. They had lived and loved, eaten and drunk, bought and sold in the tens of thousands around here. Now there were only corpses.

They had carved the bare rock of their walls to represent prominent figures from their history. Lovingly painted statues filled niches between shops. Ragnar recognised some of them: Russ and Garm and many of the others from history, fighting against daemons, beast-headed mutants and hideously mutated heretics. Of course, there were local touches. As far as Ragnar was aware neither Russ nor any of the brethren ever had pale blue skin, just marginally lighter than their armour, nor had they possessed red-glowing eyes with pupils like jewels, but that was the way the locals had chosen to depict them. Nor had they ever been quite so broad or muscular, and he sincerely doubted that any brother had ever owned fangs quite so large as these, or that their features had been quite so bestial and wolf-like.

Ragnar was not offended. He recognised the art for what it was, a form of religious devotion. The history of this world had long been intertwined with that of the Wolves. These sculpted scenes depicted the ancient struggle between good and evil, light and darkness, the Emperor and his enemies, and the Wolves depicted in them were not meant to be realistic. They were demi-gods sent by the Emperor to battle his daemonic enemies and in a way they had to look just as fierce.

Ragnar wondered if some day, when all of this was over, some Garmite sculptor might depict him, just as unrecognisably. Doubtless the inspiration for many of these figures had been some long dead brother. Long after his own death, would some stone Ragnar rush into battle with a painted daemon, or stand guard, weapons ready, over the doorway of a weaponsmith's shop?

'He's almost ugly enough to be you,' said Sven, as if reading Ragnar's thoughts. The barrel of his bolt pistol pointed to one particularly unprepossessing blue-skinned Space Marine.

'And that thing he's fighting could almost be you, save for the fact it's a little too handsome.' Ragnar pointed to a beast that possessed the head of a particularly ugly goat, and hooves to match.

'Do you two always have to fight?' asked Aenar. 'Why can we not all get along like brothers in the name of Russ?'

'I do my best,' said Ragnar, 'but he always does something to spoil it.'

Sven said, 'As ever Brother Ragnar distorts the truth to his own wicked bloody ends. I am blameless in this. I respond only in self-defence when he miscalls me.'

Trainor laughed. It was the first sign of mirth the Garmite had shown since they entered the keep. All the while his eyes had kept their haunted look, and the expression of horror on his face had increased. Ragnar guessed that seeing the conditions inside his home city-state could have done nothing for the young officer's peace of mind.

Remembering how he had felt when he looked on the ruins of his home village after the Grimskull attack, Ragnar could appreciate his feelings. There were few things in this life worse than surveying the wreckage of what had once been your home. As he remembered Ana and the friends he had left behind, something he thought he had long forgotten twisted in Ragnar's heart. Quickly he pushed it away; this was not the time or the place for maudlin memories. Soon they would face the foes responsible for this, and would pay them back in their own coin.

Ahead of him, Ragnar could see Berek consulting with the Rune Priest Skalagrim. A halo of fire surrounded the old man's nearly bald head, turning every single straggling hair into an incandescent filament. A similar nimbus tipped his staff and each of his hands.

'What is going on?' Trainor asked.

'The Rune Priest is invoking Russ and the Emperor to shield us from any divination spells used by our enemies,' Ragnar told him. He was glad that the old man was there. Many other members of Logan Grimnar's great company had been attached to the various Wolf Lords. Every single one of them had at their disposal several Wolf Priests, a Rune Priest and a clutch of Iron Priests who would control the detonation of the explosive devices.

Each of the Rune Priests was equipped with knowledge that had been plucked directly from the memories of Trainor's men, and each could contact his brother priests by virtue of his mystical powers should such a necessity arise. It made Ragnar aware of the depths of resources and

knowledge his Chapter possessed. He doubted that any
other organisation in the Imperium, save their fellow Adeptus Astartes Chapters, had access to such things. It was one
of the things that made Space Marines such deadly foes.

The old man nodded and said something to Berek. It was
obvious from the Wolf Lord's response that he had received
the response he was expecting. He glanced at Morgrim who
pawed the silver horn at his neck, as if he was just dying to
put it to his lips and blow. Instead, Berek gave the signal for
them to move. It was time for the attack to begin.

RAGNAR SURVEYED THE wreckage all around him. Dead
heretics lay everywhere. Iron Priests moved through the
remains of the massive power core, treating those brethren
who were wounded, administering the last rites to those
who would not live to see another dawn.

Ragnar glanced around at his own small pack. Considering the ferocity of the fighting they had got off relatively
lightly. Aenar had another head wound. The ceramite of
Torvald's armour had blistered and run in several places,
and he complained loudly to anyone who would listen
about the agony he endured, save when a healer was close
enough to overhear the words. Sven had a bandage
wrapped round his face, covering the empty socket where
he had lost an eye. Ragnar had heard the healer say that
he was lucky, that the nerve was still intact and that in
time a vat-grown prosthetic could be grafted on. At the
moment, a metal optical lens lay under the bandage. In
another few hours the implant would be attuned well
enough for the wrapping to come off, and let Sven see
properly again.

Strybjorn sat sullen and grim nearby, unwounded but
apparently having trouble controlling his fury. Ragnar
understood. Sometimes in the aftermath of battle, he had
difficulty remaining calm too, although it had become
markedly less common with every moon that separated him
from his joining with the beast within and his ascension to
Space Wolf.

Things had gone pretty much according to plan. The Rune Priest had spirit walked and mind controlled the men guarding the entrance to the power core into opening the massive armoured gate. The company had poured in, overwhelming ten times their number of foes in a matter of minutes. Surprised panicky men were no match for Space Marines who knew exactly what they were doing. They had been cut down with brutal efficiency. Save for a few officers kept alive so that their minds could be drained of knowledge by Skalagrim, all of the heretics had been put to death, swiftly with a single bullet. Such was the penalty for rebellion against the Imperium.

And there had been a bonus. One of Sergius's acolytes had been supervising the power core, obviously an important strategic location. Taken off-guard, he had been overwhelmed and blasted into unconsciousness by Skalagrim. When the Wolf Priests revived him, the interrogation would be fierce.

Ragnar surveyed his own body. All of his limbs were attached. He had barely taken a scratch in the attack, and he felt a little guilty about it when he considered the pain Sven was in, and the deaths of some of the brothers. Still, casualties had been light. Only two fellow Marines had gone to greet their ancestors. A few more were so badly wounded that they would be unable to fight for the next few weeks. And the enemy was about to pay.

Even now the massive extractor fans in the ceiling above were whining as they spun themselves down to a halt. The lights had flickered and gone out for a few moments until the emergency power reservoirs had cut in. Soon this whole area of the keep would be uninhabitable. And sooner than that, the massive weapons holding the Imperial army at bay would no longer have the power to fire. The keep had fallen, their enemies just did not know it yet.

'What now?' Trainor asked. He looked a little disappointed. He had not taken much part in the fighting. There was no way he could keep up with the sheer speed and ferocity of the Space Marines. He had snapped off a few shots at his enemies, but compared to the battle-brothers his contribution so far had been negligible, and it rankled. 'The heretics will soon assemble a force to retake this place.'

Ragnar smiled. Doubtless even now their enemies were massing troops to strike at them, and regain this vital strategic location. 'They will find us gone. And there will be a few nasty surprises for them.'

Ragnar indicated the Iron Priests. They had already seeded the area around the obvious entrances with proximity mines and other booby traps. Those were the least of the nasty surprises that awaited the enemy. Once they penetrated the heart of the power core the whole place was rigged to blow.

'What if they succeed in disarming the main trap?' Trainor asked. 'They'll have this place again, and all your work will have been for nothing.'

Ragnar could not miss the bitterness behind the phrase, 'all your work'. 'The core is already wrecked beyond repair. Trust me. The Iron Priests know what they are doing.'

That was true too. A few well-placed charges in critical components had seen to that. They had just left the machinery looking as if it might work, in order to lure their foes into the trap. Berek gestured for them to get up. Ragnar glanced at his troops and then at Sergeant Joris, who nodded.

'Get up,' he said. 'It's time to go.'

From a long way behind them came the sound of a chain of explosions. A moment later, the lights flickered and the floor shook, as if the keep had been hit by an earthquake.

'Looks like the heretics found our little surprise,' said Ragnar.

'Maybe it was some innocent locals,' said Trainor.

Ragnar looked at him. 'Innocent locals would not go anywhere near that power core.'

Even so, he was a little surprised that the idea had never really occurred to him. He had been so certain that what the Wolf Lord's crew was doing was right.

Up ahead, Morgrim sounded the silver horn. Its long sweet note rang triumphantly through the corridors. Somewhere in the distance Ragnar thought he heard the screams of dying men.

'Greetings, Ragnar,' said Berek. The Wolf Lord sat with his guard, giving every appearance of being a man enjoying his evening meal. The whole company was taking a rest to eat before returning to the fray. It had been a long evening of marching through the increasingly stale air. Judging by the enthusiasm with which he ate, he might have been tearing a haunch of venison from a roasted elk, rather than squirting nutrient paste into his mouth. Everything Berek did, he did with gusto,

'Greetings, Lord Berek.'

'How went the day?'

'Very well. We passed through the battle at the core with no casualties, and only the lightest of wounds.'

'Very good. You are a lucky one, Ragnar. I have heard men say they would rather follow a lucky leader than a skilled one.'

'It would be better to follow a leader who is both, surely.'

'Aye, such men are rare.' His tone left no doubt that he thought Ragnar was looking at one. For some reason, Ragnar refused to take the bait and say the obvious thing. The silence lengthened, and then Berek gave a loud laugh and spoke once more, 'You are doing well, young Ragnar. I do not doubt that sooner rather than later you and your companions will make Grey Hunter.'

In spite of himself, Ragnar felt pleased. Berek noticed his smile. 'Go! Eat! Then make ready to leave! In ten minutes we will be on the move again. Hopefully once that apostate priest comes to, we will learn something of importance.'

'ARE YOU SURE that is what the Wolf Lord said?' asked Sven for the fifth time. He was as excited as a Wolf brother getting ready for his entrance into manhood. He kept rubbing at the metal eyepiece glaring from his left socket. A rim of scab had formed around it, and seemed to hold it embedded into the flesh. It was a disturbing sight.

'Yes. He said that some of us would surely be made Grey Hunters by the end of this campaign.'

'Did he say which ones?' asked Sven.

Ragnar glanced around and sniffed the air. He did not like this place. Not only was the air unpleasantly still and humid, but it had started to stink of human waste as the recycler systems failed. And underneath it all lay the subtle, unpleasant odour of Chaos that he was starting to become depressingly familiar with.

Sven was not going to be ignored. 'Did he say which ones?'

'No – but I can give you a clue.'

'And what would that be?'

'He will almost certainly choose from the ones who are still alive.'

'Ha bloody ha!'

Strybjorn came striding up. 'I've been talking with some of the Grey Hunters,' he said. Obviously Strybjorn had news of some importance. Or at least rumours.

Ragnar was starting to suspect that any place you put two soldiers together in a campaign, you would get three rumours.

'And?' Ragnar asked.

'Seems somebody overheard Berek talking with Skalagrim.'

'And?'

'I am getting to it, Ragnar. I am getting to it.'

'Well, bloody well get on with it,' growled Sven.

'There's been a big breakthrough on the outer wall. The Guard are in.'

'About bloody time,' said Sven. 'After we did all the hard work.'

'The story of my life,' said Torvald gloomily.

'It won't be long now till the heretics are brought to heel,' added Aenar chirpily. The rest of them divided their glares equally between Aenar and Torvald.

Sometimes Ragnar could not decide which of the two was more annoying, then he saw the cynical grin quirk Torvald's lips, and realised that he was just rising to the younger Blood Claw's bait.

'It also sounds like there's some trouble two levels down.'

'Yes?' said Ragnar.

'You know, Ragnar,' said Strybjorn, 'being made acting squad leader has not made you any more pleasant.'

'Or you any less long winded.' Ragnar realised he was being a bit unfair. Strybjorn was anything but wordy. He was rarely anything but terse, but there were times when his old rival and former enemy's mere presence just annoyed him, and made him want to needle Strybjorn.

'Let the man bloody finish, Ragnar,' said Sven. Strybjorn nodded and continued.

'Seems like Sigrid's lads had some trouble with their objective, and had to be pulled out of the fire by two other companies. Berek just laughed when he heard about it.'

Ragnar was not sure that was an appropriate reaction. On the other hand, he had no doubt that if Berek had been the leader of the nearest company he would have gone to Sigrid's rescue without hesitation. He said so aloud.

'Aye,' said Sven, 'if only to have the pleasure of gloating about it afterwards.'

Ragnar glanced at Sven. He had not realised that he was capable of being so astute. 'Let's hope Sigrid feels the same way, in case we need rescuing ourselves.'

'We're the bad bloody bastards of Berek's company. What could we need rescuing from?' asked Sven.

'I am sure we might soon get a chance to find out,' said Ragnar, and as he did so a shiver of premonition passed through him.

Joris strode over. 'The heretic has regained consciousness. It's time to see what he can tell us.'

'I want to see this,' said Ragnar.

'You and half the bloody company.'

WITHOUT HIS MASK, the heretic looked somehow naked. His face was pale and pasty and his eyes glittered with a mad light. There was no stigma of mutation on him, but he reeked of Chaos and its unholy power. Even bound, and immobilised by the power of the Rune Priest, he looked dangerous. Ragnar was glad they had taken him by surprise, he was not so sure that they would have captured him otherwise.

'Talk, heretic, and your death will be quick,' said Berek. He loomed over the traitor like an angry giant and yet, unlike most men, the Chaos worshipper did not quail.

'Sergius has guaranteed me life eternal,' the heretic priest said. 'Chaos has guaranteed me life eternal, but you – you all shall die finally and forever, and after you die, your souls will be devoured by daemons. The Lord of Change will see to that.'

Ragnar had heard this phrase before. It referred to Tzeentch, the daemon god of mutation and magic. Ragnar had encountered others who worshipped the power on distant Fenris, in the caves below the mountain that had become known as Daemonspire.

'We will see how quickly you die,' said Berek.

'You can kill my flesh, but my soul will come back,' said the heretic defiantly. 'Sergius has seen to that. I will come back. They will all come back. They are all coming back.'

As the heretic spoke a change came over him. His voice deepened, his eyes glowed. The Rune Priest's face grew strained, and the nimbus of power playing around his head brightened. All of the watching Wolves tensed and readied their weapons. The temperature around them was sinking fast, and there was a strangeness in the air that made Ragnar's hackles rise. The heretic's skin aged visibly, wrinkles appeared where none had been before. His hair grew greyer.

'You are fools,' said the subtly altered voice. 'You were lured here to your destruction. The way has been prepared. The hosts have been anointed. Red Magnus will claim back his power from the Spear that wounded him, and all of his sons will return. And then you will all die.'

There was no doubt about it, the man was possessed by a daemon. Already Skalagrim had begun the ritual of exorcism, chanting the words of the ancient litany. Ragnar raised his weapon to shoot. All of his brethren did the same.

'Death waits here. Death for you and all your Chapter.'

The man threw back his head and bellowed with mad laughter. A hundred bolter shells riddled his atrophying body. He danced backwards, juddering under the impact, and then came apart. No flesh hit the ground; no blood spilled. Instead only a thick, oily vapour rose upwards and dispersed rapidly, disappearing and leaving no trace the heretic had ever been there.

Skalagrim stood there looking appalled. His mouth was open. His eyes stared into space. The strain of containing the daemon must have been enormous. Or perhaps it was something else. The old man spoke, 'I touched its mind. Before it was cast back into the warp I saw a little of their plans. I know where the Spear of Russ is hidden. We must get it now, or this whole world is doomed!'

TWENTY-THREE

'THINK THIS COULD possibly be a trap?' asked Sven sardonically, as they rushed through the darkened tunnels, following Berek and the rest of the company. They were close to the temple now. The way had been all too open. It was as if all the enemy in the area had been told to let them pass.

Judging by the scent, every heretic in this sector of the keep had passed this way, en route to the temple. What was going on?

What massive ritual was about to be performed, and what had the daemon meant when he talked of Red Magnus? He could only have meant the primarch of the Thousand Sons, the arch-enemies of the Wolves. If that Chapter of traitorous Space Marines were involved something terrible was about to happen.

'The daemon all but told us it was,' Ragnar replied.

'And yet old Berek is racing in there anyway. Makes you bloody well wonder, doesn't it? Not even waiting for the rest of the Chapter to gather.'

'If Skalagrim is right, we don't have time! Berek has broadcast the alarm. They will come as quickly as they can.'

'Aye, just in time to see Berek heroically recover the Spear of Russ, or so our beloved bloody leader is thinking.'

'Most likely.'

'You don't seem too bothered.'

'I notice you're right beside me.'

'I'm not going to let a couple of thousand heretics stand between me and becoming a Grey Hunter.'

'An admirable thought.'

All around them ran the Wolves of Berek's company. Ragnar could sense them; the smell of the vast pack was perceptible even through the filtered air of the keep, and the toxic taint of corruption swirling all around. He wondered how it had been possible for the men of Garm not to notice it. The stench of Chaos was so blatant that even a normal human nose ought to have been able to pick it up. Ragnar pushed that thought away. There was no comparison between the sensitivity of what his nostrils could detect and what a normal man could smell. It was too easy to forget that sometimes, which was alarming considering there had been a day not too far in the past when he himself could not have followed a trail by scent or picked out a faint outline in darkness.

It was strange what one could get used to. There had been a time when his sensory impressions had been so vivid and overwhelming as to be painful. Now they were merely the way the world looked to him. He sometimes wondered what things would seem like if he could be returned to his old mortal perceptions. He suspected that the world would seem flat and grey and dull. He did not want that. It occurred to him that he would not trade places with his old self even if he was given the opportunity, even if it meant he could get back Ana and his father and the whole Thunderfist tribe. That thought seemed disloyal to the ones he had lost, but it was how he had felt. Time had dimmed the pain of his memories and let him adapt to his new life. Even faced by the prospect of imminent death, and confronted by the possibility of conflict with the forces of Chaos, he realised he was happy.

Perhaps even because of those prospects. He suspected, not for the first time, that the changes wrought within him went beyond the alteration of his organs and his muscles. He suspected that his brain had been warped too, changed so that he took pleasure in danger, and thrilled to the siren song of battle.

He glanced around and saw the same expression written on the face of his squad. They too were filled with expectation as they moved forward through the dark, crouched down ready for action as they bypassed the empty strongpoints and guardposts of their enemies. He suspected that a similar expression would be etched on the features of every man in the Chapter from Berek Thunderfist on down. Another thought occurred to him. Maybe the reaction had nothing to do with the process that had turned him into a Space Wolf. Maybe it was simply one sane response to a lifetime committed to war in the Emperor's service. If you were going to fight constantly, you might as well enjoy the process.

The more cynical part of him felt that it was not likely that a thousand men would all respond in the same way without some encouragement. Even amid his old tribe there had been those who loved battle, but there had also been those who fought only when they had to, who had actually disliked it despite all the encouragement of the hero sagas. Many of them had not been numbered among the worst warriors either. Some of them had been stalwart men with an axe when they had to be.

Of course, they had not been surrounded by an organisation that encouraged them to be dedicated to warfare. They had not been chosen to fight the enemies of humanity. They had not known that the fate of worlds, and more than worlds, might rest on their shoulders. And they had not gone through the long process of selection and hardening, tempering and training that the battle-brothers had. Most of them would not have survived it.

Perhaps that was where it came from. Perhaps the process of becoming a Space Wolf was like salmon swimming upstream to spawn in the highlands of Fenris. There, only the strongest and the most determined survived to reach the breeding pools.

Perhaps with the Space Wolves the process of selection winnowed out all those who could not thrive on a steady diet of battle.

Perhaps that was where the similarities came from. Only those who actually thrived on the challenge of warfare, and enjoyed the thrill of combat could survive that long deadly process. Perhaps that was one reason why the training camps were so cruel and unforgiving and why the survival rate was so low. Perhaps that was where the real difference between Ragnar and men like Trainor came in. Perhaps it was that the Wolves really were chosen from among the most natural and fiercest of killers. No one else could survive their training. It was worth thinking about. Ragnar wondered how the guardsman was able to keep going. The Wolves would have left most men behind hours ago, unable to keep up with the killing pace set by the Marines.

All around them, the air was getting thicker and more polluted. It was not just the stench of Chaos. Even though the temple was located in an area served by different power cores than those the Wolves had destroyed, the air was still nasty. It seemed that all over the keep, the air filtration systems worked close to their capacity, and in many cases far beyond tolerable safety limits. The destruction of one part of the system caused an increased burden to the rest of it, causing polluted air to flow from one part of the building to the other. The keep was not quite as hermetically sealed as it was supposed, as the Wolves' passage through airshafts and other communicating tunnels was proving. It occurred to Ragnar that with the right sensors, it would probably be possible to trace all the breaches in the system's integrity simply by following the flow of polluted air.

Trainor and his men, reunited as their old unit now, were showing signs of wear and tear. Constantly having to live in filter masks was proving a strain even for men who had grown up under the strict air disciplines of the keep. They had to sleep in their masks, and squeeze food pastes into their mouth pieces through the same long metal straws they used to suck in the vile stagnant water. Still, they were keen to come and take the fight to those who wrecked their home.

Ragnar did not blame them. He felt the same way about taking the fight to the Thousand Sons who had desecrated the sacred soil of Fenris and who had now stolen one of his Chapter's most sacred artefacts.

'Not much longer now,' he told them in a cheery voice. 'We'll soon cleave a path of ruin through these Chaos worshipping bastards.'

'About bloody time,' muttered Sven. 'And by the way, Ragnar, you sound like you've spent too much time talking with Berek Thunderfist and his skald.'

Ahead of them the way opened into what looked suspiciously like an Imperial temple.

THEY ENTERED A vast atrium, larger than some of the islands in the world sea of Fenris. In the days before the insurrection, it must have been a place for monks to meditate and perform mass rituals. It was littered with the bodies of men, and the shattered remains of machines. Even as Ragnar watched, the crumpled shell of an aircar emitted a stream of blue sparks and consumed itself in a halo of blue fire. Ragnar could see the corpses of the men within vanish in the eerie flames. An energy pistol still dangled from the fingers of one man. His arm had been thrust out through the open window of the vehicle to allow him a better shot at his targets. Now his fingers burned black and withered. There was a dazzling flash of light as the magazine exploded, its internal energies interacting explosively with those of the damaged aircar.

Ahead of them, Berek and his Wolf Guard were already vanishing into the temple's mighty maw.

The temple was more vast than he would have believed and the deeper they went the more convoluted it became.

Massive bridges carved with hideous leering gargoyles leapt across chasms where industrial sludge flowed lava-like a hundred metres below. Enormous vaulted ceilings depicted scenes that parodied the interiors of Imperial temples and mocked Imperial dogma. Gigantic statues of cowled and masked men loomed out of the clouds of steam from the heating vents. How much of this was merely a product of monumental Garmite architecture and how much a product of the warped and feverish minds of heretical cultists Ragnar could not guess.

The air stank of Chaos. Ragnar knew that an enormous number of heretics had come this way. Why? What could be so important as to drag them down here while an Imperial army invaded their city. Why were they not up above fighting? Why were they not opposing the Space Wolves now?

Ragnar knew he was not going to like the answer when they found it.

The temple had become a maze. Archways pierced most of the walls, leading off into vast hallways full of collossal architecture. The tide of heretics had flowed this way, passed through many of the entrances. They had separated into different groups for some reason, Ragnar could not guess why. Just looking at the entrances, he sensed something sinister. It felt like bad things waited down there, that something unpleasant was just waiting its moment. He was not the only one to view them suspiciously.

'Ragnar, you and those Blood Claws check out those vestibules,' ordered Berek. 'Make sure no unpleasant surprises are going to come from there.'

Ragnar moved to obey the order, as Berek commanded other packs to check out other archways.

'I'D SAY WE'VE come to the right place,' said Sven as they passed into the vestibule. Already most of the Wolves had gone ahead. The Blood Claws had been dispatched to check out the side passages and make sure Berek and his Wolf Guard were not ambushed, en route to their date with destiny.

Ragnar saw at once what Sven meant. Intricate and disturbing murals covered the walls. Mosaics of shattered, multi-coloured glass glittered in the light of the glowglobes. It took more than one glance to appreciate their evil. They appeared to be nothing more than normal religious scenes such as might be depicted in any temple of the Imperial cult, showing men performing the normal rites of prayer and worship, wielding the usual censers, reading from the usual volumes.

But when Ragnar looked closer he saw that the faces of the mass of the congregation were twisted in blank idiotic expressions of stupidity and malice. Peering closer still, he could see the intelligent-looking ones leading the rituals had horns and hooves and the stigma of mutation. Some of the altars depicted leering daemonic faces visible only when viewed from a certain angle.

It appeared to be a commentary on the Imperial religion, a parody, suggesting that behind the façade of truth lurked the madness of Chaos, and that all of mankind's most cherished beliefs were merely a veil behind which daemons lurked, a fact that the clever ought to be able to perceive. A subtle and devious genius had gone into the production of these works that invited the viewer to join in its cleverness, to share the joke, and so be seduced to its point of view.

Ragnar could see, as he glanced at the works from the corner of his eye, how easily the Imperium could be misrepresented by its foes. After all, its mightiest organisations worked behind a veil of mystery. Its most sacred rituals were hidden from the view of the mass of its citizenry, most of whom were shielded even from the knowledge of the evil from which the Emperor's servants protected them. Was not what had happened here a subversion of what already existed?

If heretics penetrated a temple, how easily they could pervert the whole apparatus of Imperial ritual to their own foul ends. The shattered glass glittered hypnotically. Something in the pattern caught Ragnar's attention and lodged within his mind. He paused to contemplate the mural once more,

stopping in his tracks, knowing from the sound of the footsteps all around him that the others were doing the same.
An idea surged into his mind, stunning in its significance,
near overwhelming in its profundity.

Was there not an element of truth in what was being suggested by the murals? Was not the whole Ecclesiarchy a
charade? Were not all the mysterious rituals designed simply to bamboozle the ignorant and cow the credulous? Were
not those brave souls who saw the truth right to fight
against the corrupt organisation that claimed to represent
the Emperor, an Emperor whom no one had ever seen, and
who it was claimed had been imprisoned in his golden
throne for ten thousands years? Surely by now the Emperor
was dead? If he had ever existed at all. Was it not possible
that he was simply a convenient fiction created by those
who wanted to rule in his name, a promise of protection
and salvation that was counterfeit?

Ragnar contemplated these truths, wondering why he had
never seen them before. Like the sheep depicted in the picture
he had been duped. He had been lied to by those who would
use his strength and courage to further their own ends, by
those who were unworthy to lick his boots, and who by all
rights should grovel before him. Perhaps those who believed
in these childish lies deserved to be ruled over by their superiors. Certainly those who knew the truth were more worthy
to rule, had proven their superiority and fitness.

Pride in his own intellect, in the power of his own perceptions, filled Ragnar. He was a natural leader, a natural
ruler, a man destined for great things, a man who could see
the underlying pattern of existence, who saw the vast
scheme of reality in its entirety. He should forge his own
destiny. After all, everything changes. The corrupt old
regime would be swept away, and something new, pure and
shining and good would replace it, a true of commonwealth
of humanity ruled over by the elect, the greatest of whom
would be him...

All he had to do was acknowledge the profound truth that
the Changer of Ways ruled over all, and he would be given

dominion. His realms would be vast, his power great as a god. He need only kneel before Tzeentch and praise him and his reward would be eternity. Kneel, thought Ragnar, the spell suddenly slipping from his mind. Why kneel to any power? He was Ragnar, mightiest of warriors, greatest of leaders. He would kneel to no one.

Suddenly Ragnar laughed. As swiftly as the madness had come over him it passed. He saw the thoughts for what they were, a snare set by Chaos to appeal to the vanity that lurked in the hearts of all men. There was a spell worked into this glowing glass that reinforced the pride of proud men and used their strength against them. It praised the clever and so sought to win them over. It was a thing of daemonic subtlety, and in his case had been too subtle for its own good. It had puffed up his pride to the point where he would not give way to anyone, or acknowledge anything to be his superior, and then the spell had been broken, burst like a bubble, seen through like a cheap conjurer's trick. He turned to look at the others, to explain it to them, to share the joke, when he noticed by their expressions that they were taking it seriously. Hostile eyes glared at him. Weapons levelled.

TWENTY-FOUR

'IT'S A SPELL,' shouted Ragnar, glaring at the rest of his squad. 'The mural is cursed!'

He could see a look of glazed comprehension entering Sven's eyes and by their scents he thought he was getting through to the rest of his battle-brothers. He was not so sure about Trainor and his men. He knew he had mere heartbeats to act before everything exploded into violence.

Acting on instinct he threw himself to one side and lashed out at the mural with his chainsword. The blade screeched as it hit the glittering glasswork. There was a high-pitched screeching noise and then a wail like that of a lost soul in torment. Everything slowed. He sensed resistance to his attack from the enchanted mural, a powerful daemonic will pressing back against his own, resisting his blow with a force that was as much mental as physical. The strain was near intolerable: a bone-deep ache that settled on his body and made it vibrate in time with the glass, that echoed the stress he placed on it and amplified it.

Gathering all his willpower he forced his arm to straighten despite the excruciating pain, and drove the blade into the wall with as much force as he had ever used against a foe's body. For an instant nothing happened but then cracks appeared in the mural with a sound like a glacier breaking apart. An enormous explosive force pushed outwards, sending individual bits of coloured glass flying like shrapnel. They pinged off his armour and forced him to cover his eyes with his forearm. Even so bits cut his cheek drawing blood, causing a stinging, tingling pain that reminded him of poison. With every cut, images flickered through his mind like snowflakes in a storm.

He caught flashes of memory, saw scenes of an unspeakable ritual in which souls were offered up to the Lord of Change leaving a concentrated psychic residue in the glass from which the unspeakable mural drew its power. He saw cowled figures chanting around octagonal altars. He saw warriors in over-elaborate Space Marine armour that could only belong to one group: Chaos Marines of the Thousand Sons order. He saw daemons dance and caper in sealed and unholy chambers far from the sun. He saw evil rituals enacted to sanctify this place with unholy power. Once more he caught glimpses of a vast and intricate pattern, a scheme concocted by a Prince of Schemers, a lie told by a Lord of Untruth. His mind seemed to expand under the impact, consciousness streaming away into an awareness of his surroundings that was almost cosmic.

He sensed the raw evil that permeated the very stones around him, which had seeped in and tainted the place since it was a small and secret shrine, a cancer growing within the body of the factory keep, a tumour that had swollen and grown over centuries until it had metastasised and spread throughout this whole sector of a world. He saw the generations of heretics who had toiled away in secrecy in the heart of Garmite society, plotting the day they would overthrow the old order. He saw a man who he somehow knew to be Father Sergius come here but a decade ago, a hollow man, a priest of the Emperor who had lost his faith, a holy man who had fallen from sanctity. He saw the evil of the place touch the priest and fill him, and send him forth renewed with a faith far darker and far more intense than his old one. He saw the things the old man summoned and caught behind him a glimpse of what waited beyond the gates of hell.

He saw something of the old and unholy order of things, caught glimpses of distant hells in which bird-winged, bird-headed daemon princes ruled over worlds reshaped by the power of their wills, where mortal souls and mortal forms were clay to be worked on and reshaped at the whim of supremely potent masters.

He had a sense of the ancient evil power which he opposed, caught a glimpse of the sheer immensity of the enemies of mankind and, for a moment, his soul quailed. Then from somewhere far off, he sensed an opposing power, a beacon of pure shining power which pulsed unimaginably far off, and which opposed the wills of those who would destroy mankind. Its power flowed into him, and pushed him backwards and downwards into his flesh.

He felt suddenly heavy and immensely old. His limbs weighed as much as planets. His breathing was a hurricane within the immense cavern of his chest. His veins were rivers carrying cataracts of blood through the continents of his limbs.

He opened his eyes, feeling like he was uncovering the orbs of glowing suns and looked upon the face of Sven.

'You all right, Ragnar? You look like you've eaten something that did not agree with you.'

He forced himself to sit up and survey his surroundings. The mural was gone. The glittering glass now was multi-coloured ash that swirled away in the convection currents from the ventilation system. The rest of the squad were dazed and more than a little confused. The Garmites looked at once shaken and ashamed, like men who fear that they have revealed some deeply held and very dark secret. Ragnar felt a little like that himself. He has seen some truths about himself in the dark mirror of this Chaos artefact that he could well have lived without knowing.

Hardship makes us stronger, he told himself. It was an old Fenrisian proverb and useful under many circumstances.

'Don't go all mystical on us,' said Sven, as Ragnar realised he had spoken aloud. 'No need to go and apply for the priesthood just because you broke some daemon's bloody toy.'

'Did you see it?' Ragnar asked, unable quite to keep a hint of wonder from his voice.

'I only saw you smack the bloody picture as it attempted to take our souls. And a good job you did too.' For all the jovial tone of his speech, Ragnar could tell his friend was shaken. He too had felt the temptation the artefact offered. How real was it all, he asked himself?

'Too bloody real for my liking,' said Sven, and Ragnar realised that he was going to have to get a better grip on himself. He was still speaking aloud.

'You did a mighty deed here, Brother Ragnar,' said Aenar with what sounded like real respect. 'Strength is not given to every man to smite the works of darkness.'

'It is given to every Wolf,' Ragnar said. He found himself wondering about what had happened, about the beacon he had sensed, and he felt an obscure sense of sadness too at having destroyed the mural. It was an evil thing, but it had been a kind of window onto the infinite, a thing that offered a glimpse of dark wonders even in its destruction, and now it was gone from the universe.

'And a good thing too,' said Sven. 'How many men have paid with their bloody souls for those glimpses.' Ragnar swore he was definitely going to stop speaking his thoughts aloud now.

Over the comm-net came Berek's cheerful voice. +All Wolves to me. I think we have found the Spear of Russ!+

In the distance, the sounds of battle erupted, reminding Ragnar that there was work to be done. He saw that the Wolf Lord had activated his beacon. It was time to home in on it.

'Follow me,' he said. 'It sounds like the Wolf Lord has found our foes.'

In the aftermath of smashing the crystal mural, everything had taken on a surreal quality, a nightmarish air of unreality that left him not quite sure of his bearings. Perhaps it was the odd quality of his mystical experience, perhaps it was something else, but Ragnar thought he could sense all around him flows of mystical energy.

Ominous powers gathered ahead, of this he was as sure as Skalagrim had been. He guessed that whatever obscene ritual the cultists were intending, it was close to completion. From the corner of his eye, he began to catch sight of flickering outlines that flowed into odd daemonic shapes before slithering out of his line of sight. The stench of Chaos grew stronger in his nostrils with every stride. All around he could feel the presence of many foes.

They entered another vast hallway. The ceiling loomed a hundred metres above them. On the far side, steps led up into the sanctum of this temple. Now Ragnar could see battle being fought, as Berek and his embattled company fought their way into the core of the complex against more than ten times their number. The sense of cosmic evil here was almost overwhelming. The daemonic shadows had multiplied in the corner of his eyes, and seemed somehow more tangible. Ragnar could see heavy weapons fire erupt from the Wolves' position on the stairs, and see the flicker of energy as Rune Priests drew on their powers to blast aside their foes.

'Come on!' he shouted, and led his pack at a blazing sprint across the chamber. Beams of hot light seared the stones around him as las-fire erupted from turret windows above the entrance to the sanctum. Snipers, he thought veering erratically to disturb their aim, knowing there was not much else he could do at the moment. The range was too great for a snapshot.

'Nice to see some of the heretics are putting up a bloody fight,' said Sven. 'I thought they had all gone on holiday.'

'They probably heard you were coming and decided they could not let you in,' said Ragnar. At least he knew now the purpose of one of the groups the heretics had been divided into. They were guards. What was the purpose of the others?

Somehow, he made it to the stairs, and saw why the Marines were currently hunkered down there. The rise of the stairs provided cover from fire from within the temple. The enormous projecting lintel prevented snipers from firing down on them from overhead.

He heard Berek bellowing orders in the battle tongue of Fenris, and saw sergeants move quickly to see them carried out. As Ragnar arrived, Berek turned and gave him a feral grin. For all the madness and sense of impending doom about him, he gave the impression of a man enjoying himself greatly. 'Good,' he said. 'Blood Claws! Just in time. We're about to storm the door and more assault troops are just what we need.'

Ragnar nodded. Berek turned and gave orders for the Long Fangs to lay down a curtain of fire for a minute, while two supporting squads lobbed a mixture of frag, flash and smoke grenades to disorientate their enemies. Ragnar knew when the explosive screen peaked they would go. He paused for a second to take a look around at his company, suddenly aware that this would be the last time he would see some of them alive.

He breathed in the scent of the massive pack, and noticed the quick confident way in which every man moved, instinctively knowing what needed to be done, and what his part in it all was. Ragnar could see through that illusion now. The co-ordination was in part a product of long years of training, and part a product of the complex subliminal web of olfactory signals that tied the pack together.

Already the big grizzled old men of the Long Fangs were manoeuvring their massive weapons into position to send a concentrated hail of fire onto their enemies when the signal was given. Without having to be told twice the Grey Hunters were moving up with their grenades and bolters. Already the Blood Claw packs were running into positions in the fore, throwing themselves down to take advantage of cover until the moment when they would rise up and charge. Skalagrim summoned his powers. The Wolf Priests made ready to confront their foes and see to the wounded. Trainor and his men took up position amid the mass, looking as out of place as children on a battlefield.

Perhaps it was the after-effects of his encounter with Chaos, but it suddenly struck Ragnar how many more Blood Claws there were than Grey Hunters and how unlikely it was that many of them would live to be raised to the grey. Not that most of them would ask for anything different. A short glorious life and a mighty death was all most of them desired. Indeed, for men raised on Fenris where few lived to an age where they got grey hairs, it was all most of them had expected anyway.

Ragnar grinned. What did it matter when you entered Russ's halls? Every man here would die sooner or later. Nothing was more certain. What mattered was how you entered. All men wanted an end that would be worthy of a song, and a tale you could tell to the other ghosts as you swigged ale with the heroes of legend around the long tables.

In the back of his mind something niggled, though. He was not yet ready to leave this life. There were still things he wanted to do, places he wanted to see, before he passed through the grim grey portals. He pushed those thoughts back. The time and place of his falling were not his to choose. If it was ordained by fate that he die this day there was nothing he could do about it, and no way to protest. He needed to ready himself. He nodded to Berek, turned to the Blood Claws of his pack and moved towards the van, trying to get as close as possible to the centre and the front. He sensed some objections to him taking the place of heroes, and he was not about to start a fight about it at this late stage. It served him right for coming late.

Sven and the others fell into place alongside him, as the barrage of heavy weapon fire reached a crescendo. He wondered what it must be like to be on the receiving end of it. To have to face that hail of death, of heavy bolter shells, and micro-missiles and heavy las-fire, without the benefit of heavy ceramite armour, without the confidence of being a Wolf.

For a brief instant he caught a glimpse of what it must be like for ordinary men to see Space Marines coming at them. They faced an unrelenting foe that came on implacably in the face of superior numbers, a foe much faster and stronger and tougher than they were, who showed no trace of weakness. It must be like facing gods, he thought, and wondered if the spell of pride still clouded his mind, and then realised that it did not. His was an accurate assessment of the situation.

The return fire seemed to have died under the barrage of death thrown down by the Long Fangs. He risked a glance up and saw a massive cloud of smoke and thunderous explosions. Some of the wicked looking gargoyles around the entrance had been reduced to shapeless masses, chiselled away by the sheer weight of bolter shells thrown at them. Some had been melted to slag by the reflected spray of heavy las-fire. Dead bodies lay sprawled in the dirt. Chain lightning danced across his field of vision as the Rune Priests called on the fury of the heavens. It did not seem possible that anything could survive in there. And yet the sense of ominous tension had increased. Something dark and evil lay within this final sanctum. It waited for them there. A cold flash of fear flickered down Ragnar's spine.

A long, eerie, ululating cry echoed from behind him. It was the signal. The time to advance was upon them.

TWENTY-FIVE

SURROUNDED BY HIS comrades, Ragnar raced into the smoke. It billowed and swirled around him, turning his fellows into shadowy outlines. Had it not been for his heightened sense of scent he might have felt isolated, but as it was he could smell and hear his comrades and was reassured by the presence of the pack.

Like an avalanche of unleashed fury, the Blood Claws hurtled forward. Terrifying yips and howls filled the air and echoed away. As he emerged from the cloud, Ragnar threw himself flat, hoping to confuse any enemy who might have targeted him. He hit the ground rolling, and let his momentum carry him ten strides before coming to his feet again. Once more he was astonished. Only a few hundred warriors opposed them, and the Blood Claws smashed through them like a spear through a body. The heretics were no match for the Blood Claws nor the hardened Space Wolf warriors who swarmed in behind them.

Ragnar bowled over one foe, chopped down another and then the momentum of his rush carried him through the defenders and into the nave of the temple. Hundreds of ecstatic faces turned to stare at him, confused. Each belonged to a red-robed heretic whose head had been shaved and whose brow had been marked with the twisted rune of Tzeentch.

The air stank of incense and sweet perfumed oils. The cultists had the blank, delirious look of the drugged, or of zealots awaiting a manifestation of their god. At a guess, Ragnar would have said that these were the 'anointed' of which the possessed heretic had spoken.

Thousands of the cultists occupied the vast empty space within this sanctum. Huge masked figures leered down from alcoves, rebel gods spectating on what was about to unfold. The sense of gathering power that had surrounded the temple was focused on this spot, Ragnar realised. The air fairly pulsed with magical energy.

Before he had a chance to comprehend fully what was going on the battle swirled into the sanctum itself. A masked soldier aimed a bayonet at him. Ragnar cut him down with a back-handed swipe, took out two of the man's companions and looked around for his battle-brothers. In moments, the tiled and mosaic floor was taken up with the bodies of the wounded, and the surviving heretical fighters cowered away from their attackers.

No, Ragnar realised, not just their attackers. It was not merely the spectacle of the Wolves arriving that had terrified them, it was what was happening within the temple. The ritual being enacted here had seared even the sin-blackened souls of these cultists. Seeing what was going on, Ragnar was not surprised.

A dazzling aurora shimmered in the air, rainbows of multicoloured light reflected in the gleaming marble walls. At the end of the chamber, a monstrous altar, a blasphemous parody of that to be found in every Imperial temple glowed with evil might. Around it stood five men. All of them were garbed in heavy crimson robes, trimmed with gold and covered in flickering symbols of hallucinogenic complexity. One of the men held the burnished crystalline skull of some horn-headed daemon. The other held what looked like the bones of a massive hand, held together by wires of finest spun silver. The third carried a glowing orb shaped like an eye. The fourth carried a chalice of bronze. It was what the fifth man carried that drew Ragnar's eye.

He was a huge bearded old man, with the face of a prophet and the eyes of a daemon lord. It was Sergius, without a doubt. In one massive tattooed hand, the cultist held a huge spear. It was carved all of some dark wood worked with the runes of Fenris. The runes now glowed with an evil ruddy light, obviously the work of Chaos. The spearhead looked as if it were carved from the fang of a monstrous dragon. It glowed with an unearthly radiance, a chill-bright glimmer that recalled the light of Fenris's sun save that it too was being polluted by the taint of Chaos. Ragnar knew that he looked upon the Spear of Russ, and that the man who held it was the leader of this pack of heretics. The urge to face the apostate in single combat, and claim back that which he had stolen was near overwhelming. There was something about the Spear, even in its polluted state, that caused a sense of reverence in him, something that seemed to have been burned deep into his flesh, perhaps implanted within the gene-seed itself.

Sergius turned to glare at them. He was a huge man, so broad that he seemed almost obese, with arms thick as treetrunks and a neck like a bull. Under his massive cowled cloak he wore shimmering armour embossed with the eye-dazzling, stomach churning runes that were the mark of Tzeentch. Curving ram-like horns emerged from his helmet, and Ragnar was not sure whether they were part of it or actually grew from the man's head.

Above the heretic's head, a rift had appeared in reality, and through it something else was visible, a realm of shifting constantly changing lights in which Ragnar caught sight of daemon faces leering and gibbering. Even as Ragnar watched, the faces all flowed together forming one massive face, its features as yet formless save for an enormous gaping mouth and a single massive eye. Through the rift of the mouth streamers of Chaos stuff gushed out into the chamber and flickered around the room. The very light seemed tainted by the presence of daemons.

Seeing that the ritual was about to be interrupted Sergius returned to his work, chanting alien words in a deep powerful voice, words never meant to be shaped by human tongue. The words echoed within the cavern of Ragnar's skull, and brought back a flood of images from the smashing of the mural. The Wolf shook his head and fought off a momentary dizziness.

More and more streamers of incandescent radiance leapt through the rift. One of them touched a shaven-headed cultist kneeling near the altar and the man screamed as if his soul were being ripped from his body. A reddish light flickered in his eyes, and a foul frothing cloud of many colours emerged from his mouth. His body spasmed, as if he was in the grip of some powerful fit. His muscles rippled and expanded like balloons, bursting out through flesh in a tidal wave of red dripping meat, and bluish pulsing vein. With one hand, the man reached into a split in his flesh and tore it free, leaving him stripped and skinless, blood pooling on the floor near his feet. Despite a pain that must have been near indescribable, he still stood, and then, most horribly of all, he laughed, a chilling sound that rang through the chamber like the mad mirth of some demented godling.

The transformation was not over though. The possessed man opened his mouth and the stuff of Chaos slid down his throat and again his body glowed briefly, the bones glowing so bright they were visible through his flesh. As Ragnar watched, they thickened and grew denser, the joints becoming heavier as if adjusting to compensate for the additional mass of muscle on the body. The whole process was oddly familiar, and reminded Ragnar of something he had learned once before. Then it came to him – the bone structure and the increased muscle mass were almost exactly the same as the changed form of a Space Marine. The cultist seemed to be creating a wicked parody of the foes that sought to stop him.

More of the coloured stuff of Chaos flowed around the doomed human sacrifice, knitting itself into a new layer of flesh, gleaming and scaly, at once suggestive of something reptilian and something insectoid. His eyes became deep eerie pools of dancing flame that reflected the glow of the hell-lights about him. He gestured and the blood pooled at his feet washed upwards in a wave, congealing and clotting as it did so, covering him in a layer of blackened slime that hardened into a carapace very similar in appearance to the one Ragnar knew was beneath his own armour.

Another complex gesture and more and more of the scraps of Chaos stuff flowed towards him, flapping like monstrous batwings as they wrapped themselves about the man. They gleamed bright as metal hot from the forge and the man screamed once more like someone dropped into a vat of molten metal. The light surrounding him was so brilliant that Ragnar could not look at him with his naked eyes, and dropped his gaze, leaving only a horrific after-image burned on his retina. In the last second before averting his eyes, he saw what the man had turned into, and recognised it. He looked up, knowing already what he would see. Knowing that there would be recognition too in the burning gaze of the thing he faced.

A Chaos Marine stood there, clad in ornate armour of ancient design, hundreds of leering metal daemon heads emerging from his armour. He clutched a runesword that glowed hellishly in one hand, and a bolter of ancient aspect in the other. His helmet was horned. He looked much the same as Ragnar remembered from the caverns below the most accursed mountains on Fenris.

'Madox!' he bellowed, challenging the Chaos warrior he thought he and Strybjorn had killed many moons before.

'It's always nice to be recognised,' came the silky mocking voice he knew and loathed. And still the rift in the air above the spear glowed brighter. The face it had formed was more recognisably human now. Ragnar had seen its image before in the most ancient ikons of his Chapter. It was the visage of one of the greatest of all mankind's enemies, the rebel Primarch, Magnus.

More and more scraps of Chaos stuff, the souls of undying warriors, flashed out like meteors, striking cultists left and right. The glare Ragnar had seen earlier, repeated itself, once, twice, a dozen, a hundred times.

Ragnar knew in that moment that at least a company, perhaps a Chapter of Chaos Marines were warping into being all around him.

All around the heretics screamed as they were possessed, their physical forms warped, their souls displaced. Whatever they had been expecting from the ritual, this was not it. Doubtless they had been promised apotheosis, or power beyond their wildest dreams. Ragnar supposed they were getting it, just not in the way they anticipated.

Even when Chaos keeps its promises, it finds a way to break them. The shaven headed acolytes panicked and ran, but the glowing fireballs of Chaos stuff followed them, consuming them utterly and transforming them into something else. Perhaps it was his imagination, but Ragnar thought he could see the visages of long-dead Traitor Marines within each incandescent sphere. The cultists rushed past seeking to escape their doom. Screaming and bleating like frightened sheep they threw themselves headlong at the Wolves.

The rift in the air widened. The chief heretic chanted louder. Ragnar thought he could see other things swirling about within it, massive daemonic forms that sought entrance to this world. His sense of foreboding grew. It was like watching the mouth of hell open in front of him. He heard Berek shouting from behind him, 'Kill them. There will be fewer bodies for the daemons to possess!'

A cultist standing in front of Ragnar was sliced in two by a black, glowing hellblade. Ragnar found himself confronting Madox. 'An admirably brutal and ruthless thought,' he said. 'But I am afraid living or dead these bodies will serve. Of course, my returning brethren won't thank me for cutting this body in two, but I could not restrain myself.

Imagine my joy in seeing you once more. I just could not wait to greet you appropriately.'

The hellblade lashed out at Ragnar, licking towards his face. Frantically he parried with his chainsword. Sparks flew as the two blades met. The black blade moaned. 'I do believe you have improved since last we fought, youth. Excellent. This will make your death all the more satisfying.'

Madox aimed a mighty two-handed cut at Ragnar's head. Ragnar ducked and struck back, shearing a brazen skull from the Thousand Sons' armour. 'Let me show you how much I have improved, loathsome spawn of Magnus!'

'Loathsome spawn of Magnus?' The Chaos warrior's tone was amused. 'Spoken like a true Space Wolf – all mindless bigotry and unreasoning hatred.'

'Die, Chaos spawn!' shouted Ragnar, chopping at Madox with a blow that would have cut the evil Space Marine in two had he not parried. Their blades met with a crash like a hammer hitting an anvil. All around combat had become close and general as the Wolves fought with the resurrected Chaos Marines.

'I would not be so quick to condemn Chaos spawn,' said Madox, unleashing a hail of lightning fast blows that sent Ragnar reeling back into Sven. 'The longer that gate stays open, the more likely it is that you will become one yourself. Of course, you don't need to worry about that, since I will be obliging enough to kill you before you suffer what you would regard as a fate worse than death.'

The black blade gouged an enormous chunk out of Ragnar's shoulder pad. It slid free leaving the armour's internal working exposed. 'Don't thank me,' added Madox. 'Anything to oblige. Of course, when I kill you here, your soul will go straight to the warp.'

'Doesn't he ever bloody shut up?' cried Sven, suddenly stepping through the press of bodies and aiming a swing at Madox. A second Chaos Marine aimed a blow at Sven as he did so. Ragnar leapt into the breach and blocked the blow that would have killed his friend. It left his arm feeling numb. Sven's attacker was a huge brute, larger than Madox and far stronger, if a lot less skilful.

'Being dead is an interesting experience,' Madox added conversationally. 'Everyone should try it at least once.'

His blade found its way around Sven's guard and caught him at the wrist. The blade glowed more brightly as it drew power from somewhere to cut through the hardened ceramite and sever the hand at the wrist. With a howl of pain Sven fell back and the Chaos Marine's blade took him in the chest. Blood erupted from Sven's mouth. He fell forward along the blade that was killing him, trying to get his good hand around Madox's throat. The Chaos Marine headbutted him and sent him reeling backwards, blade still protruding from his chest.

'Of course, it's a little corrosive to the soul. I am not sure I would want to endure it for all those millennia like most of my brethren here. Some of them have been trapped since the Burning of Prospero and Horus's rebellion. I fear all that waiting, and wrestling with daemons has driven them a little mad and not a little vengeful. On the other hand, we will soon have every Thousand Son killed in the Long War back in the flesh, and believe me, that's a lot. True Chapters were so much larger than your puny latter day imitations. That's it, Boriseon. You almost had him there!'

Ragnar sprang backwards, away from the sweep of an enormous runic axe. Shock and anger at Sven's death filled him. He felt wild rage and anger start to fill him, a fuse burning down to an enormous keg of explosive. He knew that the relentless mocking banter of the Chaos Marine was intended to goad him but he did not want to resist. He felt that his chainsword was starting to become laden with the power of death.

'Ironic really that Russ's spear should be used to resurrect so many of those he helped destroy. It took millennia for Magnus to solve all the details and instruct our minions accordingly. I am pleased to report that I did my part spreading the word to this benighted place.' Madox strode over to Sven's recumbent form, placed one heavy metal shod foot on his chest and pulled his sword free. Over his shoulder Ragnar could see that the rift had widened, and a mighty one-eyed visage had come fully into focus. From its roaring mouth it spat the returning souls of its dead followers. Ragnar knew now that without question he was looking on the awesome visage of Magnus the Red, primarch of the Thousand Sons, a warped creation of the Emperor, who rivalled any daemon prince in power and malignity. Sensing that wicked cyclopean eye on him, his soul shrank. Had it not been for the fury burning within him, he might have quailed.

'Once we've disposed of you and your pathetic brethren we shall conquer this world. It will be the first of many. This will be the new Prospero. It sits right astride the main routes from the Eye of Terror to the Imperial hub. Still, I suppose you knew that. I say, Boriseon, that was a good one. Give me a few moments and I will help finish him off.'

The force of the giant Chaos warrior's blow nearly flattened Ragnar, even though he parried it. Ragnar stepped back and gazed at his opponent, feeling cold anger and hatred fill him. He had fought long enough to know Boriseon's weaknesses now. The huge armoured warrior was lumbering and slow. He could probably destroy a tank with a blow of his axe but first it had to connect.

Ragnar sprang forward, ducked beneath the sweep of Boriseon's axe and drove his chainsword up through the gorget of his armour, severing the brute's head. 'When you get back to hell,' he snarled, 'tell them Ragnar sent you.'

He did not wait to see the results of his attack but continued his berserk rush at Madox. His blade arced in and smashed into the blood-dripping hellsword, knocking it aside. His armoured fist connected with Madox's helmet, smashing the Chaos Marine to the ground.

But the Thousand Son was not to be so easily defeated. Millennia of combat experience lay behind his every move. As he fell he lashed out with one foot, catching Ragnar behind the knee and sending him sprawling. Before Ragnar could recover, the maelstrom of battle had flowed over them, and swept them apart. Ragnar found himself in the centre of a swirling melee where a compact mass of Wolves chopped its way through the still assembling hordes of Chaos Marines. All around the meteors of Chaos stuff fell, impacting on corpses, consuming them, restructuring them, reanimating them. Even through the rage that filled him, Ragnar could tell that things were not going well for the Sons of Russ.

Moments later, he found himself fighting alongside Berek, Morgrim and the old Rune Priest Skalagrim. The Wolf Lord and his bodyguards were overwhelming their foes by sheer ferocity but numbers were slowing them down, and for every foe who fell there was another to take their place. Amid the packed masses of screaming heretics and their trampled corpses there was no shortage of bodies to possess.

'We've got to close that gate!' Ragnar shouted at Berek.

'As soon as we get there,' said Berek confidently. Skalagrim smiled bleakly as he lashed out with his runestaff and broke a Thousand Sons' head. 'The youth is right. Those madmen do not know what they are doing. If that warp gate is allowed to run loose much longer it will break free of all control and consume the planet. This world will become a daemon world like those in the Eye of Terror.'

Ragnar shuddered. It was a fate worse than anything Madox had promised him. The daemon worlds were places where hell invaded the material universe, warped by Chaos, ruled by the whims of daemon princes. He wondered whether Magnus and the Thousand Sons had any idea what they were doing, or whether they even cared. Perhaps this had been part of their insane plan all along. Perhaps that was what Madox had meant when he had talked about the new Prospero, the planet that had been the original home world of the Thousand Sons. Perhaps Magnus intended to create a new capital here, in the image of the original, formed by his will from the raw stuff of Chaos. Could he do that? Did he really have that sort of power? Who knew what a primarch was capable of?

'We need to get the Spear. It is providing the power for the ritual, anchoring the gate to the warp, and Magnus to the gate,' said Skalagrim.

'I am open to suggestions,' said Berek. His smile was becoming a rictus of fury. His weapons dripped with the gore of dozens of slaughtered foes. He looked like a god of battle descended among mortals. Every stride took them closer to the altar, but not close enough. Ragnar raised his bolt pistol and sent a shell hurtling towards the heretics, but the air around them shimmered, a glowing sphere of light became visible and some force deflected the shells.

'I already tried that,' shouted Berek. 'We're just going to have to do this the old-fashioned way. Right lads, cut us a path to that altar.'

'If you can get me into proximity with it, I might be able to do something,' said Skalagrim.

'Always reassuring to know,' said Berek. He let out a long, low and terrifying howl and began to charge. If Ragnar had thought Berek had been ferocious before, he had a surprise coming to him now. The Wolf Lord's unleashed fury was truly awesome. He moved with eye-blurring swiftness through the mass of materialising Chaos warriors, smashing them down with thunderbolt-like blows of his blade. He fought with no thought of defence, a true berserk, living only to kill. Morgrim and Mikal Stenmark flanked him and protected him from the consequences of his all-out attack, turning aside blows intended for their war-chieftain, blocking them with their own bodies if necessary.

'Stay by me, boy,' said Skalagrim. 'Once we are close enough I will need someone to guard me while I work with the runes.'

'As you wish,' said Ragnar. 'So shall it be.'

Following the massed ranks of the Wolf Guard they cut their way through the throng of Chaos Marines, while in the air over the altar, the face of Magnus hovered like the severed head of some evil god. There was a triumphant look in that one mad eye.

TWENTY-SIX

ALL AROUND THEM, the resurrected Chaos Marines pressed hard. Ragnar fought like a man possessed, always keeping an eye open for Madox. He swore that no matter how long it took, he would pay back the Thousand Son for slaying Sven. Given a chance he would carve the blood dragon on his back.

Ahead of them the altar loomed larger, but as they closed their advance became ever more difficult. Some force seemed to be repelling them, and the numbers of the Thousand Sons increased. Fortunately, most were disoriented by their recent emergence from the warp, and this gave the Wolves of Berek's company a chance to overwhelm them while they were off-balance. Had it not been for this, Ragnar reckoned the battle would already have been lost.

He chopped down a mortal cultist, putting his chainsword blade through the back of the man's head, smashing it to tiny bits. A burning orb from the warp gate landed on it. For a moment, a field of fire limned the corpse, and then the Chaos thing withdrew, crackling with frustration. It seemed that without a brain to enter, the spirits of the Chaos warriors could not take control of the bodies.

Madox had lied about that. Now, there was surprise, Ragnar thought sourly. A follower of Tzeentch lying, how unusual. What else had he lied about?

'Shoot them through the heads!' Ragnar roared. 'That will put them down and keep them down.'

Another glance showed him something else. Where the glowing spheres landed on the fallen, they only took hold on the shaven-headed heretics with the sign on their head, and Ragnar guessed they could only possess those marked in this way. Perhaps they needed it to root themselves to. Ragnar did not know. He was not expert on dark sorcery but he knew what he was seeing and he spread the word. 'It's the rune on their foreheads that lets them be possessed,' he shouted to Berek. 'Destroy it and they cannot change.'

Berek nodded to show he understood. The order rippled out over the comm-net. His battle-brethren acted on it instantly. Perhaps it was too late now to make a difference. Perhaps too many of the Thousand Sons had already returned for Berek's embattled company to make a difference. He could not see any way in which they were going to be able to stop the ritual, or overcome the sendings of that daemonic presence hovering over the altar, and spewing out the souls of his long dead followers.

Despair almost overcame him, he felt ready to give up. Only his thirst for revenge and for a glorious death kept him fighting in that dark instant while every fibre of his being cried for him to give up.

'Fight it, lad,' said Skalagrim. 'It's the daemon's power. It seeks to overwhelm your soul with despair. Do not give in to it!'

At first the old Rune Priest's words did not sink in, then their meaning struck Ragnar with the force of a blow. He was not going to give in to the will of a daemon, no matter how powerful. He snarled and drew strength from the scent of his pack. He saw how furiously the Wolf Guard fought, and the god-like ferocity that Berek brought to the fray. They were not giving in, and neither would he. By Russ, he would prove himself worthy to fight and if need be die in their company.

Ragnar howled his battlecry and glared about him. Nearby he saw a heavy flamer held in the grasp of a fallen Long Fang. He leapt over to it, snatched it up and pulled the igniter that brought it to life. A jet of incandescent chemical fire leapt out. He squeezed the trigger and the jet lengthened. He turned it on the nearest foes, cultists and returned Chaos Marines alike. He wondered how those who had just returned from hell would like a taste of its fires.

The flames licked out, setting light to the heretics, melting the armour of the Marines. Within seconds Ragnar had burned a path forward. He advanced swivelling from the hip, clearing a channel ahead of him with the flames. Twenty strides took him within striking distance of the altar. He sensed Skalagrim at his shoulder.

'Enough, lad. Well done! I must strike now, while the heretics are distracted – while all their power goes into maintaining and controlling the gate!'

So saying he raced forward and struck at the altar with his staff. A blue flame rippled outwards. Chain lightning flared, dancing along the outside of a sphere that winked into visibility every time the bolts hit it. The air stank of ozone and death. The sphere flickered for a moment, vanished and returned. Fleeting triumph vanished from Ragnar's heart. They were not going to make it.

With a growl of frustrated rage, the Rune Priest struck again. Once more the lightning flashed, once more the force sphere flickered. This time, Ragnar was ready. He leapt forward, springing through the briefly open barrier and landing atop the altar.

An instant later the deafening hubbub dimmed. The sound of battle muted and became distant. He was within the barrier now, cut off from all aid. Before him stood the five servants of Tzeentch. Ragnar grinned. He knew exactly what he was going to do now.

Only Sergius looked at him. The others were too busy try-ing to maintain the gate. This close Ragnar could see the strain they were under. Their limbs quivered, and their knees seemed weak. He could smell their weariness and hear the harsh rasping of their breath. One of them turned to look at Ragnar and he sensed the man's fear. As he did so, the gate flickered and the sense of the awful presence of the primarch weakened a little.

'Don't let him distract you, fools. Maintain the gate at all costs. The legions of Magnus must be resurrected if we are to win our eternal rewards.'

'Your only reward will be death,' said Ragnar, leaping forward and striking the nearest cultist. His attack was a blur so fast that the man had no hope of avoiding it. Somehow, with desperate quickness he managed to raise the burnished skull he held. Ragnar's blade connected, and instead of smashing it in two as he had half expected, the blade recoiled, bounding back as if it had hit some-thing hard as diamond. Worse yet a surge of sickening pain and nausea, mingled with a bubbling daemonic energy, passed up the weapon and through Ragnar's body like an electric shock.

Overhead, he sensed something happening. The feeling of immense power intensified, became less controlled. He heard a distant roar, like surf pounding on a beach. It was as if he could hear the voices of every sailor who had ever drowned, screaming and howling within the sea's rage. He somehow knew, without being told, that he was hearing the voices of all those long dead Chaos Marines, waiting to be resurrected.

'No, idiots!' shrieked Sergius. 'Don't let your concentra-tion slip. The gate must not close until all of the Blessed Ones are returned to us.'

Ragnar gritted his teeth. 'How are you going to stop me?'

The cultist did not reply. Instead he made a twisting com-plex gesture with one hand. Trails of fire followed the intricate movements of his fingers. A small portal to some-where else appeared to open, and as the heretic pointed the raw stuff of Chaos spurted through, like water gouting through holes in the dragonskin hide of a ship.

Ragnar threw himself flat and let the stuff pass over head, not willing to risk the slightest contact with it. Doubtless it would sear through his armour like hot lead through cold butter. Such stuff was not meant to be in the mortal world. Just its presence made his skin tighten and a spasm of fear pass up his spine.

He rolled forward along the top of the massive altar, catching one of the cultists behind the leg with the blade of his chainsword. The man dropped his chalice and fell screaming.

The cord of light connecting him to the portal stretched and broke. The swirling vortex of Chaos stuff lost shape around the edges. Ragnar was not sure he was doing the right thing. If the portal ran out of control, it might swallow the world. On the other hand, he could not see anything else to do. He could not simply allow these wicked men to proceed with their ritual, not while his battle-brothers fought and died outside the shield that separated them.

He risked a quick glance outwards, to see how things were going. Not well. The resurrected Thousand Sons outnumbered the Wolves, and more and more sprang into being despite the killing and decapitation of numberless cultists and corpses by his brethren. One for one, the battle appeared to be equally matched, but soon the weight of numbers would begin to tell. It seemed too much to hope for that the rest of the Chapter would arrive in time to make a difference.

He noticed Skalagrim locked in combat with a black armoured ancient Marine. The old Rune Priest was shouting something at him. The sense was lost in the mad roar of battle, muted by the magical shield around him. It seemed to Ragnar that he should be able to understand the old man's mouthing, but he could not.

He lashed out with his foot, catching another cultist in the groin and sending him flying. The robed heretic hit the force wall surrounding them and bounced back to lie unconscious on the altar itself. Overhead, the roaring of the Chaos gate intensified. It was losing the semblance of the primarch's head and become a shapeless shimmering mass of raw, primordial Chaos. The frustrated voices of the waiting souls clamoured in anger and frustration and perhaps fear. They did not want this to happen.

A shocking pain passed through Ragnar and he looked up to see another cultist had stabbed him through his shattered shoulderpad with a black, rune encrusted dagger. The agony was intense, poisonous magic swirled away from the wound. Ragnar used the butt of his chainsword to smash the man's skull. It collapsed like an eggshell hit with a hammer, splattering Ragnar with gooey jelly and fragments of bone and blood. Knowing he might only have seconds to live, Ragnar came to a quick decision. Two lightning fast strikes killed two more of the ritual workers and left him face to face with their leader. He struck at Sergius's head but the hulking man leapt back and Ragnar's blow succeeded only in ripping the helm from his head and leaving a dripping, bone-deep cut on his brow. Even as Ragnar watched the wound closed. It was true then, – mortal weapons could not harm the daemon lover.

The poison in the wound slowed him now. He could feel his limbs grow heavier and stiffer with every heartbeat. Whatever it was, it was no normal venom. Even his altered Space Marine body was unable to cope with it. Perhaps it was not poison at all but magic. And if it was magic, it could be resisted by the strong of soul, Ragnar told himself. Offering up a prayer to Russ, he drove himself onwards by pure force of will.

The arch-heretic looked at him and snarled. His mouth was a red gash. Most of his teeth were small and white and very sharp but two of his canines were as long as Space Wolf fangs. 'You fool,' he said. 'You know not what you do! You have doomed us all, and this very world.'

'It would have been doomed anyway, if the Thousand Sons returned.'

'It would have lived an eternity in glory. I would have lived an eternity in glory, sitting at the right hand of Magnus. Now there will only be ruin and destruction.'

'There will always be that,' said Ragnar, circling, looking for an opening. The cult leader held the Spear of Russ in his right hand, as if considering throwing it at his assailant. Inwardly Ragnar quailed. His armour would not be able to withstand that legendary weapon even if wielded by a heretic. The Chaos worshipper came to his decision. He drew back his arm for the cast. Everything slowed. Everything became perfectly clear.

Ragnar could make out every little detail of the man's movements, the way his weight shifted from front foot to back foot and then returned. The way his cloak swept back over his shoulder and fluttered in the wind. The mad melee was visible behind the man, frozen for a split second, a tableau of mayhem in which Berek's company fought the black armoured minions of Chaos.

Sergius threw. Ragnar could feel the death in the weapon, sense the weight of it, knew that when the weapon struck a life would end. It hurtled towards him like a thunderbolt cast by an angry god. He watched it come, knew that on its current trajectory the glittering point would pierce his heart.

Still he stood, watching like a man who sees his death approaching but whose wyrd is upon him and can do nothing. At the last moment, he reached out and snatched the Spear from the air, catching it just behind the head. He felt its momentum and its mass, far greater than anything he could have expected. He let the weight of it turn him around in a half circle, bringing him to face the heretic once more and with a snap of his arm he set it onwards to bury itself in the Chaos worshipper's chest. Even Sergius's vast, sorcery riddled body could not withstand the weapon that had wounded Magnus himself. It passed right through him and almost out of the other side.

At that moment, the force wall dropped and the roar of battle flooded in, temporarily drowning out the sound of the portal. The screams of the dying, the bizarre chants of the Chaos Marines, the howls of the Wolves warred with the blast of bolters, the thunder of grenades and the grating whine of chainsword on armour. The scents of blood, excrement, incense, ceramite, explosive charge and the raw stuff of Chaos assaulted his nostrils. The air vibrated with the power of the Chaos gate and the detonation of munitions.

Overhead the gate blazed with power, gouting forth the souls of Thousand Sons and the raw stuff of Chaos in equal measure. As Ragnar watched it started to widen. Shimmering coruscating light flickered across the chamber, reflecting off armour and stained glass and marble, limning everything in hellish light.

Ragnar stared at it in awe and wonder and terror. He could see things moving up there. He could see the outlines of daemons coalescing and fading along with the faces of the damned. All of them appeared to be components of a greater face that leered down on him, the one-eyed face of Magnus the Red. At times that greater face lost shape and the gate grew wider. At other times, the features swam together and he reappeared and the gate appeared to stabilise.

All of the time, the swirling mass of lesser faces and beings seemed somehow to be components of the primarch's face, as if somehow contained within him. The primarch's face now showed the strain, and it occurred to Ragnar that wherever he was, and whatever he was doing to perform his part in this insane ritual, Magnus did not want the gate to give way, any more than Ragnar did. Ragnar could only guess why. Perhaps he did not want the gate to open until all of his warriors were resurrected, or perhaps interrupting the ritual had somehow placed the gate outside even his god-like control.

For whatever reason, it was obvious that the renegade primarch was under enormous strain. The eye that glared down balefully on Ragnar contained a measure of uncertainty, of doubt. Perhaps the primarch had tied himself to the gate and now as it ran out of control, the unleashed energies were capable of destroying even him. It was an awe-inspiring thought to contemplate the death of a being coeval with the Emperor, who had lived for centuries.

Ragnar shook himself. This was getting him nowhere. This was not his field. He was a warrior not a priest. He glanced around for Skalagrim, to see if the old man was doing anything about the gate, but the old man was locked in combat. Ragnar was about to spring to his aid when a blast of mystical energy washed over him and the whole gate began to shimmer and pulse, expanding and contracting uncontrollably. The tide of Chaotic energies seemed about to wash in and over them, and Ragnar knew that if that happened they were all doomed.

There must be something he could do, but what? He glanced around frantically, praying for help from the Rune Priest but none came. Instead, he found his eye irresistibly drawn to the Spear of Russ. This was the anchor, the focus of the ritual, the thing from which the dark ones had drawn their power to open the gateway. Surely it was the key to undoing it.

Ragnar was not sure what inspired him to his next action. Some instinct sent him springing to the corpse of the chief heretic. He wrested the ancient weapon from the body, hefted it and then threw it with one perfect cast, directly into the one mad eye of the primarch. The spear vanished into the raw stuff of Chaos, sinking slowly from sight like a stone vanishing under water. The scream of a god in agony filled the temple, booming across the room with such force that Ragnar had to cover his ears with his hands. The voice of Magnus seemed to contain the voices of all that multitude beyond the gate, and in it, underlying it, he could hear echoes of all their prayers, entreaties, threats and promises. It was like listening to the voice of pure undiluted madness, and for a moment his own sanity teetered on the brink.

Then came a moment of shocking silence. All combat ceased. The air around the gate began to shimmer and swirl, spinning inwards like a whirlpool. The blazing fireballs that were the souls of the Thousand Sons were drawn back into the vortex. All of the air was sucked out of Ragnar's lungs.

His armour's life-support systems kicked in automatically to compensate. A terrible gravitic pull began to lift Ragnar from his feet to suck him upwards into the collapsing gate. Desperately he clung to the edges of the altar. He knew that if he let go he would be sucked into the maw of Chaos to join all of those other damned souls there.

The pull became near unbearable. He saw several men – Chaos Marines, Space Wolves and cultists alike – sucked upwards and inwards. Anyone nearby was being drawn in, as the Chaos gate gave way. They vanished into the gaping mouth of hell leaving barely a ripple amid all of those leering faces. The corpse of Sergius hit the gate and vanished into the depths. Ragnar felt his legs being lifted and grasped by something and kicked at them. He did not look back, but kept his eyes locked on the ground below him, as if that would anchor him as surely as his gauntleted grip on the altar.

Slowly, inexorably, he felt his grip slip as the very stones crumbled beneath his fingers. He knew that he did not have a moment longer to live. The stone gave way and he felt the terrible suction lift him upwards towards the waiting gate. He snarled in defiance and then felt his wrist gripped by a strong hand, and looking down he saw Berek gazing up at him, his massive metal hand braced on the altar.

A moment later there was a thunderclap of inrushing air and the gate closed. The drag was gone and Ragnar fell to the altar, his armour clanging on the stone like some great bell.

He glanced around. There were still Thousand Sons here, and the battle raged on, but now there seemed to be far more Wolves. Looking over at the entrance he could see Logan Grimnar and the rest of the Chapter had arrived.

'How is it going?' Ragnar asked a battle-brother he did not recognise, someone from Redmaw's company.

'It is all but over. A few of the Thousand Sons may have escaped into the tunnels, but we will hunt them down.' The man turned and walked away with a curious unfriendly expression on his face.

Ragnar nodded. He was as weary as he had ever been in his life. The two hours' rest he had had since the battle ended was not nearly enough. The fighting after he had closed the Chaos gate had been gruelling and deadly. Try as he might, he had not been able to find Madox, which galled him, for the thirst for revenge was strong in him, and hatred of that evil Space Marine burned bright. His wound pained him, and he was weary as no Wolf ought to be.

He caught a familiar scent and turned to confront Morgrim Silvertongue. There was a curious grim expression on the skald's face.

'Thunderfist wants to see you,' he said. 'Come with me to the field hospital.'

The hospital was small and isolated, the apothecaries and priests dour and determined. They looked as if they had entered a personal conflict with death, and battled every step of the way to deny him. Judging by the number of bodies being carried away, they were being less successful than the Wolves had been against the remnants of the Thousand Sons.

One of them, a grim faced ancient called Wothan, looked at Ragnar as he entered the small chamber. There was a look of awe and revulsion on his face that Ragnar had come to recognise on his march to the chamber.

'This him?' asked the priest, running a medical sensor over the area of Ragnar's wound. He already knew the answer, Ragnar could tell. He was speaking only to have something to say.

'Looks clean. The hellblade has left no taint, I would say.' He sounded oddly disappointed.

Of all the men he had seen so far, only Berek looked at him with unrestrained friendliness, and the man whose bed the Wolf Lord knelt beside. It took Ragnar a moment to realise that it was Sven. Relief warred with guilt. Relief that Sven was still breathing along with guilt for not having visited his friend sooner. Berek seemed to read his thoughts and shook his head.

Sven was pale. Sweat beaded his brow and there was a distant look in his eye as if he contemplated worlds beyond this one. The stump of his hand was bandaged. He looked as if he had aged twenty years. His hair was greyish, and his face lined. Once more Berek seemed to read his thoughts. 'It takes a lot of a man's strength to recover from a hellblade wound. Even with the help of Rune Priests it is draining.'

'Ragnar,' said Sven weakly. 'I might have known you would show up to take all the credit. Lord Berek was just telling me that it is certain that we will make Grey Hunter. Once I'm back on my feet, I'll get a new hand fitted and then I am going to go and find that Madox and stick my blade up his–'

'I get the picture, Sven.' Ragnar could barely conceal his joy that his friend was still alive. His voice came out gruff but he could tell by Sven's expression that he understood. Berek gestured for Ragnar to come closer.

'I would have summoned you here sooner had I known myself, but I had other duties to attend to.' For some reason the mention of other duties made the Wolf Lord look embarrassed. It was an expression as out of place on his confident features as guilt on the face of a lion.

'Now Ragnar we have matters to discuss, you and I. None of them pleasant. Walk with me.'

'What is it, Lord?' Ragnar asked. Berek continued to look grim as they strolled through the ruined corridors beneath the temple.

'You have set our brother priests and our Great Wolf quite a conundrum, Brother Ragnar.'

'And what would that be, Lord Berek?' said Ragnar trying to match his liege in formality.

'You closed the gate and most likely saved us all from being dragged into hell, and to be frank for this I would see you rewarded. If I had my way you would have been made a Grey Hunter at the same time as Brother Sven and Brother Strybjorn.'

'But–'

'Yes, Brother Ragnar there is a "but". It is this: you have destroyed one of our most sacred relics, an act which some of our elder brethren in the priesthood consider quite blasphemous.'

'It was not my intention to do so, lord.'

'I know, Ragnar, I know.' Berek sounded almost kindly now. 'You must understand though that the Spear of Russ was a most precious and sacred thing. It was created for Russ, Lord of Lords, Wolf of Wolves. It contained part of his power. It is said that on the day of his return he would claim it and use it to smite the Great Evil One in the last days. I think he will find that a bit difficult now.'

Ragnar felt a deep-rooted sense of shame take him. He thought he had been a hero. He thought he had been saving the world. He thought he had made the right decision. Instead he had committed an act of blasphemy and sacrilege. A sudden flash of anger passed through his mind. No – he had made the right decision, the only decision under the circumstances. He had stopped the Chaos gate running out of control. He had stopped this world being overrun by the raw stuff of Chaos. If called upon to do so again, he would. He said as much to Berek.

'And I agree with you,' said the Wolf Lord. 'And I was there. Unfortunately not all of our brethren were. Some of the priests are not so sure that the gate would have run out of control. Some of them feel that it would have collapsed harmlessly in on itself once the summoners were slain. And who is to say that is not true? I am not an expert on such things. Are you? The only man who might have said so for sure was Skalagrim and he was so badly wounded he is not expected to recover.'

Ragnar shook his head. Perhaps he had been presumptuous after all. Perhaps things would have turned out well without him.

Was it possible he was really going to go down in the annals of the Chapter as the man who had destroyed the Spear of Russ? He would most likely become the most reviled brother in the history of the Chapter. It was not a pleasant thought.

'Regrettably there are other influences at work here too,' Berek added.

'What do you mean, lord?'

'In any mighty organisation there will always be politics, Brother Ragnar, even among the Russ's Wolves. There are those who see discrediting you as a means of discrediting me. After all, it means my company goes from being the one which saved the world of Garm well-nigh single-handed to being the one which lost our Chapter's most precious relic.'

'You mean Sigrid is behind this.'

'In part, he and his allies are behind this. I am sure of it. They are pushing for punishment and exile. Some of our more... devout... brethren wish to see the blood eagle carved on your back.'

'If such punishment is deemed fair by the Great Wolf, I will face my destiny like a Space Wolf.'

'Spoken like a true Son of Russ,' said Berek. 'We go to face Logan Grimnar now.'

EPILOGUE

'WHAT HAPPENED THEN?' blurted Mikko from the crowd of rapt faces, forgetting his status in his eagerness for the tale to continue. The Blood Claw had an expression on his youthful face that made it plain he wanted to hear so much more. As the tale had continued, the young Blood Claws had joined the circle of veterans, barely daring to make a sound. 'I mean, lord, would–'

Ragnar shook his head and looked around, almost as if seeing his battle-brothers arrayed before him for the first time. The sounds of the encampment rose up around him once again. The day had passed and his throat was dry as dust. The old memories of comrades long dead had come flooding back and filled him with memory and sadness and a sense of loss. Just as the day had ended, so his desire to revisit those dark memories had faded.

'That is a tale for another day,' Ragnar said, rising from beside the fire. 'Besides, if we do nothing but tell tales of what has already been, how will we create the heroes to be talked of tomorrow? Brother Mikko, you are anxious to learn what it is like to be made a Grey Hunter, but I do not think you need hear of such an occasion from another's lips. Form up your squad. We must see if the brotherhood will accept you and your comrades into their pack.'

He could tell by the young warrior's face how delighted he was, and Ragnar envied him that, never having experienced it himself. The Space Wolf was silent for just a moment longer, then he gestured for the men to follow him to the place the priests would have purified for the ritual.

As he walked, Ragnar thought of all the men he had known who had been worthy to be Grey Hunters and had never undergone the ritual because they had died too soon. Brave warriors all, now lost, fallen upon one gore-strewn battlefield or another. And he thought about himself, and wondered at what he had lost by never undergoing it, and all the strange adventures he might have missed if he had done so.

ABOUT THE AUTHOR

William King was born in Stranraer, Scotland, in 1959. His short stories have appeared in *The Year's Best SF, Zenith, White Dwarf* and *Interzone*. He is also the author of seven Gotrek & Felix novels: *Trollslayer, Skavenslayer, Daemonslayer, Dragonslayer, Beastslayer, Vampireslayer* and *Giantslayer*, four volumes chronicling the adventures of the Space Marine warrior, Ragnar: *Space Wolf, Ragnar's Claw, Grey Hunter* and *Warblade*, as well as the Warhammer 40,000 novel *Farseer*. He has travelled extensively throughout Europe and Asia, but currently lives in Prague.

MARK OF THE WOLF!

The Space Wolf novels by William King

From the death-world of Fenris come the Space Wolves, the most savage of the Emperor's Space Marines. Follow the adventures of Ragnar, from his recruitment and training as he matures into a ferocious and deadly fighter, scourge of the enemies of humanity.

'Paints a bleak but compelling portrait of life in the 41st century'
Publishers Weekly

SPACE WOLF

On the planet Fenris, young Ragnar is chosen to be inducted into the noble yet savage Space Wolves Chapter. But with his ancient primal instincts unleashed by the implanting of the sacred canis helix, Ragnar must learn to control the beast within and fight for the greater good of the wolf pack.

RAGNAR'S CLAW

As young Blood Claws, Ragnar and his companions go on their first off-world mission – from the jungle hell of Galt to the polluted hive-cities of hive world Venam, they must travel across the galaxy to face the very heart of evil.

GREY HUNTER

When one of their Chapter's most holy artefacts is seized by the forces of Chaos, Space Wolf Ragnar and his comrades are plunged into a desperate battle to retrieve it before a most terrible and ancient foe is set free.

WOLFBLADE

When Ragnar takes up his duties on ancient Terra, he soon becomes embroiled in an assassination plot that reaches into the very depths of Imperium!

More Warhammer from the Black Library

The Gotrek & Felix novels
by William King

THE DWARF TROLLSLAYER *Gotrek Gurnisson and his long-suffering
human companion Felix Jaeger are arguably the most infamous
heroes of the Warhammer World. Follow their exploits in these
novels from the Black Library.*

TROLLSLAYER

TROLLSLAYER IS THE first part of the death saga of Gotrek Gurnisson, as
retold by his travelling companion Felix Jaeger. Set in the darkly
gothic world of Warhammer, this episodic novel features some of
the most extraordinary adventures of this deadly pair of heroes.
Monsters, daemons, sorcerers, mutants, orcs, beastmen and worse
are to be found as Gotrek strives to achieve a noble death in battle.
Felix, of course, only has to survive to tell the tale.

SKAVENSLAYER

SEEKING TO UNDERMINE the very fabric of the Empire with their arcane
warp-sorcery, the skaven, twisted Chaos rat-men, are at large in the
reeking sewers beneath the ancient city of Nuln. Led by Grey Seer
Thanquol, the servants of the Horned Rat are determined to overthrow this bastion of humanity. Against such forces, what possible
threat can just two hard-bitten adventurers pose?

DAEMONSLAYER

GOTREK AND FELIX join an expedition northwards in search
of the long-lost dwarf hall of Karag Dum. Setting forth for
the hideous Realms of Chaos in an experimental dwarf airship, Gotrek and Felix are sworn to succeed or die in the
attempt. But greater and more sinister energies are coming
into play, as a daemonic power is awoken to fulfil its
ancient, deadly promise.

DRAGONSLAYER

IN THE FOURTH instalment in the saga of Gotrek and Felix,
the fearless duo find themselves pursued by the insidious
and ruthless skaven-lord, Grey Seer Thanquol. *Dragonslayer*
sees the fearless Slayer and his sworn companion back
aboard an dwarf airship in a search for a golden hoard –
and its deadly guardian.

BEASTSLAYER

STORM CLOUDS GATHER around the icy city of Praag as the
foul hordes of Chaos lay ruinous siege to the northern lands
of Kislev. Will the presence of Gotrek and Felix be enough
to prevent this ancient city from being overwhelmed by the
massed forces of Chaos and their fearsome leader,
Arek Daemonclaw?

VAMPIRESLAYER

AS THE FORCES of Chaos gather in the north to threaten the
Old World, the Slayer Gotrek and his companion Felix are
beset by a new, terrible foe. An evil is forming in darkest Syl-
vania which threatens to reach out and tear the heart from
our band of intrepid heroes. The gripping saga of Gotrek
and Felix continues in this epic tale of deadly battle and
soul-rending tragedy.

GIANTSLAYER

A DARKNESS IS gathering over the storm-wracked isle of
Albion. Foul creatures stalk the land and the omens foretell
the coming of a great evil. With the aid of the mighty high
elf mage Teclis, Gotrek and Felix are compelled to fight the
evil of Chaos before it can grow to threaten the
whole world.